THE UNEXPECTED PEACEKEEPER

THE INSCRUTABLE PARIS BEAUFONT™ BOOK 9

SARAH NOFFKE

MICHAEL ANDERLE

LMBPN Publishing
PMB 196, 2540 South Maryland Pkwy
Las Vegas, NV 89109

Version 1.00, October 2021
eBook ISBN: 978-1-68500-473-6
Print ISBN: 978-1-68500-474-3

THE UNEXPECTED
PEACEKEEPER

THE UNEXPECTED PEACEKEEPER TEAM

Thanks to the JIT Readers

Zacc Pelter
Dave Hicks
Diane L. Smith
Veronica Stephan-Miller
Jackey Hankard-Brodie
Deb Mader
Dorothy Lloyd
Jeff Goode
Angel LaVey

If we've missed anyone, please let us know!

Editor
The Skyhunter Editing Team

For my Hemingway—I love you, Craig.

— Sarah

To Family, Friends and
Those Who Love
to Read.
May We All Enjoy Grace
to Live the Life We Are
Called.

— Michael

CHAPTER ONE

The desperation clung to the air like mold spores as sweat poured down the magician's face.

"It's enough money," Whitney Ives demanded, leaning across the countertop and immediately regretting it. The smell of tobacco and poor hygiene on the gnome shop owner hit her in the nose, making her pull back.

"That's a statement when it really should be a question." The fat old gnome laughed through a mouth full of blackened teeth. "Is it enough money, you should have asked, and the answer is no. No, it's not even close."

Whitney gritted her teeth, sensing that Sidney Beater or Courtney Montgomery standing behind her wanted to intervene. However, they'd decided that only one of them would do the talking so they didn't look like immature young girls, haggling outside their comfort zones—although that's what they were. This was almost all their money and negotiating with the criminal before them wasn't something they often did.

They'd decided that as the magician, Whitney would lead the negotiations with the gnome known as Driftwood. It most likely wasn't his real name, since gnomes often went by nicknames. It was also common knowledge that they preferred dealing with magicians over fairies, as they didn't trust the whimsical creatures who were often viewed as overly emotional.

"It's all the money we have," Whitney argued, the sweltering hot shop feeling more like a sauna than a place that sold illegal and dangerous items on Zhuang Alley.

"Then get out," the man ordered flatly. "Go make more money and come back when you can pay up. The price is twice what you have, and that's that."

"How do I know that you're selling me the real stuff?" Whitney challenged, fisting her hands on her hips.

The dirty gnome's eyes skipped to her waist, tightly covered in her usual black leather corset, before looking her in the eye. The stool where Driftwood sat on the other side of the countertop made it so they were eye-to-eye although he would've been much shorter than Whitney if he were standing.

"I'm the only place where you can get demon blood." He indicated the dusty bottle of black liquid sitting on the counter between them. "You're gonna have to take your chances, sweetheart. If you and your friends want the stuff that badly, then pony up the money. Otherwise, get outta here and don't tell anyone you were here. I don't need a reputation for selling to tooth fairies. They'll laugh me right off Zhuang Alley."

"We aren't tooth fairies." Whitney's eyes narrowed.

"No, I heard about y'all." Driftwood chuckled. "You're tooth fairy dropouts. Your faces are plastered all over Roya Lane, I heard. I guess it's better that criminal tooth fairies were in my shop than the good ones, although let's admit it, all your kind are rejects. Not like those sweet fairy godmothers." He laughed again. "Now imagine finding one of those pretty little things in my shop. That would be a sight."

"Would you shut up!" Courtney yelled, stepping forward, vibrating with anger.

"Court," Whitney seethed, a warning in her voice. "I've got this, remember?"

"You be Virginia Montgomery's daughter," Driftwood said, his one good eye studying her, the lazy one taking a break. "I heard you ruined the family's reputation when it came out that you were at Loose Teeth College." He laughed once more. "Bet it makes it difficult for your mum to look down her nose at others now."

"Whatever," Courtney fumed, pulling her broken wand—which didn't look broken—from the waist of her black tutu and slamming it down on the countertop. "We'll take the demon blood in exchange for this wand."

Three things happened in quick succession: Driftwood's eyes widened with surprised delight, Whitney shot Courtney a murderous scowl, and Sidney yelled, "No!"

"It's fine," Courtney urged, glancing back over her shoulder at Sidney. The old witch Courtney had paid to fix her broken wand made it look like it hadn't ever snapped in half. The magical instrument didn't work properly, but it would be enough to pass the dumb gnome's test.

"Now you're talking." Driftwood greedily grabbed the wand and eyed it speculatively. "I could get big bucks for this."

"Court, that's your wand," Sidney urged, stepping up next to her, eyes wide.

Courtney shook her head, her pigtails hitting her in the side of the face. "It's fine. I'm not going to need it."

Driftwood probably thought that was because she was a tooth fairy dropout and not because the wand was most likely beyond repair. The real truth was that soon Courtney wouldn't need one even if it worked. If they got the demon blood and were successful with the next phases of their plan, it wouldn't matter. The Knees, as the authorities were calling them, wouldn't even need separate clothes because they would share—they'd be one.

The tooth fairy dropouts had found a mad scientist who said he could help them combine their powers. That's what they'd decided needed to happen to beat Paris Beaufont.

As a halfling with demon blood, she outmatched them. Paris had broken Courtney's wand, exposed her secret and made her lose her trust fund, got rid of Bloody Mary, then got the three kicked out of

Loose Teeth College. On the run and desperate, the Knees had to admit that to beat the halfling, they would have to become like her.

The Frankenstein scientist they'd found said that using some freaky magitech, he could fuse the three women making them one person. Then they'd be two parts fairy, one part magician, and have a bit of demon blood—like Paris Beaufont.

Admittedly, the halfling was more powerful due to her uniqueness. That's when the three decided that to defeat her, they needed to become the shadow version of her. It would require each of the women to give up their individuality, but then they'd be more powerful than ever.

Currently, as fugitives, everyone was looking for their faces. If there was ever a time to change appearances drastically, it was then. FLEA was looking for three women too, a magician and two fairies, not a brand-new hybrid with demon blood.

That last part was crucial. That's why the three knew they had to do whatever it took to get the demon blood. Without that, fighting Paris wouldn't be a decisive win. However, the Knees believed they would own the power granted by the demon blood, whereas Paris most likely fought it, weighed down by her conscience.

"You don't have to do this." Sidney eyed Courtney intently.

Although the wand didn't work right, it still worked and was Courtney's last connection to her old life. The three women knew that. They were all giving up their identity for this but had decided to hold onto some parts of themselves. Fairy wands, even if they didn't work right, were a symbol of power.

Not to mention, that's the only way the fairies could draw magic from the Fang Wellspring, and that would be necessary for completing the fusion. However, Courtney figured that Sidney, who still had her wand, could supply that.

"I have to do this," Courtney urged, turning her attention to Driftwood. "Will you take the wand in exchange for the demon blood?"

He grinned, showing more gaps than teeth in his mouth. "You got yourself a deal, sweetheart."

With a sigh, Whitney grabbed the bottle of demon blood before the dirty gnome could change his mind. Also, they needed to get out of that shop as soon as possible—before Driftwood figured out the wand didn't work completely. That would happen as soon as he sold it and the customer returned madder than hell. Then not only would the three women be fugitives, but criminals would hunt them.

CHAPTER TWO

"I don't understand." Faraday scratched his head with the tip of a small, squirrel-sized screwdriver. "Are you trying to make Wilfred laugh or cry?"

Paris rolled her eyes at him. "I'm trying to make the man laugh. Why would I want him to cry?"

Faraday shook his head, returning to the science project he was working on. "You're so bizarre. He's a piece of state-of-the-art magitech and not an audience member at a comedy club. He's not supposed to laugh."

Paris Beaufont sighed, looking between the talking squirrel sitting on a workstation in front of a strange contraption in his lab and the magitech AI butler in a three-piece suit and looking very British. "Wait, how am I the weird one here? I'm simply trying to bring joy to the world. What's the problem there?"

Wilfred shrugged, his white gloves in the air beside him. "I'm simply not wired that way, Paris Beaufont. I don't understand humor or why one would laugh."

"Because it feels good," Paris argued. "And because my jokes are awesome."

"Although the first part is true, the second one is debatable," Faraday stated.

Paris narrowed her eyes at the squirrel. "Come on. It was a good joke. Why did Bill hate astronomy?"

Faraday went back to his work, his eyes on the strange contraption. "Yeah, yeah, because he thinks black holes suck. It wasn't funny the first time."

"Well, you didn't like it because it was a science joke," Paris said.

Faraday straightened, combing his paw over his chin speculatively. "Maybe that's what you need. We all like jokes about things we relate to."

"Well, you didn't, and you love science," Paris stated.

"Again, the joke wasn't good...at all..." Faraday muttered.

"Hey, interesting fact. Did you know that t-shirt is short for 'Tyrannosaurus shirt?'" Paris deadpanned. "It's because of the short arms!"

"That science joke also wasn't good." Faraday went back to work. "My point is that maybe you need to come up with a joke that's relatable to Wilfred."

She glanced at Wilfred. "Do you mean butler jokes? British ones? Artificial intelligence?"

"It goes to reason that he's more likely to laugh about something he understands rather than randomly horrible jokes," Faraday answered.

"My jokes are amazing," Paris argued. "But fine. I have jokes for all of those things. Just let me think of one."

"While you're quiet, I can think." Faraday squinted to read a panel on the side of his contraption.

"Hey, what are you doing?" Paris asked.

"Winning the quiet game," he seethed, obviously trying to focus.

"Oh, I'm so sorry for interrupting your work," Paris joked. "Are you trying to steal Wi-Fi or cable from the Seelie?"

"I don't think the Seelie..." Faraday shook his head. "You weren't serious, I'm guessing. Anyway, I'm trying to track down a lead on that scientist who created the drones the Dragon Elite couldn't shoot down."

"Still?" Paris argued. "Have you heard that if you don't succeed, you quit?"

"That's not how the phrase goes."

"I'm certain it does," she stated. "If at first you can't find what you're looking for, you sit and Netflix until you forget that you were ever trying...I'm sure that's how the adage goes."

"Actually..." Wilfred interrupted in his dutiful voice. "The phrase you're referring to says—"

"No, Wil, you don't get to play," Paris interrupted. "You laugh at my jokes, and you get to interject your Internet wisdom. That's the deal."

He coughed uncomfortably, glancing to the side.

Paris looked at the squirrel. "So you're pretty obsessed with this scientist or scientists or whatever it was that created the drones then?"

"I'm not obsessed," Faraday corrected. "I have good reason to believe that whoever is behind the drones will return and probably not in a way that we'll find favorable. They employed undefeatable drones to protect a satellite that served to corrupt the world. Either they have evil agendas, or they can be bought by those who do. Either way, I must track them down and keep an eye on them."

"You might be more effective if you keep both of your eyes on them," Paris teased.

"I think Faraday meant that in the figurative sense," Wilfred interjected.

"Hey, my friend has hired a butler without a left arm," Paris said casually.

"Oh, really?" Wilfred asked, arching a curious eyebrow at her.

She nodded. "Yeah, serves him right."

Faraday groaned. Wilfred shot her a confused look.

She nodded. "Yeah, I expected those reactions."

"If you want a laugh, you could try increasing the funny factor of the jokes," Faraday offered.

"Hey, you said to tell a joke that Wilfred can relate to," Paris argued. "I told a butler joke."

"A joke he relates to that's good," Faraday amended.

She tapped her boot impatiently and folded her arms. "Okay, well, I'll need time to come up with a good AI-slash-butler-slash-British joke."

"I look forward to hearing it," Wilfred said in a dignified manner, bowing to her.

"So you can look forward to something, but you can't laugh?" Paris muttered. "I simply don't get you."

"Looking forward to something isn't an emotion," Faraday explained. "It's a behavioral plan."

"You're a behavioral plan," Paris spat, continuing to tap her boot.

"Good one, Pare."

"So where are you with tracking down this diabolical scientist or organization?" Paris asked. "Need my help?"

"I'm not certain that you could be of much help until I get this signal tracker working," he answered.

"Have you tried turning it off and back on again?" Paris deadpanned.

"I don't think that will...oh, you're not serious again," Faraday said. "I've been able to isolate a few strange signals that are akin to the drones. So the idea is to track them down, which should give me a lead on where they came from, or lead me straight to the facility that manufactured them."

"That's when I swoop in and invade this place and teach Mr. Crazy Scientist a lesson." Paris punched the palm of her hand with her fist.

"Or Miss Crazy Scientist," he corrected. "Also, you have quite enough to fill up your time right now."

Paris nodded in agreement. "It's true. Between finishing my final project, negotiating for peace between the Seelie and Unseelie, and tracking down the Knees so Queen Helena MacGillie will clean the Fang Wellspring, I don't even have time to eat."

"Well, don't neglect your nutrition." Faraday looked up from the signal tracker device and glanced at Paris, checking her over. "You have to take care of yourself, or you won't be of help to anyone."

Paris let out a long breath. "Yeah, I need to visit Papa Creola. I still can't believe that I'm the one who he stated would forge peace between the Seelie and Unseelie finally."

"You can't believe that?" Faraday asked. "You're a halfling with demon blood—one of a kind and also prophesied to save the fairy godmothers, somehow. You can't believe that you'll have other history-changing tasks ahead of you?"

She shrugged, slipped her hands into her pockets, and kicked a stool beside a workstation. "I don't know. I'm only a girl in a leather jacket who tells bad jokes and gets in trouble."

He sighed. "You're a Beaufont, the daughter of the most famous Warrior for the House of Fourteen, who saved magic worldwide. Your Aunt Sophia was the first female dragonrider in history and respawned a new population of dragons right before their extinction. Your Uncle Clark helped to uncover the forgotten history when mortals weren't able to see magic. And you can't believe that you'd settle a war that's been going on for hundreds of years? Really?"

"When you put it that way...yeah, no, I can't," Paris admitted. "I still don't get how I'll save the fairy godmothers. They seem to be doing okay with Saint Valentine taking back power from the bullying FGA board."

"Yes, but the fairy godmothers also have three dangerous women who want nothing more than to take them down." Faraday referred to the Knees who were on the run after the Bloody Mary incident.

Paris seethed. The aftereffects of the haunting were still evident around the college. "Yeah, one of my top priorities will be to track those evil goth creeps down and turn them over to Queen Helena MacGillie. I'm certain that the punishment she has in store for them will be painful and something they deserve."

"Maybe capturing the Knees will be how you save the fairy godmothers," Wilfred offered, having been listening to the conversation.

"Maybe," Faraday chirped. "I think there's more to it than that. Pare is a change agent. Even with Saint Valentine establishing his power over the board, I think that to survive and bring more love to the world, there's going to need to be an evolution at FGA."

Paris' stomach rumbled as the smell of bacon and oatmeal wafted up from the first floor, enticing her senses. "Yeah, so no pressure then. I guess I better go fuel up for the revolution-slash-witch hunt-slash-peace negotiations I have to accomplish."

"Don't forget about the farm-to-table restaurant you have to launch for your final project to graduate," Faraday imparted.

Heading for the door to the science lab, Paris groaned. "Thanks. I'd forgotten and wasn't having a full-on panic attack for a moment."

"Don't worry, I believe you can accomplish all this," Faraday sang proudly.

"I do too," Wilfred added, also giving Paris a look of encouragement.

She smiled over her shoulder as she pulled back the door. "Well, thanks. With friends like you two, I have better chances."

"Thanks, Pare. One last thing before you go," Faraday called before she left.

"Yeah?" Paris paused and glanced over her shoulder at the talking squirrel.

"Try to stay out of trouble," Faraday offered. "I believe you can accomplish all that you have before you, but one more problem might tip you over."

"I think we know that I don't go looking for trouble," she said with a laugh. "I'm a magnet for it."

"That you are," Faraday agreed. "Which is probably why you'll do so much good in your time. You can't fix the world's problems if you can't find them."

"Good point," she conceded. "Good luck with finding your crazy scientist, but also, take your own advice and try to stay out of trouble. We both know that I don't have the time to come and save your tail."

"I'll do my best, but no promises." Faraday waved as she exited the lab.

Hunger led Paris downstairs, although she wasn't looking forward to seeing the aftermath of Bloody Mary.

CHAPTER THREE

The mood in the dining hall at breakfast was understandably still somber. When the Knees had let Bloody Mary loose on the college, she'd taken ten students and staff members. According to all sources, there was no known way of returning them.

The only consolation was that the evil spirit had been trapped in the attic of the fairy godmother mansion and therefore couldn't come through mirrors anymore and steal people's souls...or whatever she did, which was still unclear.

Paris' stomach had been rumbling with hunger pangs a moment prior. They quickly stopped when she approached her usual spot at the dining table. She glanced down at her plate of breakfast sausages and avocado toast and promptly lost her appetite for eating it. Although the many mourning fairies poking at their food was sad to see, the real reason that Paris suddenly wasn't hungry was because of whose gaze she'd caught.

Hemingway's blue eyes held regret as his gaze connected with hers.

"Hey," he said when Paris took her customary seat next to him.

"Hey," she replied, sliding her plate onto the table and quickly away from her.

"How are you?" He studied her face.

"I'm staying busy." She shrugged, avoiding answering the question.

Christine leaned over, inviting herself into the conversation. "What's going on between you two?"

Paris pushed back in her seat, rolling her eyes. "What do you mean?"

Christine pointed her finger between them, giving them a scrutinizing glare. "There's something wrong between you two."

Paris pushed her plate a little farther away. "A few days ago we faced a horrible evil. I think everyone is pretty upset, not only us."

"Yeah," Christine drew out the word, looking between the pair. "This is different. There's something going on with you two." She glanced up at Chef Ash and Penny beside him. "You both see it, don't you?"

Chef Ash quickly stuck a biscuit in his mouth and pointed at his mouth as he chewed, nonverbally saying, "I can't talk right now."

Penny glanced nervously at her plate as though it suddenly demanded her attention.

"Oh, you two are cowards," Christine complained, scoffing at them before looking back at Paris. "So why are you upset at Hemingway? What did he do?"

Paris' eyes widened. "Nothing. Nothing at all."

Christine didn't believe her based on the expression she flashed. Pursing her lips, she glanced at Hemingway. "What did you do?"

Paris was about to defend him when he nodded. "It's probably not so much about what I did. More about what I'm going to do."

Chef Ash and Penny both looked up suddenly. Now they weren't pretending not to be involved in the conversation.

"What are you going to do?" Chef Ash wiped crumbs from his mouth.

"Well, I was going to tell you all this afternoon, but I guess now is as good a time as any," Hemingway began, looking at Paris for a moment, seeming to need her support.

She offered him a sympathetic, tender smile and a nod of encouragement.

"I believe Paris is disappointed because she knows that I'm soon leaving the college," Hemingway continued.

"What?" Christine slapped the table in front of him, leaning across Paris to do it. "Details, Mr. Noble. I want them now."

Hemingway smiled and looked at Paris. "Of course, I was only assuming that was why you were...different, since you know I'll be leaving soon. You might be happy and looking forward to getting a Magical Gardening instructor who allows you to use your magic for shortcuts."

She sighed. "Obviously, I'm upset that you're leaving, you fool. And I use my magic to speed up gardening projects all the time when you're not looking."

He snickered. "The fact that you think I don't know is truly entertaining."

Again Christine rapped in front of Hemingway. "Would you two stop being cute with each other and answer my question? Where do you think you're gallivanting off to, Mr. Gardener? Who said you could leave the college? I'm mad at you too!"

Paris groaned. "I'm not mad at Hemingway for leaving."

"Well, no, and you all will be leaving soon too, hopefully if you graduate at the end of this term," Chef Ash offered, his voice catching for a moment—his eyes connecting with Christine's briefly.

"Yeah, but we'll be fairy godmothers at FGA," Christine argued. "We'll be connected with Happily Ever After College. Why do I get the impression that Hemingway is leaving for good, off to another planet where he can't come back easily?"

Paris restrained from punching her very observant friend in the face. As flippant as Christine acted, she was very intuitive.

"It's true," Hemingway admitted at once. "I've decided to take a job as a contractor, searching out unique magical plants. My adventures are supposed to take me away for long periods to distant places. I'll return, of course, but I suspect the missions will keep me gone for extended times."

Christine pushed back from the table and folded her arms. "You really are a selfish and awful friend, Hemingway...if that's even your real name."

He laughed at this. "That's definitely my real name. Why would anyone choose to share a name with that famous author? I realize that it sounds like I'm abandoning you all, but the whole thing is brand-new, and it might not be as demanding as I'm making it sound."

"Congratulations, man." Chef Ash extended his hand across the table, offering it to Hemingway with a genuine smile. "That sounds like a great opportunity for you."

Before Hemingway could take his hand, Christine knocked Chef Ash's away. "Don't be happy for him. He's blowing off his friends to go hunting for four-leaf clovers. Not to mention how it must make Paris feel when she so obviously has a crush on him."

"You know I have demon blood that could make me impulsively act from rage, right?" Her friend casually sat back in her seat, not showing her embarrassment.

"I think," Hemingway said, daring to put his hand on Paris' arm, his touch warm, "Paris knows I feel the same way about her, although crush is an understatement."

Now it was impossible to keep the blush off her face, so Paris was grateful when Christine stole everyone's attention with a squeal. Many around the table looked over at them. Most eyes darted to Hemingway's hand on Paris, their curiosity evident. It was no secret that many students had crushes on the rugged, handsome guy beside her. However, Hemingway hadn't shown interest in anyone...until Paris. Now she felt his affection for her, and it made everything worse.

Hemingway was leaving. They all knew it now. What Paris hadn't wanted to admit had been said aloud. His job working for Astrid would take him away for long periods. He'd be in distant lands where it would be hard to communicate or portal back.

Paris was obviously in love with Hemingway, and everyone knew it. She might've been the last one to see it, but there was no avoiding it now. However, this was the heartbreak the prophecy spoke of. To save the fairy godmothers, she'd have to fall in love and have her heart broken.

The first part had happened over laughs in the greenhouse or treks through the Bewilder Forest and long conversations on the Enchanted Grounds over the last several months. The next part, the heartbreak, was happening right then, slowly and in front of everyone.

Hemingway's fingers tightened on Paris' arm. She brought her gaze up to meet his. "I won't be gone forever, but I'll miss you, more than I can say."

"What about me?" Christine asked, and Paris was grateful for her intrusion, breaking the tension.

"I'll miss all of you." Hemingway grinned wide and looked at her, Chef Ash, and Penny on the other side of the table. "It's just that I feel like this is something I have to do. I've been at Happily Ever After College all my life. Not until recently had I left the grounds. This is something I'm passionate about that will take me around the world, seeing things that I've only ever dreamed about.

"Hopefully, I'll be doing work that makes a difference. I've always admired that's what you all do as fairy godmothers. I love teaching, but I want a chance to make real change in the world."

"I think that's commendable," Penny said softly.

"Definitely," Chef Ash added.

"Sounds sappy," Christine teased. "When do you jet-set off, Dora the Explorer?"

Everyone laughed, Paris again grateful for her friend's sense of humor making things easier.

"Soon," Hemingway answered. "My replacement should be here today. My new employer is throwing a party to celebrate my new venture tonight, and I'll set off tomorrow."

"Seriously, if I had Paris' demon blood, I'd have cut you already," Christine stated, offended. "When were you going to tell us about this?"

"Well, when my replacement got here," Hemingway answered.

"Which is?" Christine asked.

"That's the really cool part," Hemingway began, excited. "With Saint Valentine's permission, Willow has offered my teaching position to a non-fairy."

"What?" Chef Ash's eyes widened in surprise. "That's unprecedented."

"It's the start of something hopeful," Paris remarked, knowing that if Hemingway ever wanted to return to his teaching position, he wouldn't have to worry about anyone finding out he wasn't a fairy. She was sure someone would divulge that bit of information soon.

"It definitely is." Hemingway smiled at her, his hand still on hers. "The headmistress has hired the giant, Rory Laurens, to replace me."

"That's great!" Penny exclaimed, her voice uncharacteristically loud.

Hemingway nodded. "Yeah, he has to finish up his projects working on Paris' restaurant and farm, but partnering with Chef Ash, we've been able to make a lot of progress."

"Yeah, the farm and restaurant have come along fast," Chef Ash said proudly.

Paris gulped, feeling the pressure of her final project. Her friends and experts like Rory had banded together, and it was almost ready to be launched. That would be the true test of how successful the venture was and whether it was worth everyone's efforts.

"Yes, thanks to Paris' quick-growing spells, the produce is almost ready," Hemingway explained to Penny. "Quiet, Ainsley, and Maddy are almost ready for service. The buildings are all built with Chef Ash's supervision. Bermuda Laurens' animals feel at home. It's amazing to see it all come together. I wish I could be here for opening day."

"Yeah, but you're abandoning us for some Indiana Jones baloney," Christine jabbed. "You won't even be here for our graduation, well, if we graduate. We might fail because our faculty member quit on us at a crucial time, deserting our education."

Hemingway shook his head, not deterred by Christine's many insults. "You all are going to be fine without me. Besides, Rory Laurens is an expert on plants and magical gardening."

"Great, have Astrid give him this opportunity on distant planets or whatever," Christine insisted.

"Rory doesn't want it," Hemingway stated. "Plus, he needs to be available to help Paris with the farm, work on his novels, and advise the House of Fourteen on giant matters."

"What about small matters?" Christine joked.

Everyone laughed.

"I'm happy for you," Paris finally said after a moment of quiet, looking Hemingway in the eyes. "It's the perfect opportunity for you. We'll all be rooting for you."

"Not me," Christine added quickly, making everyone giggle again.

"Thanks, Pare," Hemingway said, pulling his hand off her finally, regret flicking to his eyes for a moment before he glanced at the others. "I hope you all will join us tonight on Roya Lane. Apparently, Astrid has a surprise for me."

Chef Ash and Penny nodded. Christine sighed and shrugged. "I have to wash my hair."

"We'll all be there," Paris amended, knowing what the surprise was since she'd designed the elaborate cake for Hemingway's bon voyage party.

CHAPTER FOUR

The subdued mood followed Paris to her Art of Love class, where many of the students were simply sitting quietly—looking blankly at a projected quote on the front wall of the room. The quotes rotated and changed every few minutes, inspiring their lively discussions on love and romance in the class.

Paris didn't catch the last quote before it changed to one that seemed meant for her. It read,

"If you love someone, set them free. If they come back, they're yours; if they don't, they never were." – Richard Bach

A pang of emotion shot through Paris' chest, filling her with heartache. She knew that she had to let Hemingway go, but what if he didn't come back? What if in a decade she heard about his adventures and the family he had? Or worse yet, what if Paris was assigned to be his matchmaker as a fairy godmother?

She couldn't even fathom the task of pairing him up with some Cinderella who wasn't her. Yes, it was time to admit that she adored the man and had from the beginning. He was so down-to-Earth. So calm and positive. He was everything she never knew she wanted.

Paris tried to remind herself that soon, hopefully, she'd be leaving Happily Ever After College and taking a full-time position at FGA. The department she got as a fairy godmother depended on how her final project went, how much it affected the love meter, and her final performance on the last exams.

Although Paris was more accepting of the idea of being a fairy godmother than when she first started reluctantly at the college, a part of her didn't think that role was right for her. Fairy godmothers worked in the field, doing individual cases.

Conversely, Agents for FGA assigned the cases and handed down the strategy of how the godmothers would work them. That involved a more holistic approach that appealed to Paris. However, women were fairy godmothers and men were agents for no discernable reason that Paris could tell. Headmistress Willow Starr's shrug had met her complaints about this. However, Mae Ling had winked at her during that same meeting—as if she was encouraging her to keep fighting the FGA's current structure. Paris planned to.

Taking her seat next to Christine, Paris read the next quote that replaced the last. It was by the same author. "True love stories never have endings."

She instantly liked that quote better and wanted to believe it was true. Was there ever really an ending to anything when life continued? It was some deep subjects that Paris was bordering onto lately, but she guessed that was due to everything coming to a head.

"Do you want me to cook up a 'Break A Leg Cake?'" Christine asked her in a low voice.

Paris shook her head, scowling at her friend. "Those make people break a leg, don't they? Why would there be such a magical recipe and how do you know it?"

"Sometimes people want to break a leg," Christine argued. "Like, if they need a reason to get out of a marathon they signed up for but forgot to train for."

Paris lowered her chin, regarding her friend with a curious expression. "You did that, didn't you?"

"I had to," Christine explained. "Then once I'd been dismissed from the race and got my money back, I whipped up some 'Mend-The-Fences Pudding.'"

"That fixed your broken leg?" Paris was impressed but tried to hide it.

"Well, when it's about to rain, my knee gets sore still," Christine admitted. "But yep. I can make you a cake for Hemingway. Then he won't be able to trek through the Amazon rainforest."

Paris shook her head. "No, but I know your heart is in the right place. However, he needs to do this, and I'm happy for him."

"That's a load of pixie poop," Christine teased. "People say they're happy for someone in that situation so they don't look like selfish jerks. We're happy when the ones we love are with us, not when they're abandoning us for some exciting opportunity where he's probably going to contract some rare disease."

"Unsurprisingly, you're not making me feel any better," Paris joked. "This is Hemingway's dream. How can I not be happy for him?"

Christine shook her head. "Wrong. His dream is doing what he loves in the same zip code as the person he loves, which everyone knows is you and has been from the minute you marched onto this campus."

Paris blushed, diverting her gaze from her friend's. She didn't say a word, which was fine since Christine was on a roll.

"Isn't it obvious that Hemingway is doing this because soon you'll be leaving Happily Ever After College?" Christine asked. "This place won't be the same when we're gone. I wouldn't want to stick around here without you so why would he? I'm sure that he thinks you're going to pop off to FGA and get a fairy godmother position in one of the top departments and forget all about him and his dirt-stained hands and dashing blue eyes."

"That's not what's going to happen—at all."

"It is," Christine chirped simply.

"Look, he needs to take this risk," Paris argued. "Like he said, he's not been outside of these grounds much. How will he ever know what he wants unless he gets out there and explores?"

"It's cute that you think exploring the world is how we find what we want," Christine said with a wise glint in her eyes. "We usually know what we want but exploring tells us what's in our hearts that we can't live without."

CHAPTER FIVE

Headmistress Starr swept into the classroom as another quote flashed onto the front wall. It read,

"Being deeply loved by someone gives you strength; loving someone deeply gives you courage." – Lao Tzu

To Paris, there was a lot of truth in those words. As a girl who hadn't been much interested in love and spent most of her life repulsed by the idea, she thought that secretly, she was grateful Hemingway wasn't sticking around. If he were, she'd have to do the one thing that was harder than letting him go—love him.

Paris had overcome a lot, but she wasn't sure if she was ready for that...ever. That kind of love seemed fit for other people. It would be her job as a fairy godmother to create that for Cinderellas and Prince Charmings.

"The mixtape has long been a way for a potential suitor to show his affections to a girl he's courting," Willow began. "Not only are they clever devices for creating warm feelings of love because they use the art of music. But also they can poetically express messages that a lover might be reluctant to say in their own words, with their voice."

"My ex-boyfriend once made me a playlist with all AC-DC songs," Christine joked, making many students laugh.

Willow looked grateful for the interruption rather than irritated. The headmistress appeared more stressed than usual, dealing with the aftermath of Bloody Mary and the missing students and staff members. "I think for some, that could be considered romantic. The key is that the songs are picked based on the taste of the person receiving them. Today, we're going to create romantic playlists that will create budding feelings or express untold emotions."

"Shouldn't creating a love playlist be the job of the Prince Charming?" Becky Montgomery asked in her usual snotty tone.

"Or the Cinderella," Willow added. "Yes, in an ideal world, Prince Charmings would take the initiative and create playlists or purchase flowers or spend the effort to make a romantic gesture. However, sometimes they need a little push, and that's our job. The magic of fairy godmothers is about working behind the scenes, setting up the right atmosphere for love, or coordinating getting two people together."

"So we make a romantic playlist based on the personality of our Cinderella, let's say," Christine began, "and then what, we leave this mixtape lying around for Prince Charming to find? Do we take a time machine back to the 1980s first? Or maybe we leave an 8-track and go back to the '70s."

The class laughed again, making Willow smile with relief.

"Well, I think we rely on current technology," Willow stated. "Now, how you leave this playlist of perfect songs for your charges to find is up to you. Maybe you simply orchestrate playing the songs randomly throughout the day for them to hear."

"Oh, kind of like you're giving them the idea to make the playlist," Paris guessed.

The headmistress nodded. "Exactly. Or you could make a playlist on Spotify and figuratively set up to have it dangled in front of their attention."

"This is a waste of our time," Becky complained.

Paris assumed she didn't know when to stop.

"Why is that, traitor?" Christine dared to ask, turning in her seat to face the other fairy, showing her a pursed expression.

Becky scoffed. "I'm not a traitor. This is a waste of time because the couples we should be matching don't need silly playlists. They need invites to the same social engagements and the seating charts to place them together and maybe for Cinderella's ride to cancel and Prince Charming to be her only way home."

"Right." Paris drew out the word. "Because the coach turned into a pumpkin. You do realize that people don't all meet at balls while wearing gowns and lining up to kiss the king's ring, right?"

Even though Paris wasn't looking behind her at Becky, she could've sworn that she heard her eyes roll with annoyance. "I contend that we should direct our efforts at those of social status who attend balls or the like, golf tournaments or galas or premiere red carpet events."

"Well, traitor, what about the other ninety-eight percent of the population?" Christine asked. "Do we ignore them and hope they have enough hope to get through the day so they can clean these people's houses and do their dry cleaning so they can go to these social engagements?"

"Stop calling me a traitor," Becky nearly yelled. "It's not my fault that tooth fairies attacked the college!"

"Isn't it though?" Christine challenged. "It was because of the knowledge that Courtney, your twin sister, got from you and your mother about Happily Ever After College that allowed her and the Knees to get here, correct?"

There was a long silence as Christine waited, as if she was curious to get Becky's real answer. No one said a thing, not even Headmistress Starr. The details regarding the Knees, the Montgomerys, and the feud with Loose Teeth College had become mostly public knowledge with the big events related to Bloody Mary.

"I didn't tell Courtney how to get into Happily Ever After College," Becky finally seethed in a low voice, obviously working to corral her anger. "And I didn't help Whitney Ives or that other tooth fairy. Courtney simply snuck around until she figured out what she needed to know to get them in here."

"But as her twin," Paris began, turning to face Becky finally, "you probably know where your fugitive sister is? Maybe your family is even harboring her."

Becky looked up suddenly at Willow as if hoping that she'd put an end to this. The headmistress, Paris noticed with a glance, seemed genuinely interested in the reply, not intervening.

Becky let out a long breath. "No one in my family has seen Courtney or her friends. She drained her bank account as soon as she got wind that Mother was cutting her off, but she didn't get much since she's only paid a monthly allowance at a time."

"The Montgomerys have it hard." Christine laughed and turned to face the headmistress.

Paris joined her, shaking her head. "Yeah, why don't you focus on pairing up the posh elites, Bec. The rest of us will focus on the commoners."

"That's fine by me," Becky replied.

Willow forced her usual polite smile, which didn't quite reach her gaze as she glanced at Becky. "Do let me know if you hear anything about your sister or the Knees' whereabouts. That's important information that we need to resolve further matters."

Headmistress Starr was referring to the fact that for Queen Helena MacGillie to clean the Fang Wellspring, they had to turn the three tooth fairy dropouts over to the Seelie. However, they couldn't do that unless they knew where to find them.

Becky simply grunted in reply to the headmistress. Willow didn't seem bothered or surprised by the retorts. She directed her gaze to the rest of the students, her expression relaxing. "Go ahead and get to work on crafting a playlist that you think could appeal to a young couple—something not overly sappy or affectionate, but elicits the feelings of fondness. Something that will lead to more flirtatious interactions between the two."

Paris couldn't help but think of Hemingway and the kind of songs she would put on a playlist for him. Right then, they might include a lot of mixed messages since she didn't want to fall anymore.

However, the projected quote changed suddenly. She caught her breath, surprised by the author of the phrase and the perfection of the words.

"No one you love is ever truly lost." – Ernest Hemingway

CHAPTER SIX

Most of the students were making noises that would have dogs howling. The high-pitched squeals made Paris cover her ears when she entered the ballroom, although she was glad to see the students excited about something rather than sad about all the missing women.

Many of the fairies were holding up their ballgowns and twirling around as if pretending they were dancing in the dresses right then. Juergen had finished with many of the outfits. That meant Paris would have to try on hers finally.

She flashed a look of gratitude at the tailor when he handed her the garment bag with her dress. Paris slung it over her shoulder and glanced around the room for an open area of the floor. She needed to practice the final dance number that everyone expected her to have mastered for graduation.

"Well, let's see it." Christine tugged on the bag on Paris' shoulder.

She shook her head. "Haven't you heard? It's bad luck to see a fairy godmother's dress before the graduation ceremony."

Christine laughed, waving around the ballroom with excited students showing off their dresses to one another. "Then we're going to have a lot of bad luck. Come on. You need to see if it fits and what shoes you're wearing with it."

"These," Paris said simply, indicating the black combat boots she was wearing. "And my leather jacket. If it doesn't fit, I'll wear these pants and blame my carb addiction."

"No, you're not wearing combat boots with that dress." Christine put her hands on her hips. "That will ruin the whole effect."

Paris lowered her chin, flashing a rebellious look. "Or will it make it that much better?"

"You're ridiculous."

"I'm glad you finally realized that," Paris sang. "Now, I need to go practice, or I'll be hanging up this gown until next term when I get another chance to graduate."

"Oh, you're going to graduate, no problem," Christine encouraged. "You passed the previous exams, and your project is off the charts. Again, you're giving me more reasons to hate you, making my fashion consulting business look like a lemonade stand on the side of the road."

Paris laughed. "Your project is great and will bring love. I mean, think of how much better the world will be when you're not angry because people are wearing bangs or mom jeans."

"Why?" Christine asked, her passion igniting. "Like, why do seemingly normal teenagers wear jeans up to their rib cage and disgrace their foreheads with bangs? There's only one reason someone should have bangs. His name is Harry Potter, and he's covering up a revolting scar. No one else has an excuse."

Paris chuckled again, heading over to the corner of the room that was mostly open and Wilfred was supervising various students practicing. "Anyway, your business will be great. You've got this dance down. I, on the other hand, need a lot of help."

"Well, you're not going to fail if you don't have the dance down," Christine offered. "It's a cumulative score with the main project weighing the heaviest. The dance, signature dish, and scores on practical exams are all a smaller percentage. However, in years past, women have failed graduation because they missed a few points on each of the requirements, so it's important to try to do as well on as many as possible."

"Which is why I'm politely dismissing you." Paris waved her friend away.

Christine rolled her eyes, shaking her head at her. "You have nothing to worry about. You're not only going to pass but pass in the shortest amount of time of any student in history, sealing your fate as someone I truly loathe."

"I look forward to getting all the hate mail from you," Paris sang, winking at Christine as she retreated in the opposite direction.

She then glanced at Wilfred, hoping that he'd help her practice. He wasn't who she'd prefer to dance with for her graduation ceremony, but Hemingway most likely wouldn't be in attendance, so the magitech AI butler would have to do.

CHAPTER SEVEN

U sually, Paris would long for the fresh air and open grounds around the greenhouse on a day where many were so depressed from recent events. Not on that day, though.

It was Hemingway's last day teaching at the college and word had spread about it, making people even more somber. She realized now why he didn't want to tell anyone until the last moment. He wasn't one to want attention.

Paris was bitter as she overheard other students expressing their regrets about Hemingway leaving the college as they strode over to the greenhouse. She couldn't imagine that their pain over this loss was greater than hers. She knew that was unsympathetic but couldn't stop herself from feeling that way.

The only thing that made her feel better was the sight of the giant standing outside the greenhouse when she approached. Rory Laurens looked so out of place next to Hemingway, who was much shorter than him. He also appeared out of place on the Enchanted Grounds as an instructor.

His mother, Bermuda Laurens, had visited the college to catalog animals in the new Bewilder Forest. Sophia, a dragonrider and magician, had been to Happily Ever After College several times. However, a non-fairy was there to teach, which made things feel like they were changing.

If a giant was teaching Magical Gardening, what would happen next? Would fae soon be teaching music lessons and elves pottery classes? It was a hopeful change, which most welcomed with the knowledge that the college was losing a staple—Hemingway Noble.

"As many of you have heard," Hemingway began when the class had gathered around him. "Today is my last day teaching at the college."

This was met with many groans and sounds of regret.

Hemingway offered a sympathetic and slight look of gratitude in reply before holding up his hands to quiet the class. "Don't worry. This is going to work out in your favor. You aren't even going to miss me—"

"That's impossible," some fairy who wanted Paris to give her a nosebleed interjected.

Hemingway smiled politely. "I've been hogging the role of faculty when there was someone else who is much more qualified for the position." He turned and held a presenting hand at Rory Laurens, who immediately turned a light shade of pink and tucked his head to his chest.

The giant's hands were deep in his jean pockets, and his curly brown hair caught snatches of the afternoon sunlight. "Hey," he said a bit sheepishly. "It's nice to be here."

"We have a giant as an instructor?" Becky asked. "The board will never allow such a thing,"

Hemingway's light expression dropped. "The board has already been overruled on the matter by Saint Valentine."

"He can't do that," Becky complained, her hands on her hips.

"He can because of the board's inability to pivot when facing challenges like agents turning on the leader of FGA," Hemingway said sternly. "The board is undergoing evaluation and many of its members being removed. In the meantime, Saint Valentine is making sweeping changes to the organization, starting with the college. There is no reason that a giant or any other magical race shouldn't be able to teach at Happily Ever After College."

"He's not a fairy," Becky stated, her face flushing red. "That's enough reason."

"He's a specialist when it comes to magical plants," Hemingway argued. "His mother is the foremost expert on magical creatures. Either we're going to evolve as an organization by employing the very best, or we'll stay limited and stuck in the Dark Ages. Don't forget that our main goal is to promote love, and the best way to do that is to arm ourselves with knowledge and tools. Rory Laurens, your new Magical Gardening instructor, is the person to help you to become better fairy godmothers."

Becky didn't appear to have a ready response to this.

After the uncomfortable silence passed, many of the students offered welcoming words and waves to the giant. When Rory smiled, his green eyes lit up, and his nervous expression fell away.

"I'm looking forward to teaching this class," Rory began in a squeaky voice that didn't seem to belong to a giant. He cleared his throat and sounded more normal when he continued speaking. "I've long wanted the chance to explore the grounds of Happily Ever After College. My mum, Bermuda Laurens, says the Bewilder Forest is quite the sight and had some drastic changes to it lately."

Rory's gaze drifted to Paris for a moment, and he almost seemed to wink before he glanced back around the class. "Although I'm not a fairy, I do know a lot about growing magical plants and using them for many different purposes. The giants' element is the earth after all."

"That's right," one student said in an excited voice.

"Who better to teach this class," another student added.

This put a damper on Becky's disdainful mood, Paris noticed as she sulked toward the sidelines as other students moved forward. Many of them had their hands up and curious expressions on their faces.

"Mr. Laurens, can you tell us the best way to get hydra-moss to grow in desert conditions?" a student asked. "My mother lives in Phoenix and can't get the stuff to grow."

"Call me Rory, and yes, I have some tips on that."

Paris didn't hear what the giant said next because Hemingway gliding over in her direction stole her attention.

"Hey," he whispered when he arrived beside her at the back of the class. The other students had all moved forward and were gathered around Rory, listening intently to his explanations.

"Hey." She realized they were pretty much having a repeat of their conversation from breakfast.

"Tonight, after the party, I hope you'll stick around for a minute or two," he began, nervousness making his voice sound weird. "I have something I want to ask you in private."

Paris felt like this was the perfect opportunity to make a joke or say something sarcastic, but when she looked into Hemingway's eyes, she couldn't do it. "Yeah, I can do that."

"Good," he chirped, trying and failing to look light.

"Will you miss the Enchanted Grounds?" Paris asked although the answer seemed obvious.

"Of course." He proudly looked around at the glistening green grass. "I mean, I'm going to places that have seasons. I might even sweat in the locations that get hot."

Paris laughed. "Yeah, it's going to be weird to be somewhere that's not the perfect seventy-five degrees all the time."

"It will be, but I'm looking forward to exploring and seeing places that aren't perfect. I mean, don't get me wrong, it's amazing having been raised and lived my entire life in a bubble that's always green, with a gentle spring breeze and the food is delicious, and everyone is always smiling…but…"

"It's just that, it's a bubble," Paris imparted.

He nodded. "It's time I see the real world and places that aren't perfect. I'm the first one to admit that I'm sheltered. Although I've loved my time with the fairy godmothers, I think it's overdue that I see the real world."

"I'm proud of you," Paris said after a long pause. "It's not easy to give all this up for an unknown potential, but you don't win anything new if you don't take a risk."

The dimple on his left cheek surfaced when he smiled. "That was my thought too. I can stay here my whole life and live a comfortable life, but it will be just that. Thanks to a certain halfling, I don't *just* want comfort in my life. I want bliss and adventure and to follow my passion."

"You got all that from me?" Paris' chest suddenly tightened with emotion.

"It's funny. I've lived my whole life in a place that promotes love, but I never really understood it until I met you." Hemingway appeared to struggle to swallow suddenly. "You don't do anything with half your heart. Even if it gets you in trouble, which is often the case, you do everything as if your life depends on it."

"Usually it does," Paris joked, grateful to break the tension for a moment.

Hemingway chuckled. "My point is, I can't stay here being comfortable when I know that outside this bubble is something that will make my heart sing. I want to throw myself into something new and find a passion like I see on your face when you're taking on a new adventure. I want to do something that I love. I want to be like you and do something that makes a difference."

"So you're doing this because of me," Paris stated, rather than asked—hating herself suddenly.

"I'm doing this because you gave me the courage and inspiration." He drew in a breath, an unmistakable desire in his eyes—all devoted to Paris. "If I never met you, I wouldn't even know what was feasible in my life. I wouldn't know that it was conceivable to have big dreams and to follow them...or that it was possible to feel so inspired and enamored by someone that you want the rest of your life to be as amazing as them."

CHAPTER EIGHT

"Man, I can't wait to be out of this place." Christine mopped the back of her forearm over her brow to wipe away some rogue flour.

"You love Happily Ever After College," Paris remarked, stirring her secret ingredient into her cheese ball. It was the recipe she was making for the final ceremony. She was all too aware that her signature dish was overly simple, but she believed it would wow the faculty —earning her a passing score for graduation.

"Yeah, but I also like being with who I want," Christine said in a low voice, sliding her cornbread muffins into the open oven and closing the door. Her gaze went to the corner of the demo kitchen. On the far side of the room, advising some students on how to make their tomato soup more savory, was Chef Ash. "Isn't he so dreamy?"

"I guess," Paris said, endeared to the chef's easy grin and positive demeanor. She wasn't attracted to men without hair. She found Hemingway attractive. She liked the strong, rugged look and guys with soul.

How could she not be proud of Hemingway for following his passion and doing what made his "heart sing?" She hadn't gotten over the irritating fact that it had been her who unknowingly encouraged him to take this new risk and venture into the unknown.

"I know you only have eyes for Dimples," Christine said, again being perceptive and seemingly reading Paris' mind. "As soon as he's gone tomorrow, you two can officially be together."

Paris rolled her eyes at her friend and grabbed a handful of parsley from a nearby plant. "Yeah, except that whole part where he'll be hiking up Mount Everest."

"You think he'll have to do such crazy things?" Christine asked.

"Well, if there's a certain plant that only grows at that elevation, then yes."

"Man, he could die…"

"You know, just a tip, don't become a therapist. You aren't good at this whole counseling business."

Christine shrugged. "I tell it like it is. I'd make a great therapist. I'd fix people's problems and make them better dressers. I'd love the opportunity to tell people how to live their lives. Like you, for instance. You have to tell Hemingway how you really feel about him before he leaves. Like, really how you feel—not only implying that you want to wake up to see his blue eyes every morning."

Paris grabbed a knife and chopped the parsley. "You're such a romantic. I don't think the time to tell someone your deepest feelings for them is right before they head off for an unknown period."

"If not then, when?" Christine challenged, setting a timer for her cornbread muffins. She kept burning them, probably because she couldn't take her eyes off Chef Ash. "How else will he know that he needs to return unless he knows that you love him?"

The "L" word made Paris shudder.

Christine pointed at her. "I saw that."

"Shush it." Paris grabbed some walnuts to chop and add in with the parsley. That was the mixture she rolled the finished cheese ball into, covering it and making it look somewhat decorative and like a human brain.

"I'm just saying that you need to be honest with him." Christine sounded a bit more sensitive now. "You don't want to have any regrets. After today, you two can be together and not worry about that no staff members dating students rule."

Paris looked up suddenly. "That's a real rule?"

Christine nodded. "Gosh, why do you think I haven't jumped that man's bones already?" She nodded in Chef Ash's direction.

"I thought that for once in your life, you were showing a bit of restraint."

"Yeah, right." Christine laughed. "No, it's because I'd get kicked out or he'd get fired. After I graduate, well, then we can be together officially."

"How does he feel?" Paris asked.

"He's crazy about me," Christine answered at once. "How could he not be? I'd date me if I could."

"I feel like you sort of do."

"The silver lining to Hemingway leaving when he does is that you two can be together," Christine stated.

"You have, like, a five-second memory," Paris remarked. "Remember that he's leaving. I have a lot going on. Romance isn't something I should be concerned with right now with so many things happening."

Christine shook her head. "There's always time for love. It's why we're here after all."

"We're here to create love for others," Paris argued.

The fairy sighed. "Quit being so literal. I meant that as human beings. We're here to love each other. It's just that we have the privilege as fairy godmothers of sparking it for people. That doesn't mean you can't have it too. I think that as fairy godmothers, we make the best lovers."

"You would," Paris teased, although she knew that her friend was right. She felt that her capacity to love had grown exponentially since coming to Happily Ever After College. Her life had expanded tenfold since she'd found her parents and family and made friends. A relationship with Hemingway, well, the kind she wanted, didn't seem in the cards right then. Maybe one day…

CHAPTER NINE

"Is there any particular reason that I had to step over Cat to get into the bakery?" Paris asked Lee, pointing over her shoulder at the door she'd come through.

The baker assassin glanced up from the Nintendo Switch she was playing. "Does there need to be a reason?"

"Call me crazy, but I think so," Paris replied.

"Crazy," Lee spat, returning her attention to the video game. "Go away. I'm busy."

"You're playing a video game," Paris pointed out.

"Minecraft isn't a video game. It's a cult, and I'm proudly a part of it. Now go away."

Paris chuckled, amused rather than offended by Lee, who was always trying to be as offensive as possible. "I will, right after you give me the cake you made for Hemingway's bon voyage party tonight."

"I didn't make it," Lee muttered, moving the controls on the hand-held game, really focused on the screen.

"What? But you promised!" Paris exclaimed.

"Ask my wife. I often break my promises," Lee said unaffected.

"How could you not make the cake?" Paris was suddenly fuming. "This was important, and Astrid asked you to do it for Hemingway."

SARAH NOFFKE & MICHAEL ANDERLE

"But you don't want Hemingway to leave," Lee stated matter-of-factly.

"That's not true…I mean, of course I don't, but it's a great opportunity." Paris tripped up on her words several times, vibrating with frustration.

"Fine, you want me to whip up a poisoned cake?" Lee asked. "Something that makes Hemingway less ambitious and therefore decline the job offer?"

"No," Paris said at once. "And it's too late. I can't believe you let me down."

Lee glanced up from her game, no remorse on her face. "Join the club. My wife is the president."

"You know, sometimes you can be a…a…a…" Paris paused short of finishing her sentence, her hands fisted by her side.

"A what?" Lee challenged. "What can I be?"

"A jerk!" Paris exclaimed. "I was counting on you, and this was something nice I wanted Hemingway to have before he left. I had designed it with him in mind, hoping that he loved it. Now he won't see the thoughtfulness I put into the cake."

To Paris' surprise, Lee grinned. "I knew it. You love him."

Paris' eyes widened with horror. What was going on here? "That's none of your business. And you don't know anything."

Lee grinned victoriously. "I know that the kind of cake you designed for Lover Boy was extraordinary and showed not only how much you know him but how much you wanted him to like the cake. I know that with true love, you want what's best for the other person, even if it's not best for you. So you went above and beyond, designing a cake that would make him happy for his going-away party even though the last thing you want is for him to leave."

She lowered her chin, giving Paris a challenging look. "Please tell me, am I wrong on any of that?"

Paris opened her mouth to argue but knew it was futile. "Well, you didn't make the cake so what does any of it matter?"

"Of course I made the cake. I wanted to see if you'd get mad."

"He's my friend, and I was supposed to get the cake. Of course, I'd get mad."

"Friend, that's cute. That's the thing about you Beaufonts," Lee began. "You all are cool under pressure. However, mess with someone you love, and you all turn into angry little demons that scare even me...well, you're pretty much a demon, so you become more of one."

Paris let out a long, steadying breath. "So you made the cake...really?"

"Really," Lee answered. "I had it delivered to the Glowing Orchid for the party. It's massive, and I didn't think you wanted to risk something happening to it transporting it to Astrid's."

"Okay, thanks," Paris said with relief and added, "That was a nasty trick."

"Well, I hope it helps you to admit your feelings."

Paris sighed. "Why does everyone want me to express my feelings?"

Lee suddenly looked at her with a serious expression. "Because sometimes if you don't, you wind up regretting it. Take it from me, kid. You don't want to look back and wish you told someone how much you care about them. Sometimes you don't get a second chance."

Paris sucked in a breath, getting the distinct impression that Lee was talking from experience. She didn't know how to respond, but thankfully King Rudolf Sweetwater came through the door a moment later, wearing his usual wide grin. He then ran his gaze over Paris, and his light expression dropped.

"Who hurt you?" he asked in a rush. "Tell me, and I'll kill them this very minute."

CHAPTER TEN

"I'm fine," Paris said at once, trying to fix the expression on her face that gave it away that she was upset.

"She's heartbroken," Lee said on the heels of her statement.

Paris swung around, her mouth popping open. "I am not!"

"You're going to be," Lee argued. "My psychic intuition tells me that your giant Beaufont heart is going to break minutes after the party ends tonight."

Gulping, Paris remembered that Hemingway had asked Paris to stay after the party was over that night. What was it that he wanted to ask her, she wondered with sudden great tension. "You're a baker and a bad assassin," Paris remarked, trying to dismiss Lee's statement.

"Oh, now the claws are coming out," Lee countered with an amused laugh. "Be glad I'm a bad assassin, or you'd be dead, halfling. You know how many people on Roya Lane have had it out for you?"

"All bullies who can come after me if they have a problem with someone serving them justice," Paris replied.

"Said like a true Beaufont," Lee sang as Rudolf came around into Paris' line of vision.

"Are we going to talk about this heartbreak?" the fae asked, a sensitive expression on his face.

"I'm going to dodge that question like Lee did when I asked her why Cat was lying in front of the door outside," Paris answered.

"Oh, that's obvious," Rudolf chirped, a smile surfacing on his face.

"Not for those not on drugs," Paris remarked dryly.

He turned to face Lee. "I'm guessing Cat is protesting customers coming into the bakery yet again."

"Yes, but it hasn't worked," Lee affirmed. "Like you two Interrupters-of-my-Game, people step over her and come in here with their demands."

"Talk about rude," Paris said sarcastically. "I bet they try to buy things with real money."

"Yeah, talk about the nerve." Lee huffed. "At least Cat is making a valiant effort to deter them. Either that or she's fallen and can't get up…"

"She seemed fine to me," Rudolf stated. "I hope it's okay that I wiped my feet on her. At first, I mistook her for a doormat."

"That's fine," Lee answered. "She treats me like a doormat all the time."

Rudolf swung back around and focused on Paris. "Now this heartache. Is it because your father is the worst human being in the world…if one could even call him that?"

Paris laughed, always entertained by King Rudolf's incessant disdain for her father. It was purely out of jealousy but endearing nonetheless. "No, and I'm totally fine."

"It's that boy who's leaving on an expedition for Astrid," Lee cut in.

"Oh, Faulkner?" Rudolf asked.

"Hemingway," Paris corrected. "He's not a boy. He's a man and a very talented one. It's normal for people to be sad when their friends are leaving."

"That's normal," Lee added. "But heartbroken, well that indicates a different level of intimacy between you two."

"Will everyone get out of my personal affairs!" Paris exclaimed, totally fed up with all the unsolicited advice.

"Yes," Rudolf said at once. "But at least let me try to do something to cheer you up."

"I don't want a Pegasus," Paris said at once, remembering the last time Rudolf had seen her stressed and offered to buy her one.

"No, I know. I have another idea. It shouldn't be hard to pull off in time for the party.." King Rudolf made for the door, looking like he was on a sudden mission.

"Wait, you're coming to the party now?" Paris wasn't sure she liked the idea.

"Of course. And I'll be bringing your favorite person," he replied.

Paris didn't know who Rudolf thought that person was, but she was almost sure he'd be wrong.

CHAPTER ELEVEN

"See, I told you that she'd be here today." Papa Creola leaned against a counter in the Fantastical Armory when Paris came into the shop.

"I know," Mama Jamba replied, sitting in the pink armchair in the corner. "I saw the t-shirt you were wearing."

Glancing at Father Time's tie-dye shirt, Paris read it aloud. "She had the soul of a gypsy, the heart of a hippie, and the spirit of a fairy."

"And don't forget, evil demon blood," Subner said, not looking up from the book he was reading, as usual in his spot behind the back counter.

"So you knew I was coming here today, then you know what I'm going to ask," Paris stated.

Papa Creola held up his hand, ticking off fingers. "Yes. Because. And you're not going to like it."

"I think I missed part of the conversation," Paris muttered, running her eyes over the hippie elf's stringy hair and trying to understand the riddle he'd thrown at her.

"Those are the answers to your questions," Papa Creola answered.

"Oh," Paris chirped. "So yes, it's true that I'm supposed to be the peacekeeper between the Seelie and Unseelie. Your answer to my question about why you didn't tell me is 'because.' That's annoying—"

"You're annoying," Subner interrupted.

"Drop dead, Subner," Paris remarked, not taking her eyes off Father Time.

"When you're around, I want nothing more," the grumpy store owner replied.

"And in regard to what I have to do to fix things between the Seelie and Unseelie, the answer is, I'm not going to like it," Paris said to Papa Creola. "What is it? Or is that in riddle form too?"

"You have to go to the king of Unseelie and ask him what he needs to mend things with Queen Helena MacGillie," Papa Creola imparted.

"But he's the angry sort and will try to kill you on the spot," Mama Jamba added, thumbing through a magazine on her lap, her legs crossed and foot bouncing. She was wearing a purple tracksuit and Skechers sneakers.

"I figured as much, if the Unseelie are the evil ones between the two," Paris stated. "I met the Seelie, and they were whacked."

"You're one to talk," Subner mumbled as if he was a part of the conversation and not reading his book—or pretending to.

"So, do you have a note that I can give King Hamish Abernathy that says not to kill me?" Paris asked Papa Creola.

"I don't," he answered simply.

When he didn't expand, Paris let out a loud, annoyed sigh. "Well, does anyone have advice on how I can stay alive long enough to find out what the Unseelie king wants to stop warring with the Seelie?"

"I don't," Subner repeated. "I say you show up and see what happens."

"Thanks, but that sounds like a death sentence," Paris remarked.

"I have something," Mama Jamba offered, setting down her magazine.

"Thank the angels." Paris sighed. "What is it? Does it involve a riddle or obtaining something impossible?"

"Take King Hamish Abernathy this." She held out her hand, and a large, green avocado appeared in her palm.

Paris blinked at Mother Nature, wondering why these two god-like people had to mess with her constantly. It was like their form of entertainment. "You want me to take an evil, murderous king of the Unseelie an avocado, and that's supposed to keep me alive long enough to ask my question."

"Yep," Mama Jamba said simply as if that was a suitable answer.

"Can I ask why?"

"Because long ago, I forbade the Seelie and Unseelie from having avocados by not allowing them to grow in their realm," Mama Jamba explained. "Since those fairies don't like to leave their bubble, they've gone without avocados."

"So you punished them by withholding guacamole from them. Is that right?" Paris asked, still half-believing this was a joke.

"That's right," Mama Jamba answered. "The Unseelie king adores avocadoes. If you bring this special one to him, he can plant the seed and avocadoes can grow there once more. He'll be so happy that he'll give you the minute you need to tell him who you are and ask your question."

"So why did you forbid avocadoes from growing in their realm?" Paris had to ask.

"Oh, because King Hamish Abernathy insulted me at a dinner party a few centuries ago." Mama Jamba looked into the distance and recalled the memory. "That rage-filled nincompoop said that the Big Dipper was a boring constellation and I could've done something a bit more elaborate."

She shook her head of grayish-blue curls. "I'd like to see him create a solar system and make every single star pattern create a shape. I mean, that was a Tuesday, and I was already spent from a busy Monday and the prospects of a busy week. Creating Orion's belt the weekend before had drained my creativity, so you all got the Big Dipper."

Paris nodded. "That settles it. I've lost my mind."

"You're figuring that out only now?" Subner muttered.

"So you took avocadoes away from the Seelie and Unseelie?" Paris asked.

"Yes, I did," Mama Jamba answered. "But I'm the forgiving type so I'll let them have them back. You tell that fairy if he insults me again—and I will know about it—I'll ensure that all that grows in his realm is Brussels sprouts. He loathes those delicious little cabbages."

"I might leave out that part since it sounds like the Unseelie king has anger management issues," Paris remarked dryly.

"Well, and besides giving him a second chance, if you die, that messes up a whole host of things," Mama Jamba added.

"I don't suppose you'll give me any heads-up on these things, will you?" Paris asked.

"You're important," Mama Jamba stated. "You've figured that out by now. But no, I'm not giving you any hints. I'll ask you to take this avocado so I can get back to my magazine."

Paris strode over and took it from Mother Nature with a smile. "Well, thanks. Wish me luck. It sounds like I have a crazy man to meet."

"That you do," Mama Jamba sang and pulled a handkerchief from the table stationed beside her. "Oh, and take this too."

Paris took the embroidered handkerchief, which had her initials G.P.B. as if it belonged to her. "Why do I need this? Is the Unseelie king going to make me cry?"

"Probably not," Mama Jamba answered. "But someone else will."

CHAPTER TWELVE

The Glowing Orchid seemed empty even with all the people in the plant shop. Astrid had cleared out many of the flowers that usually filled the space to make room for Hemingway's cake—which was enormous. Lee and Cat had done an incredible job, really bringing to life the design that Paris laid out for the bon voyage cake.

The round, three-layer cake was widest at the bottom and decorated with sea life, making it look like an under the ocean scene. They'd used blown sugar to create a surface that formed waves around the cake. On the two layers atop the ocean, a waterfall rushed down a mountaintop, cascading into the sea.

There were colorful plants and flowers that were unique in shape and appearance. It was such a visual masterpiece that Paris could hardly believe her eyes. The bakers had done it. They'd created a scene that showed the landscapes under and above the ocean.

"It's an unbelievable work of art." Hemingway's eyes were wide as he paced around the cake, taking it all in from every angle. There were so many details that Paris thought it might take hours to notice them all—but they didn't have that long.

"It's the most amazing cake I've ever seen," Astrid agreed, standing near a serving table stocked with napkins, plates, forks, and drinks.

"Lee, you and Cat outdid yourselves," Paris remarked, looking across the shop at the assassin baker. Her wife was still lying in front of the bakery, warding off paying customers.

Lee shrugged, picking her teeth with a toothpick and seeming disinterested in all those gawking at her creation. "I slapped it together."

"No, you didn't," Rudolf interrupted, shaking his head. "You were working on it for ages and kept saying that you had to do justice to Paris' design for the cake."

Hemingway whipped his head in Paris' direction. "You designed this cake? I thought it was Astrid."

Paris blushed, lowering her chin and averting his gaze. "She asked me to do it."

"Well, it made sense," Astrid stated. "She knows you best."

"That's true, especially after looking at this," Hemingway said, his gaze intently on her, although she refused to meet it still. "You couldn't have designed anything more perfect for me than this."

"I'm glad you like it," Paris said in a low voice, aware that everyone in the shop was looking at her. "It was really Lee's brilliance, though."

"The cake is Betty Crocker," Lee joked, still picking her teeth. "Oh, and when you slice into it, keep an eye out for a razor blade. I might've accidentally dropped one into the batter."

"Well, good thing I'm on a diet and not having any cake," Ramy stated with a shiver. "I don't want to die today."

Rudolf slapped him on the back. "I'm sure you'll make it through the day without dying, Ramy-Cans. Today, the only version of you that's going to die is that one." He pointed at the piñata that was hanging by a rope in the corner of the shop. It had an incredible likeness to Ramy. Apparently, that was King Rudolf's way of trying to cheer Paris up. At the last minute, he'd had a nearly life-sized piñata of Ramy made and filled it with candy.

"I'm not sure I like the idea of you all beating me." Ramy shook his head as he gazed at the large shape.

"Come on," Rudolf encouraged. "Everyone loves a piñata, and it isn't a birthday party without one."

"It's not a birthday party," Paris corrected.

The king of the fae waved her off dismissively. "Of course it is. It's the birth of something new. That ruggedly handsome man is taking a job, meaning that I have less competition for being the most attractive person on Roya Lane, and therefore the birth of more happiness."

Most chuckled.

"Leave it to you, Ru, to make this party about you." Lee pulled a large ax from a holster on her waist.

"Well, I tried to make it about Ramy since I know he didn't want to die today," Rudolf stated. "When I was trying to think of ways to cheer Paris up, I thought, who would she want to beat senseless? The answer was obvious."

"I don't want to hit Ramy," Paris argued.

"Even after I tell you that he's the one who gave Astrid the idea that she should hire Hemingway to seek out rare plants?" Rudolf asked, curiosity in his eyes.

Paris' mouth popped open, but she tried not to look unnerved by this admission.

"Really?" Hemingway looked between Ramy and Astrid.

"Well, like King Rudolf said," Ramy began. "When you're on Roya Lane, he gets all angry because he doesn't think he's the most attractive person here and he's a worse boss. So I thought if I got rid of you for good, my life would be easier. When you were staying on Roya Lane, he killed me every hour to let off some steam."

"Wow, I didn't realize that my looks were causing such problems," Hemingway joked, shaking his head.

"It's a curse I've lived with all my life," Lee said flatly. She held up the ax. "Ready to chop up the cake?"

"It's too pretty to cut," Hemingway said. "I want to preserve it forever so I can always look at it."

"Oh, it's a cake," Lee scoffed. "They're for eating. And I'm hungry and want to eat one of those dolphins." She indicated the cake where the sea creature was leaping out of the water, making an arch.

"How about we do the piñata first," King Rudolf offered. "That gives everyone more time to enjoy looking at the beautiful cake."

Lee narrowed her eyes at the ax in her hand. "Fine, but the next person who says something about the cake gets cut. If word gets out that I make such masterful creations, I'll have customers throwing gobs of money at me to make them something."

"I always tell everyone that your baked goods make me sick," Rudolf offered, picking up a bat and doing a practice swing with it.

"Thanks, Ru," Lee sang. "I knew I could count on you."

The fae handed the bat to Hemingway. "All right, although I would rather swing this bat at your pretty face, why don't you take the first hit since it's your party."

"I'll take that as a joke and not a direct threat." Hemingway chuckled, taking the bat.

"Take it how you want," Rudolf muttered. "Let's break Ramy open so you can high-tail it out of here."

Hemingway took the spot right in front of the piñata and held the bat to the side before swinging it cleanly at the stuffed Ramy's midsection. When it connected, there was a loud *crack* as the piñata swung through the air and back again, but it didn't take any damage.

"Wow, Ramy, you're tough to crack." Hemingway handed the bat to Paris. "You want to take a hit?"

"Sure." Paris averted her gaze as she took Hemingway's spot.

"Hit him hard," Rudolf encouraged. "It's a great way to get out emotion. Hitting the real Ramy is good for that too, but he also cries."

"You're so weird." Paris looked over her shoulder at the fae.

He shrugged. "Hey, he can't die, so why not."

"I can't die easily," Ramy corrected. "One day, my luck could run out."

Paris swung the bat through the air and hit the piñata, which she thought might be wood rather than cardboard or papier mache, which was the typical construction material. It flew toward the far wall and back, again not taking any damage.

"Man, you got a hard head, Ramy-Cans." Rudolf took the bat from Paris and handed it to the shop clerk for Heals Pills.

Ramy shook his head. "I don't think I can swing a bat at myself. That would be weird."

"Oh, don't be such a baby," Rudolf stated. "Maybe this will break your curse, and you won't die every day. If we kill piñata-Ramy, you might get the day off."

A spark shot to Ramy's eyes. "That's a good point. Okay, I'll give it a try."

"Hit it like your life depends on it," Rudolf cheered.

"After him, I'm going at it with this ax," Lee added. "I contend that bat won't do the job. Ramy is too thick."

"Okay, like my life depends on it." Ramy lunged low, holding the bat far over his shoulder. Then he wound up in a full circle and whacked the piñata with his likeness so hard that it shot in the opposite direction and knocked into the wall. Instantly and with great force, it swung back and raced at him. Ramy froze and didn't even duck as the large piñata rammed into him, knocking him to the floor where his head hit the side of the serving table, killing him.

"Whoa, is he dead?" Hemingway rushed over.

"Yeah, he appears to have hit the table in exactly the right place with his head." Lee looked down at the dead man's body. "Or wrong place. That takes talent. It's a hard pressure point for even a skilled assassin to find on a victim."

Rudolf sighed. "Well, it appears that Ramy has ruined yet another party with a senseless and totally avoidable death."

Lee held up her ax. "Speak for yourself, King Rudolf. Who wants cake?"

CHAPTER THIRTEEN

Everyone had left when Hemingway was pretending to sweep the floor of Astrid's shop for the third time. Paris had nothing left to clean so she was simply leaning against the door, waiting until he asked her what he wanted to. Currently, she was simply studying Hemingway and how he moved as he brushed the broom around the floor. She wasn't pretending not to watch him, and he wasn't pretending that he didn't notice her eyes on him.

Even with Ramy dying, the party had been nice...as nice as it could be with the notion that it was sending Hemingway away. The cake, when they'd finally hacked into it, was good. It was beautiful inside and outside, and thankfully no one got a razor blade in their slice. After Lee took a turn on the piñata with the ax, it had finally split open, and the flood of candy had rained down.

If the party hadn't been about Hemingway leaving and Ramy hadn't died, it might've been fun, but for Paris, the truth couldn't be shaken away with frosting from a cake and laughs after a piñata broke open.

She knew that the only thing that was breaking was her heart. Still, she reminded herself of the phrase on her locket from Uncle John that had reunited her with her parents: "You have to keep breaking your heart until it opens." Maybe the magical power of that phrase wasn't over, and Paris needed to keep breaking her heart...this time for others. She had to save the fairy godmothers, but why did that have anything to do with her heart and Hemingway?

"You had a question for me," Paris quietly began when Hemingway looked ready to start polishing the wood floors. She didn't want him to ask this question. She didn't want for the next part to happen because she knew it ended with goodbye. However, they couldn't delay any longer. Paris had to move on...there was a whole fate waiting for her.

Hemingway paused and pushed the broom to the side as if it had annoyed him as he sighed. He looked up at her with a raw truth radiating from his eyes. "Yeah, I have something serious to ask you. And I'm so worried about what you'll say."

"So no pressure, then." Paris tried to sound light but didn't feel it.

Hemingway nodded, leaning the broom up against the wall and quickly making his way back to her. Within seconds, his hands held hers in front of him, and his eyes stayed pinned on hers. Paris felt like she was being held hostage, not by the man before her but rather by her feelings. This was new. This was different. This felt like something she hadn't wrestled with before.

"Pare..." Hemingway's voice broke on her name. He swallowed and tightened his hands on hers. "I've needed to leave Happily Ever After College all my life. But it wasn't until I met you that I had the confidence to do so. Now, because of you, I want to see the world..." He paused.

Hemingway paused so long that Paris thought he'd finished speaking, and that was it.

So without an indication of more or a question, she squeezed his hands and forced a smile. "I want you to see the world."

He shook his head. "I want to see the world with you."

Her hands untangled from his without her realizing. It was a reflex. "I can't. I have school. Then I'll be assigned and—"

"You have school, but it will be over soon," he interrupted.

"You forget that I'm at Happily Ever After College fulfilling a sentence to erase my criminal record," Paris stated. "I have a service that I have to provide."

"Oh, come on, Pare. You've saved the fairy godmothers from Agent Ruby and fought a tooth fairy. You're going to settle the score with the Seelie and Unseelie and Loose Teeth College. I'm sure that after that, FGA will dismiss your record. Then you'll be free."

"And what?" Paris challenged. "What did you have in mind?"

"Well, I have this contract with Astrid," Hemingway explained. "I'm traveling the world on expeditions. I thought that when you could, you'd join me. We could see things together. We could go to Rome and Edinburgh and Bali and Paris… We could do it all together. We could be together."

Paris hated that moment. The one where she got everything she wanted, everything she thought she wanted, but then changed her mind and didn't want it the way she would have if she were who she used to be.

"Hemingway, I didn't think I wanted to go to Happily Ever After College," she began in a low voice. "I did it to keep Uncle John out of trouble. To keep me…"

"I know," he said at once.

"But now," she continued, "I've changed in a way I didn't expect."

"Oh…"

"Yeah," she went on. "I thought that creating love for others would be gross. But now, I can't think of a better mission in life."

"You want to be a fairy godmother?" he asked in surprise.

She shook her head. "No, I want something bigger than that, but I'm trying to figure out how to get there. My point is that I want to work for the fairy godmothers."

"So then you wouldn't want to travel the world with me?" Disappointment lay heavy in his voice.

"Hemingway, these expeditions finding rare plants is your dream…mine is different."

He nodded. "I shouldn't expect you to give up yours for me."

"And I can't ask you to give up yours to stay with me," Paris remarked.

"Then that means we're going in different directions," he stated morosely. "With no path back to each other."

Paris reached out, taking his dangling hands, gripping them with tenderness. "There can always be a path back to each other."

"How?" Hemingway asked with a sincere, lost look.

"I-I-I love you," Paris said, her words sounding so unlike her but right. "I'm in love with you, and I think it all started the moment I fell out of a tree, and you nearly caught me on my first day at Happily Ever After College." She laughed, thinking that he would too. That he'd say something. But he didn't. Hemingway simply looked down at the floor, his hands limp in hers.

Finally, he pulled his fingers from hers and slid them into his pockets, his gaze not meeting hers. "I better close up the shop for Astrid."

"But…" Paris didn't know what to say. She felt suddenly rejected. So hurt. So heartbroken. "Yeah, I get it. Well, goodbye…" Paris turned and made her way for the door, realizing there was nothing left to say if Hemingway wasn't going to reply. She reasoned that she'd misread things. Or that she'd hurt him by not taking his offer. They weren't in the right place at the right time. It wasn't meant to be.

Tears already spilled down her cheeks. Her heart already felt like it was shattering into a million pieces and falling to the floor at her feet. Each step felt like enough to end her, but Paris made her way to the door, knowing that Hemingway's eyes were on her back.

Not wanting him to see her cry, Paris held up her head and subtly glanced over her shoulder. "Good luck with everything, Mr. Noble."

His eyes were marked by regret when Hemingway nodded. "I'm going to need it, Miss Beaufont. Without you, I'll need more than luck."

Paris and Hemingway stole one last look in their peripheral vision. However, when he didn't say anything more and didn't return the sentiment she'd expressed—those three simple words—she turned and marched out of the shop, her heart breaking with each step.

CHAPTER FOURTEEN

It was obvious what Paris had to do at that point: drown herself in projects. Thankfully she had a lot to soak up her attention and keep her mind off her heart and its problems.

The clean Colorado air was a welcome relief when Paris stepped through the portal to the grounds of Little Pleasures the next day. She could hardly believe that the farm with its various buildings was the same plot of empty land that Mama Jamba had given her.

Hemingway had done as he'd promised and planted the seeds that Astrid had given to Paris. As promised by the Glowing Orchid's owner, the seeds were fast-growing and had quickly produced brightly colored vegetables and lush fruit trees. The berries were huge and plump, and the lettuce patch was overflowing with leafy greens.

Quiet and Maddy Laurens had made quick work of harvesting the ripe produce. It filled several bins that they'd transport to the farmhouse where Ainsley would transform it into the various recipes that Chef Ash had created for the menu.

Even more impressive than the farm that had seemingly sprouted overnight was the large farmhouse next to the trees. Rory had built it based on Chef Ash's design. Of course, Rory had done the heavy lifting, but it was Uncle Clark's renovation magic that made it possible to construct the two-story restaurant in such a short time.

The red house reminded Paris of a barn with its white trim and high, pitched roof. She half-expected a horse to poke its head out of the windows framed with shutters or a goat to jump onto the metal slat roof.

"You outdid yourself," Paris said to her uncle standing next to her, proudly surveying the house in front of them. She was astounded at the level of talent of the people around her.

"Thank you." Clark blushed. "It was nice to work on something outside of House of Fourteen business. Oh, but I did forget something important." He twirled his hand in front of him, and above the double barn-like front doors a sign appeared that read, Little Pleasures.

A pang of tenderness hit Paris in the chest. It was all coming together, and she could hardly believe it. The farm had produced not only delicious vegetables and fruits but ones with superior nutrition. Ainsley and Maddy were almost ready to open the restaurant.

Hanging plants dangling from trees and twinkling lights sparkling in the branches overhead filled the outdoor picnic area around the farmhouse. A cute little shop on the side of the restaurant that sold Heals Pills and produce and other things from the farm topped it off.

"I do have to warn you," Uncle Clark began in a cautious tone. "As I mentioned, renovation magic makes things a bit unpredictable. We didn't build the house so much as we grew it from spells mixed with materials."

"So what does that mean?" Paris tensed.

"It means that the house, like a living and breathing creature, has moods and feelings, and it reacts to its environment."

"But it is the environment," Paris argued.

He shook his head. "No, who's inside the house becomes its environment. The farmhouse, you might notice, is temperamental at times. If it doesn't like someone, it could eject them. Conversely, if it likes someone, it might not let them leave."

"I think I'll get in trouble if my restaurant is holding customers hostage or throwing them out without warning."

Clark gave her a sympathetic look. "Well, we were up against the clock, so I had to employ a lot of renovation spells, which means the house is more magic than it is wood and nails. I took the idea from the name and implemented many simple pleasures throughout the place. The house will smell different to each person. It will be whatever reminds them of fond childhood memories."

"That's amazing," Paris gushed, impressed by her uncle's skill.

He nodded proudly. "It's neat magic. I was also able to make the furniture so it conforms to the person's unique stature. So if a tall person sits in a chair, it will be higher and adapt for their body."

"Wow! That's going to make customers more comfortable."

"And," Clark said, drawing out the word and smiling. "The spell I'm most happy about is the 'right decision' one."

"Right decision? What's that spell?"

"Well, customers inside the farmhouse always feel that they made the right decision no matter what," Clark explained. "So they'll be happy with what they order, who they're with for dinner, or their reply to the conversations."

"I can't believe it," Paris remarked. "With spells like that at work, the farmhouse is going to love everyone inside it because all the customers will be happy."

"That was the goal, right? You wanted to create love, and this place is sure to do that. Get ready to really wow Saint Valentine."

Paris pulled her shoulders up to her ears, pressing her hands together. "I really hope so. My goal is that Little Pleasures creates love for people of all types—families, friends, and couples. But I fear I've bitten off more than I can chew."

Uncle Clark put his arm around her shoulders and pulled her in tight. "I think you went big and it's going to pay off for you big. You're a Beaufont, after all, and we don't do anything small."

"I hope you're right." Paris regarded the grounds with intense pressure but also a renewed sense of hope. When she rotated halfway around, she caught sight of Bermuda Laurens standing in front of the fenced-in area where they kept the animals. She was waving Paris over with a serious expression.

The giantess had said that soon the farm animals would be ready to go, and she'd let Paris know when that was. It appeared that they might be—which meant that Little Pleasures was almost ready to open.

CHAPTER FIFTEEN

"The animals are ready?" Paris asked as she trotted over to Bermuda Laurens.

The giantess nodded, unlatching the gate to the fenced-in area. "Yes, we have eggs, milk, and honey. Everyone appears to have settled in. They're happy with their new home."

"You were worried about the animals all getting along," Paris began, looking around for the creatures but not seeing any. "Are they okay together?"

"They are because they don't know each other exists," Bermuda explained. "I wrestled with the idea of putting them together, but sometimes it's better to have borders and keep those who will fight away from each other."

"Why would they fight?"

"Well, because the drunken cows, as the name suggests, are always drunk and therefore a bit belligerent," Bermuda explained. "My observation is that they're angry drunks instead of happy ones because they're large and can't move easily."

"I'm not sure I'm following you," Paris stated. "We have drunk cows? Are you feeding them whiskey?"

"Of course not." Offense filled Bermuda's expression. She peeled back a flap to a large tent and waved for Paris to follow her. "The cows are naturally always buzzed based on their magical DNA. Because of that, they produce milk that has a very high alcohol content. We can use it to make all sorts of drinks that are both nutritious and also have the inebriation effect."

As Paris' eyes adjusted to the darker tent, she saw a row of stalls. In each one was a black and white cow eating hay or lounging or completely passed out. One was on her stomach and belching what sounded like the alphabet.

"Those are drunken cows?" Paris pointed at the farm animals. "They're all drunk?"

"Yes," Bermuda answered. "Which is why we're not going to make this tent a place that customers can visit. A drunken cow can either be your best friend or worst enemy depending on their mood, so it's better to keep them away from others. Quiet will milk them each day and will be the only person allowed in here."

"Okay." Paris followed Bermuda back out of the tent, glad to get away from the deranged cows. Although it was pretty funny that the patrons of Little Pleasures could have a white Russian cocktail without Paris stocking any liquor.

"Over there in the coop, we have the surprise chickens." Bermuda indicated a small building that looked like a replica of the farmhouse.

"What?" Paris watched as a normal-looking chicken poked its head out the front of the coop, stalked down the ramp, and began pecking around the yard. "How is it a surprise? It seems normal to me."

Bermuda shook her head. "Does no one read the updated version of my book, *Magical Creatures*? The sixtieth edition was published a few days ago with details on surprise chickens."

"I've been a bit busy," Paris replied.

Bermuda *harrumphed* and grabbed a seemingly normal egg from a basket hanging on the side of the pen. She handed it to Paris. "Go ahead and break it."

Paris took the egg and gave the giantess a confused look. "Won't I have a bunch of egg mess to clean up?"

"Oh, do what I said, would you?"

Shrugging and turning to the post closest to her, Paris tapped the eggshell against it until she heard it crack. Then she pried it apart with both hands, expecting a thick liquid to spill out. What Paris didn't expect was for a small stalk of broccoli to fall from the shell.

Stunned, Paris turned the two pieces over, thinking the egg had to be in there still. However, the shell was empty, the green stalk of broccoli sitting on top of the post.

"Surprise chickens," Bermuda said simply.

"In each of those eggs is something different?" Paris pointed at the basket.

"Yes, and it's always a surprise," Bermuda confirmed. "I figured you can serve them at the beginning of patron's meals and they can get a nice surprise. Well, hopefully it will be nice. I guess it depends on whether they like what they get."

"That's incredible." Paris picked up the stalk of broccoli. "Are the surprises edible?"

"Try it for yourself." Bermuda encouraged Paris to take a bite. She did and was again surprised by the crunch and authentic flavor of the broccoli.

"Wow, that tastes like the real thing."

Bermuda rolled her eyes. "That's because it is." She strode for a set of boxes on the other side of the tent.

Paris squinted in the direction of the large white boxes, wondering what she was looking for. Something black swooped through the air, flying past her and disappearing into a hole in the side of a box. The creature's wing had grazed Paris' face, making her duck suddenly.

Covering her head, she looked up at Bermuda. "What was that?"

"A bumble bat," the giantess answered. "They're harmless but don't like the surprise chickens, so it's best to keep them on opposite sides of the yard."

"Why don't they get along?"

"Because they're both winged creatures and they're always in direct competition."

Paris nodded. "And the cows are offensive. It seems like these animals need therapy."

"They do not," Bermuda said at once disapprovingly. "They simply have a lot of ego due to their magic. The same thing happens to magicians."

Paris ignored this. "So the bumble bats, what do they do?"

"Isn't it obvious?" Bermuda said as another small black creature streaked through the air and disappeared into the white box. "They make honey."

"Wow, bats that make honey." Paris was impressed. "What's the special thing about the honey? Does it make patrons happier or healthier or sweeter?"

Bermuda pursed her lips. "No, it's regular honey made by bats. Things don't always have to be unique."

"Right," Paris chirped. "Well, this is amazing. Thanks for all your help setting up the animals. I'm sure Quiet will have his hands full with them and tending to the farm."

"Quiet is more than capable of managing it all," Bermuda stated. "You'll have a tough time replacing him when the time comes."

"Yeah, after I graduate," Paris said, remembering that Mama Jamba had told her that Ainsley and Quiet would only help until she launched the restaurant. Then she'd have to find employees to replace them. "I guess it will all depend on how they grade me on this effort. The final project is crucial for graduation."

"Get ready to write your ticket into whichever department you want at FGA." Bermuda sounded proud as she looked around the farm. "I suspect that this venture is going to be wildly successful, creating so much love."

CHAPTER SIXTEEN

W illow had advised Paris on where she should go once she entered the Seelie and Unseelie realm. She'd offered to go with her to meet with King Hamish Abernathy, but reading the hesitation in the headmistress' eyes, Paris had declined. She reasoned that if the king was likely to kill her on the spot without the avocado, they shouldn't push their luck.

Paris was supposed to negotiate peace between the Seelie and Unseelie, not Willow Starr. The headmistress had her hands full trying to track down leads on the evil tooth fairy dropouts.

So far, there'd been rumors of sightings of three goth fairies on Zhuang Alley—a place full of criminals and illegal magic. The crafty lawbreakers were always moving the magical street's location, making it difficult for the House of Fourteen to track it down. Paris' mother and father had offered to devote their efforts to it, but she didn't think the Knees were hanging around there.

Therefore they'd enlisted Mortimer at the Official Brownie Headquarters to keep an eye out for the three criminals. Hopefully, it was only a matter of time before they were in custody and turned over to the Seelie queen. Then peace could reign once more between the fairy godmothers and the tooth fairies, and the Fang Wellspring would offer only pure, good magic. Win-win-win.

In the meantime, wanting to stay busy and keep her mind off her thoughts, or rather her emotions away from her heart, Paris decided she'd visit King Hamish Abernathy. Papa Creola had said she wouldn't like what the Unseelie king requested to end the war with the Seelie, but Paris wasn't going to get any closer to getting it until she found out what it was.

Not wanting to rely on a hot air balloon or a dragon every time she needed to get to the vortex on the far side of the Bewilder Forest, Paris moved the medicine wheel. She hadn't known that was an option, but Mae Ling suggested it.

It stood to reason that with the Bewilder Forest connected to Paris, it would bend to her will—so she simply intended that the medicine wheel was inside the entrance to the Bewilder Forest, close to the Enchanted Grounds. It was a risky move since it meant the tooth fairies or the Seelie or Unseelie could come through and attack Happily Ever After College without the issue of crossing the forest.

However, it was a risk the fairy godmothers had decided to take. Hopefully, they'd be mending ties with the tooth fairies. Paris was working presently to end tensions between the Seelie and Unseelie. During all her peace negotiations, she couldn't be trekking across lava pits, sunflower fields, and juniper forest to get to the different realms.

Paris was still surprised when she entered the Bewilder Forest that afternoon to find the medicine wheel with the four quadrants sitting inside the line of trees. The large circle of stones on the ground seemed out of place in the shady forest, but it was close, and Paris was grateful that she didn't have to hike to reach it.

She still couldn't get over the idea that the Bewilder Forest was her —in essence. That meant, if she really wanted to, she could make it do almost anything. The thing was, she didn't know what she wanted it to do. Mae Ling explained this was also trickier than she would expect. It was like the human body. People could control theirs, but that didn't mean they did.

Often, bodies were a result of people's unconscious thoughts. So it was with her forest, Paris realized when she looked around, feeling like she was in a haunted woods. Although the sun was shining overhead, it was dark, and the trees filled with ominous glowing eyes.

Paris decided that she didn't want to meet any of the creatures the eyes belonged to. She knew she was in a dark place in her life, having been rejected by Hemingway and facing failing her graduation projects. She didn't need a reminder of the stress by meeting her subconscious in the Bewilder Forest in the form of goblins and ghouls.

Quickly, Paris took her spot on the vortex quadrant that led to the land of the Seelie and Unseelie, the avocado in her hands. She hoped the fruit was enough to keep her alive. Having been in the strange fairy realm once already, Paris knew that her challenges started well before she met the Unseelie king. Although Willow had advised her on where she could find King Hamish Abernathy's court, getting there without incident wasn't likely.

CHAPTER SEVENTEEN

L ike the first time Paris had visited the strange land of the Seelie and Unseelie, snow falling from the purple sky greeted her. That would've been bizarre on its own, but it was falling on beautiful green grass and spring flowers and fertile land with lush trees where it melted immediately. The temperature was warm like a hot summer day, although the snow made it feel like winter.

The land when Paris stepped through the portal was as diverse as the weather with rolling green hills around her, snowcapped mountains in the distance, a stream that jutted back and forth and disappeared over a cliff to the west, and a dense forest to the east. Where she'd come through at the vortex door, there was desert sprinkled with cacti of varying sizes and shapes.

Unlike the first time, Paris wasn't surprised when she heard a patch of daisies passionately discussing education reform at the local level. Their little faces showed their interest in the subject as their argument got more heated.

Paris averted her eyes from a pair of bunnies playing Yahtzee, heeding Willow's warning that they were gamblers. They'd try to get unknowing visitors to play with them, but the furry little creatures cheated, taking everyone's money.

According to the headmistress, the most harmless animals were the raccoons, although they could always be found smoking in a tree. To Paris, this was a health and a fire hazard, but according to Willow they kept to themselves and didn't try to trick others.

Also, from her first visit, Paris knew to ignore the owls, who were pathological liars. It seemed like a psychedelic world where one should expect the unexpected. Paris shook off the strangeness and made her way to the stream, which should lead to the Unseelie court, to Willow's best recollection.

It didn't fill Paris with a lot of confidence that she was taking very uncertain directions to find a place where the king might kill her on the spot. She tightened her grip on the avocado, nearly laughing at the strangeness of her life depending on the existence of a fruit.

When Paris was close to the stream, she noticed something poke its head out. Reflexively, she tensed, ready to defend herself. She thought she should be on guard once she realized what was peering at her from the water's surface. However, then the alligator raised its head out of the stream and grinned awkwardly at her. If that wasn't strange enough, then it was what the creature said next.

"Well, if it isn't a Beaufont. Am I glad to see you! I'm starving!"

CHAPTER EIGHTEEN

"I'm sorry, not sorry, but you can't eat me." Paris backed away from the stream, putting some distance between her and the massive alligator.

"Oh, I'm not going to eat you," the strange talking alligator said.

Hadn't everyone been paranoid about Faraday because animals weren't supposed to talk? Paris had met a lynx who waxed on about philosophy, a dragon who told bad jokes, lying owls, and now a strangely pleasant-sounding alligator. Apparently, that rule on talking animals didn't apply to her experiences.

She tugged the avocado closer to her. "Well, I'm sorry, but you can't have this. It's not for you."

"Oh, I'm not starving for food," the alligator replied good-naturedly. "I'm starving for conversation. My name is Smeg, and I love to talk, and here, well, conversations are dangerous. The owls tell me things that tend to be wrong. The bunnies are always wheeling and dealing. Don't even get me started about the daisies. Geez, they always have some political agenda they're going on about. Why can't we discuss simple things like interstellar colonization on a small-scale location?"

"Yeah, really," Paris muttered sarcastically. "How do you know that I'm a Beaufont?"

"Well, you look like your mother, Liv," he answered. "Or is your mother Sophia? You look more like Liv."

"Wow, you have quite the eye to have noticed the resemblance," Paris replied, impressed. "Yes, my mother is Liv Beaufont. I'm Paris."

"Pleased to meet you, Paris Beaufont. Besides the resemblance, only a Beaufont would venture into the Unseelie realm, knowing that they don't welcome outsiders. You all are very brave."

"So you know my mother and my aunt?" Paris felt very strange talking to the alligator.

"Oh, yes. They're both excellent conversationalists. Your mother and I had a very stimulating discussion on antidisestablishmentarianism. What are your thoughts on church and—"

"Although I'm sure this will be an interesting topic, I'm on a mission right now and can't talk," Paris interrupted, feeling remorseful when the strange alligator craved conversation.

"Of course," he croaked. "You're a Beaufont. Of course, you'd be on a mission. If I can offer any help, Smeg is at your service."

Paris sighed, grateful for the friend she'd found. She trusted him because he really couldn't have made all this up and did seem to know her family. Only her mother would have a discussion with a talking alligator about antidisestablishmentarianism and probably while on a dangerous mission.

Paris pointed ahead, the way the stream flowed. "Is this the way to the Unseelie court?"

"Why yes, but you really shouldn't go there," Smeg answered. "I know you must be brave and strong like the other Beaufonts, but King Hamish Abernathy is a mean ruler who will try to kill you before you even take a breath in his court."

Paris held up the avocado. "I know. That's why I brought this."

The alligator's eyes widened, and Paris thought it was because he didn't believe that an avocado could save her. Then something leapt over her shoulder in a blur, grabbed the avocado from her grasp, and dove into the stream—disappearing under the surface.

CHAPTER NINETEEN

"What?" Paris exclaimed. "That was my avocado."

"Which is why the stupid lutrinae stole it." Smeg instantly sounded defeated as he started to mope.

"The what?" Paris looked between the alligator and where the thief had disappeared into the water. "Who stole my avocado?"

"It was a lutrinae," Smeg repeated. "You probably thought they were otters, but they're magical creatures that are part that and part human. More importantly, they're thieves who will steal anything they think someone else wants."

"I needed that avocado so I don't get slaughtered when I go to see the Unseelie king." Paris knelt and looked into the water below, hoping to glimpse where the otter-thing had disappeared.

"Well, I can try to draw them out if you like," Smeg offered. "I mean, I'm not a match for a lutrinae, but I can try to use my intimidation factor."

Paris regarded the alligator with contempt. "You're a cold-blooded predator. How can you not be intimidating to an otter?"

"I'm not the violent type," he explained. "I'm a vegetarian because I don't like hurting innocent animals."

Paris sighed, realizing that of course, she had to meet the only vegetarian alligator in existence. She shook off the frustration, already vibrating with stress over losing the avocado to a thieving otter-slash-human. She hadn't gotten a good look at the creature, but it had seemed entirely like an otter. Hopefully, she'd get a closer look…when she was giving the jerk a knuckle sandwich.

"Yes, can you please dive and try to find that lutrinae and scare it up here?" Paris asked in a rush.

"I'm on it, Paris Beaufont." Smeg disappeared under the surface, making the water splash upward.

She scanned the stream, looking for movement below. The seconds felt like hours as Paris waited to see something break the surface. She didn't want to consider what she would have to do if she lost the avocado. It was a special one, given to her by Mama Jamba. She didn't think the older woman would be too happy if she had it stolen from her…by a strange creature.

A head popped up a few feet away in the middle of the stream. It wasn't Smeg. At first, Paris didn't know what it was. It took her a moment to realize what she was looking at. The head was brown and covered in fur like that of an otter's. However, it had a human child-like face. That's where the similarity to humans began and ended.

Pulling its body up and lying on the surface of the water, the creature held the giant avocado in its webbed paws. Paris was about to use magic to retrieve the object when another head popped up several yards away. She expected it to be Smeg, but it wasn't.

To her horror, it was another lutrinae. The creature held out its paws as the alligator surfaced between the two sea animals. Then, as though playing a dumb game of keep away, the first lutrinae volleyed the avocado through the air in the other's direction.

The fruit passed over Smeg's head before colliding into the paws of the second otter-like animal.

"Oh, come on, guys!" Paris pleaded. "Give that back! I need it!"

In a strange show of grace and agility, Smeg jumped into the air when the avocado passed over his head again. However, his efforts weren't successful, and the first lutrinae grabbed the avocado.

Paris gritted her teeth and was about to use a telekinetic spell to grab the fruit when Smeg swam fast in the thief's direction, making water go all over—obscuring the scene. Heart racing, Paris almost launched herself into the water. She had to get that avocado back. But currently, she didn't know what was going on with all the splashing and thrashing around.

"Get it, Smeg! I'll talk to you for ages!" Paris yelled, trying to make herself heard over the commotion.

The other lutrinae had disappeared under the water's surface, and Paris watched as the current indicated the creature was retreating in the opposite direction. Smeg and the thief appeared to be wrestling. Paris hoped the nonviolent alligator was okay. She'd spied claws and fangs on the lutrinae, similar to ones that an otter would have.

The two creatures disappeared, and the splashing ceased at once. Paris held her breath—as if she was underwater too. She searched for movement. They appeared to be moving in the stream but not as close to the surface anymore.

Paris pictured that Smeg and the lutrinae were wrestling close to the bottom. She knew that the alligator was larger and stronger, but the otter-like creature would be faster and more agile, able to maneuver out of positions and dodge attacks.

The waiting was starting to get to be too much and again, Paris considered diving in. However, in the Unseelie realm, who knew what flesh-eating creatures could be waiting to attack her.

Paris straightened suddenly when something large shot up over the water and nearly landed on the bank by her feet. To her relief and total astonishment, the talking alligator had the avocado gently pressed between his teeth, offering it to her.

CHAPTER TWENTY

"Thank you so much!" Paris exclaimed, taking the avocado from Smeg's mouth and wiping the drool off it and onto her jeans.

"You're very welcome." He panted. "How could I not with an offer for conversation? Those mean lutrinae are so rude, always taking things that don't belong to them for the thrill of it."

Paris held the avocado in both her hands, looking around for another thieving otter-like creature. She indicated the stream that snaked toward the Unseelie realm. "You want to accompany me most of the way? Then we can talk like I promised."

"Yes, of course." Smeg dove back into the stream, his tail swishing behind him as he began to swim. "What should the talk be about? The meaning of life? Life after death? Our favorite foods?"

Paris laughed, striding along the stream, keeping an eye out for potential enemies. "Quite the diverse discussion topics. Whatever you'd like to discuss."

"I think I was an earthworm in my past life," Smeg began. "I always dream that I'm burrowing in soil and have an inexplicable affinity for composting."

"That's interesting," Paris remarked.

"What do you think you were in your past lives?"

"I never really thought about it."

"You should start observing the things that are compelling to you," Smeg advised. "I took a class on past life assessment, and it's a fascinating thing. Do you realize that all of your experiences from every past life are locked in your subconscious, and you can access them through deep meditation?"

"Wow, I didn't. I hope that in one of my past lives I was a quick-talking negotiator because I'm going to need it for this interaction with King Hamish Abernathy."

"You seem to speak really well, so I think you'll do fine," Smeg offered. "And you have your avocado so that will hopefully buy you some time and goodwill from the Unseelie king."

Paris was walking at an even pace, realizing that she wasn't in a hurry to get to the actual court. Still, she realized as they came to a huge stone archway surrounded by dense trees that she'd arrived. It was time to find out what King Hamish Abernathy wanted to end the war with the Seelie. She gulped, offering Smeg a tentative look.

The strangely thoughtful alligator winked at her and grinned. "Good luck, Paris Beaufont. Hopefully, we shall meet again soon. I look forward to more stimulating conversations with you."

Paris tried to reply but found her mouth dry and her throat tight. She simply nodded, waving at Smeg as she continued forward, entering the Unseelie court.

CHAPTER TWENTY-ONE

S kinny, bendy trees filled the darkness behind the stone archway. Although the trees were devoid of leaves, they blocked out the light overhead, casting Paris in blackness. Low fog clung to the ground, making it difficult to see the path. However, Paris noticed a clearing up ahead. As she neared, she spied stone walls, similar to the archway she'd passed under.

The sounds of panting and cries of despair met Paris' ears as the fog cleared and a stone path met her feet. The trees disappeared as Paris stepped into a courtyard with three walls, very similar to the one where she met the Seelie queen. Along the walls were fairies all dressed in dark clothes—wearing hostile scowls.

Paris took in the sights at rapid speed. Unlike the Seelie court, this one appeared to be more a part of the forest, the branches overhead creating a ceiling of sorts. Many of the closest fairies pulled swords and pointed them at Paris. A lion sat casually in the corner, his mouth open and a man's head inside it. Three fairies were dancing on the far side of the court—as if their lives depended on it. In the center of the space stood one of the most attractive men Paris had ever seen.

King Hamish Abernathy flashed her a murderous glare and Paris felt a cold chill cut through her as if his gaze could stab her. Before he could give the order to kill, she thrust her hand into the air, holding the avocado, and yelled, "Don't kill me. I bring gifts."

CHAPTER TWENTY-TWO

Everyone in the Unseelie court froze. Paris held her breath, her hand shaking as she held the avocado over her head. The lion's eyes slid to gaze at her, a casual look on its face like it didn't have its mouth gaping open and a man perched beside him with his head between its jaws.

The three fairies kept dancing although there wasn't any music and sweat was pouring down their red faces. The other Unseelie around the court all held weapons pointed in Paris' direction, but no one attacked. Their eyes flickered between Paris and the king.

He wore a black velvet suit with long tails and a high collar. His jet-black hair came to his chin and was swept to the side, partially obscuring his forehead and one of his piercing blue eyes. His pale skin contrasted against his black suit and his pointed chin lowered as he regarded Paris with keen interest, his black wings fluttering at his back.

"Is that an avocado?" His Scottish accent was thick, like how Queen Helena MacGillie sounded.

Paris nodded. "Yes, it's from Mother Nature. She said that if you don't kill me, you can have it and she'll forgive you. You can take the seed and plant it in your land and have avocados once more."

"Why?" he asked with a sharp growl. "Who are you to trespass into my court? Your kind isn't allowed in our realm."

"I know." Paris was distracted by the man shaking as he uncomfortably stood with his head in the mouth of the lion. "Queen Helena MacGillie has permitted me to enter because—"

Gasps ran around the area as the fairies continued to level their weapons at Paris.

"You dare to say that revolting name," King Hamish Abernathy spat, shaking his head. "Who are you? Tell me at once. Make sure it includes why you smell like something different."

"I'm Paris Beaufont. I'm a halfling who is both magician and fairy."

He sniffed the air. "That's not all. There's something else about you."

"I have demon blood."

At this he smiled wickedly, showing fangs like a vampire would possess, and nodded to his court, making them lower their weapons. "Oh, how very nice. Why are you here, Paris Beaufont? The avocado has kept you alive thus far. Let's see if it stays that way based on your reasons for trespassing."

"I'm here because Father Time has foretold that I'm the one to stop the war between the Seelie and Unseelie."

This produced more gasps from around the courtyard—these more horrified than the last.

"What if I don't want the war to end," the king stated matter-of-factly.

"Well, that's why I'm here," Paris began, finding it hard to focus with the three fairies dancing and doing a very poor job of it like their legs were about to give out on them. "I'm here to find out what it is that you need to end the war with Queen Hel—I mean with the queen of the Seelie. There must be something that will end the dispute."

"You brought me this avocado from Mama Jamba as a gift?" King Hamish Abernathy asked. "So I'm supposed to let you live and answer your question regarding a truce, is that right?"

"I think that was the idea," Paris said, finding it hard to concentrate.

King Hamish Abernathy noticed her distraction, her eyes skipping between the dancers and the lion with the man's head inside its mouth. He chuckled, amused. "Go on, then, but before we proceed, ask your burning questions regarding the activity in my court while I consider my terms of ending the war."

Paris didn't know if it was a good idea to challenge the Unseelie king on why three fairies seemed ready to dance themselves to death or why another looked close to getting his head chomped off by a lion. However, her curiosity, as it was prone to, got the better of her.

CHAPTER TWENTY-THREE

Paris pointed at the lion with its mouth open. "I'm sure there's a perfectly reasonable answer, but why does that man have his head inside the lion's mouth?"

The Unseelie king snickered, pressing his hands behind his back. "Is that your only burning question?"

"Well, I also wonder why those three are dancing nonstop and look ready to pass out." She indicated the three fairies on the far side of the court.

He nodded, seeming to have expected that question. "I'm a man of efficiency and therefore wanted all your questions at once since their answers are a part of the same thing." King Hamish Abernathy grimaced in the direction of the dancers. "Those three losers are my court poets. I asked them to write me something so very sad that it brought me pure despair."

Paris nodded. "I get that. Sometimes I turn on West Coast folk music and lie on my bedroom floor, wallowing in my pity over the self-destructive poetic lyrics regarding lack of worth and fear of rejection."

She was totally sarcastic, but the Unseelie king apparently didn't have a radar for such a thing. A sadistic smile graced his pink lips. "You and I could make beautiful music together."

"I don't play an instrument," she said at once with a sad sigh.

"These poets are a disappointment as well." He grimaced in their direction, their feet hitting the floor repeatedly, but no grace in their movements. "They all wrote me rubbish poetry that didn't make me feel one ounce of sadness."

"So their punishment is to dance," Paris guessed.

"Their punishment is to dance happily for as long as I tell them," he answered. He clapped his hands in the dancers' direction, and fake smiles full of pain sprang to their faces suddenly. "There's a fine line between happiness and sadness, so I believe that once they've graduated from true bliss, they will fall into the depth of sorrow."

"Flawless reasoning." Paris turned her attention to the lion and man. "And the reason for this? You said the answers to my questions were part of the same thing. Did he also write a rubbish poem?"

"No," King Hamish Abernathy answered sullenly. "Wolfgang wrote me something so sad that I wanted to kill myself. Alas, I can't do that, so he will have to die."

Paris took note that the Unseelie king punished those who failed and succeeded at what he wanted. One couldn't win with this guy... but she needed to. "It seems that he did what you asked him to. If you kill him, you might only feel worse."

"I do not think that is possible," he said morosely, looking off as if trying to plan a funeral. "Since I'm a man of efficiency I decided that since Wolfgang needed to die that he'd be the lion's dinner—he's sure to be hungry soon. Once he is, then he simply has to close his mouth, and Wolfgang is no more."

"Although I'm a fan of efficiency, maybe we get the lion a steak, and Wolfgang is assigned to write you something that perks up your spirits," Paris offered. "You wouldn't want to get rid of a talented poet."

Wolfgang was simply vibrating, the precarious position with his head inside the lion's mouth no doubt uncomfortable.

"But I don't want to feel better," the king whined like a lost school child. "I just don't want to feel as sad as his poem made me. There's a fine line."

"Right," Paris chirped. "You mentioned that before."

"That was the fine line between happiness and sadness!" he exclaimed suddenly. "Don't taunt me, demon halfling."

Everyone in the court fell deadly silent. Paris tensed. The dancers kept dancing.

"I didn't mean—"

"The range of emotions is a map, and they all border each other," King Hamish Abernathy interrupted her. "You can't live in two lands at once, but one must simply take a step to find themselves in a new place."

Paris didn't think this was a good time to say she was bad at geography so she averted her eyes to the dancers who were starting to fall into each other. They looked ready to pass out.

She couldn't fathom how long this had been going on or how much longer it would. Paris knew she had to stop this torture, although King Hamish Abernathy didn't appear to be the type for compromise. That meant peace negotiations between the Seelie and Unseelie might be more difficult than she envisioned.

Although she was sure that other horrible acts went on regularly in the Unseelie court, Paris simply couldn't leave knowing that she hadn't done something to stop that which she witnessed. However, she also reminded herself that the fairies in this realm chose to be there.

According to Willow, these weren't the solitaries who had split from the Seelie and the Unseelie. The ones that remained in their original land liked the whimsical nature of the place and the arbitrary laws created by the rulers. Also, they gave up certain freedoms to have a life of indulgence and debauchery—something that wouldn't be allowed in the regular world.

Regardless, Paris was going to do something to save the four fairies currently being tortured—even if they'd brought this on themselves. She didn't know what it would be.

"Have you considered," Paris began, thinking out her approach, "that you might feel worse if you kill Wolfgang? Maybe give him another chance to write a poem with the right level of sadness."

King Hamish Abernathy shook his head. "Killing someone always makes me feel better." He then looked around the court of fairies—all of their attention on him. "Tell me, peasants, when will you ever get a second chance from me?"

In unison, they all dropped into low bows. "Never, our lord, since we are unforgiving of such things," the fairies sang together, a nice chorus of voices despite their words.

Sorry, Wolfgang, Paris thought, her eyes flicking to the dancing fairies. She didn't know how she was saving them either if second chances weren't allowed.

"You feel sorry for them," King Hamish Abernathy observed, seeming pleased by the idea.

Paris bolstered herself, shaking her head—knowing that pity wouldn't help the fairies. "No, not at all. I simply think their dancing is bad and a bit distracting. I can't even remember why I'm here...I'm so put off by bad moves."

"Should I kill them then?" King Hamish Abernathy asked. "That's the idea anyway. If they stop dancing, they die. If they don't stop dancing, they will die."

"Clever," Paris said, deciding to focus on saving the Seelie at the very least. She held up the avocado. "So you can grow this fruit once more. Would you like to have it?"

"Of course." He combed his hands through the air. "Hand it to me, and I'll tell you my terms for ending the war with that repugnant, self-indulgent, tyrannical little witch of a queen."

Paris pulled the avocado back to her chest, her instinct leading the way. She knew that crossing the Unseelie king in his court was dangerous. However, she'd come all this way and had to use the leverage she had. She was, after all, watching his people dance themselves to death and lay their heads in the mouth of a lion. If she wasn't a bit cautious, she might end up regretting it.

"First, I want you to tell me your condition for ending the war," Paris stated, holding the avocado to her chest.

Many of the drama-hungry fairies in the court gasped again—since that was their favorite reaction, it seemed.

Paris rolled her eyes and cut off the Unseelie king before he could object. "If I hand this over, you'll have what you need and no reason not to kill me or answer the question I risked my life to come here for. So at least you'll tell me the terms, and we'll agree on me delivering them. Then I'll give you the avocado, and you'll allow me to leave here, knowing that you'll get what you asked for. Otherwise, the war will wage on...that will be our agreement. Understood?"

If her boldness put off King Hamish Abernathy, it didn't surface in his blue eyes. Instead, a delighted smile whisked to his mouth. "What makes you so confident that I won't have my court seize you at once and take the avocado from you that I so desire?"

Paris huffed like she was hot stuff. In actuality, she was scared to her core and shaking inside, but she knew better than to show it. Now was the time to talk a big game and beat King Hamish Abernathy at his play. "I'm a halfling with demon blood. You haven't met anything like me, I assure you. So do you think your court stands a chance against me?"

"How am I to know?" He casually shrugged.

"Well, how many others have strode into your court and risked their lives?" Paris challenged, still trying to keep her voice neutral.

"None, so you might be a match for my court," he countered. "But few have something I want so desperately." His eyes flicked to the fruit in her hands—or at least that's where she thought they landed. "I'll do anything to get my hands on what I want."

"Well, I got this back from a lutrinae so I think I'll take my chances at this point." Paris tried not to sound flustered.

The Unseelie's eyes widened. His mouth popped open. Many around the court looked around in alarm. Even the dancers paused, but only momentarily.

"The lutrinae are back!" King Hamish Abernathy exclaimed. "This means war! I want my best soldiers out there, hunting those thieves immediately!"

CHAPTER TWENTY-FOUR

Paris expected many members of the court to rush from the area, carrying their weapons. She expected that the Unseelie king would order the strongest man of them to go after the naughty lutrinae. What she didn't expect was that the lion would back up, gently pulling his mouth away from the head of Wolfgang and work to try to close his jaw, like it was difficult to shut after all that time open.

Then the lion shook his mane like a dog after a bath, his tail also flying in the air.

"Sawyer," King Hamish Abernathy said, addressing the lion directly.

The lion blinked at him—definitely at attention.

"You are to go and hunt down the lutrinae," King Hamish Abernathy ordered. "Do not return until you've killed every one of those creatures."

Without a growl or a motion of acknowledgment, Sawyer majestically marched toward the entrance to the court and away.

Wolfgang crumpled to his knees, obvious relief flooding his being as he sank to his hands, huffing and puffing after having his breath stolen by the giant lion.

Not taking notice of the relieved court member, King Hamish

Abernathy turned his attention back to Paris with a delighted smile. "Well, it seems that you're more help than one would have anticipated. I had no idea that the lutrinae had dared to enter our lands. That means we'll have extra meat at our feast tonight."

"So you don't like the lutrinae," Paris guessed.

"They stole my dignity on more than one occasion," he answered.

"And here I thought they went after handheld objects," Paris muttered.

"The little beasts take that which is of most value," King Hamish Abernathy continued, not having heard Paris. "Those monsters once stole all the ammunition from our weapons the night before a battle. Do you know what happened when the Seelie marched up with their white flag, ready to declare surrender to us after two hundred years of battling and we went to shoot them down cold?"

"Nothing," Paris guessed.

"Nothing," King Hamish Abernathy stated like she hadn't already said it. "My soldiers pulled the triggers, and there was a round of *clicks*. The queen of awfulness thought we'd accepted her terms of peace. Thankfully, I had a cannon the lutrinae hadn't gotten to and fired it at the unarmed men, killing many on the spot, winning the battle."

"I bet you felt great about yourself," Paris remarked dryly over the king's laughter.

"I did," the Unseelie king said, still laughing. "Anyway, I've been looking for a way to get rid of the lutrinae and punish them for their misdeeds ever since."

Paris was starting to feel bad for the Seelie, being tortured by the evil Unseelie for centuries. However, Willow had said they weren't so different. Opposites, yes. But they were two parts of a whole, one more extreme than the other. There was something she didn't fully see about the situation, and she would need to know more before she could negotiate peace, she reasoned.

"So can you tell me," Paris began. "what started this feud between the Seelie and Unseelie? More importantly, what will it take to resolve it?"

CHAPTER TWENTY-FIVE

The king of the Unseelie snapped at Paris—a loud commanding sound. "I've had enough of your demands. Give me the avocado, and you won't die. That was the gift given from Mama Jamba in exchange for your life, was it not? I will promise not to kill you...ever. How about that? The avocado is quite the gift, I will admit. However, I don't have to answer your question about my feud or what I want to end this war."

He was right, Paris thought. The avocado was to grant her entrance. She didn't have any way to make King Hamish Abernathy answer how to make a truce with the Seelie. For that, she'd need something more, she realized.

Paris stepped cautiously forward, drawing in a measured breath, and held out the fruit for him. "Fine, but Mama Jamba also offered the avocado in exchange for me to ask my question. You don't have to answer it, but here is my promise if you do—I will find a way to grant your request to end the war, one way or another."

That was a huge wager. Paris knew it. But she was turning over her bargaining chip.

"So all I have to do is simply answer your question, and you'll find a way to give me what I want?" King Hamish Abernathy took the avocado, eyeing it hungrily for a moment. "That's all? What's the catch?"

"There isn't one," Paris stated. "I can't resolve this war unless I give you what you want to fix things and I can't do that unless I know what it is. Papa Creola told me that much. So unless you help me out, I can't proceed…and I need to proceed."

"Why?" he asked bluntly. "Why do you want to intervene with us?"

"Well…because it sounds like you've had a senseless war for centuries and many have died," Paris answered. "My job as a fairy godmother will be to promote love. I can't do that unless I end war and suffering and all the things that come from it. So this is part of my job…and also, my demon blood makes me want to end battles, rather than promote them."

"That sounds really annoying," he spat.

She nodded. "It can be. I don't sleep a lot."

The Unseelie king was quiet for a moment while he considered things. The dancers were still going, their arms knocking into each other and their faces flooded with sweat. They looked past the point of exhaustion.

"You're telling me," the king began in a slow, calculating voice, "that I simply tell you what I want to end a war that means no consequence to you and you'll do whatever it takes? That's it? You don't need anything in exchange?"

Paris didn't think it was necessary to tell the mischievous king that she'd promised Queen Helena MacGillie that she'd put all her efforts into this. Instead, she decided to play a fairy game and use her leverage. "Look, I don't have a lot to benefit from your war halting. However, if I must make demands, I will."

"After careful consideration, I feel that you must," he answered. "I'm going to tell you what I need to end a long war that doesn't concern you. You've promised to give it. How can I trust that you'll honor it unless you first request something of me? Only then, and once I've given it to you, will I know that no matter what, you'll honor what I want for a truce."

Paris couldn't believe it. She'd gone from nearly getting killed to the Unseelie king asking what her demands were in exchange for his own. She swallowed, straightened, and let out a long breath.

"So be it," she began. "But I don't have one demand to fulfill yours to bring peace."

"Oh?"

Paris shook her head. "No, I have two."

CHAPTER TWENTY-SIX

G asps echoed around the court. Paris turned and scowled at the fairies. "Oh, would you get a new reaction to things? That's getting a bit old."

"I've been telling them that," King Hamish Abernathy admitted, suddenly sounding bored. "Maybe I should kill them all on the spot."

"No, I don't think that's necessary," Paris said at once. "Order them to have different and varied reactions."

He waved dismissively at the court of fairies. "As she said, have diverse reactions. Huff or exclaim or make whispered remarks."

"What?" someone said in shock.

An exasperated breath shot from someone else.

At the back, two fairies whispered tersely to each other.

"Good on you all, taking direction," Paris called over her shoulder to the court of Unseelie.

"These two demands," King Hamish Abernathy said, bringing her attention back to him. "What are they?"

Paris turned to him. "I ask them of you, and you'll honor them without question?"

He nodded, almost too quickly, a smile hiding under his eyes. "Yes, and in exchange, you must do whatever it takes to honor mine to create a truce with that horrid queen."

"Sounds like you're well on your way to creating peace," Paris said dryly.

He waved. "We will be. All she has to do is give me the one thing I want."

"Which is?" Paris asked.

The Unseelie king shook his head. "Oh, no, you first. You make your demands. Then me."

"Fine," Paris replied. "The first is that they stop dancing." She pointed at the fairies, who looked like their legs were close to breaking.

Quickly she added, "Nothing happens to them. They simply get to stop dancing, but no other bad punishment for their bad poetry."

King Hamish Abernathy glanced at the fairies and pursed his lips. "Is that all?" He waved his hand dismissively as if pulling a spell from the Unseelie. They all staggered and nearly fell to the floor. They caught each other and moved off into the crowd, not wanting more torture.

"Fine. They stopped dancing. Like I care...although I'm bored now without any entertainment." He looked around the court. "Will someone else do something I disapprove of so I can make you do something to entertain me that's cruel?"

Paris took a step forward, blocking the Unseelie king's vision. "No, and I have another request, so let answering that be your entertainment."

"Fine." He appeared uninterested. "Let out with it. What's your second demand?"

"Tell me why you're battling the Seelie." To her annoyance, everyone in the court gasped—as if they were very, very slow to learn.

CHAPTER TWENTY-SEVEN

"Seriously?" Paris held her arms wide and turned to face the court of Unseelie fairies. "I thought the king informed you to come up with unique reactions. No more gasps."

"We don't ask about the reason for the war," one of the nearby fairies muttered.

"It's true." A woman leaned forward.

"No one knows why we battle the Seelie," another informed Paris.

She turned, crossed her arms, and regarded the Unseelie king with annoyance. "Your people have been battling the Seelie for centuries, and they don't know why?"

He drew in a breath and simply nodded. "They don't ask questions since they prefer to live."

"That's crazy," Paris argued. "How come they put their lives on the line every day without knowing why?"

"Because they love me," he answered.

"Fear," Paris corrected. "You're confusing the words love and fear."

"They love what they fear," he said, waving her off. "It's semantics."

"Not really," she stated. "My request is to know why you're battling the Seelie and also what you want to end the war. Those are the terms of our agreement. Then I'll get you whatever you want."

"Fine," he stated matter-of-factly, regarding his nails like they might need a manicure. "But my terms have changed."

Paris scoffed. "You can't change the terms!"

"Of course I can," he said simply. "We haven't started to honor the agreement. We're still ironing out the details. So now that I know what you want, I'm changing what I want."

"That's really conniving," she said, narrowing her eyes at him.

King Hamish Abernathy laughed indulgently. "Yes, I know. But I didn't realize you'd ask for so much."

"So much?" Paris questioned. "I'm asking to know what it will take to end your war with another party and why you're warring with them. My job will be to give it to you. I don't see how I'm asking for a lot."

"It seems that this means a lot to you," he countered. "So you'll give me two things in exchange for your two requests."

The Unseelie king was protecting himself, and Paris knew it. However, he'd called her out. This meant a lot to Paris. She'd promised to do this for Queen Helena MacGillie.

If she didn't resolve things, she couldn't get the Seelie queen to clean the Fang Wellspring for eternity. Without that, the battle between the tooth fairies and godmothers wouldn't end. Paris had to give the Unseelie king what he wanted, and she'd prepared to do that. She only hoped it wasn't going to cost her more than she had to give.

CHAPTER TWENTY-EIGHT

"Okay, fine. You stopped the fairies from dancing as I requested. So it seems that you should tell me what you need to end the war." Paris put her hands on her hips with a defiant expression.

The Unseelie king wagged his finger, also with a look of defiance. "Oh, no, no. You get what you want first. That's a gentleman's way. Tit for tat. And you want to know why we war the Seelie after hundreds of years."

"Well, yeah," Paris remarked. "It seems like it would be important to know…and maybe help in all this."

He pressed his hands together in front of him. "It might in fulfilling my second request."

"Sounds like a riddle," Paris replied dryly. "Are you going to tell me what you want?"

"Not yet," he said simply. "But I will tell you why I've long slaughtered the Seelie—"

"Or rather had your fairies do it," Paris interrupted.

A grin sprang to his lips. "I like you, Paris Beaufont. Few would be as bold as you. Fewer would live to hear me say that. But you're different."

"Flattered," Paris said blandly. "So I requested two things. None do

I benefit from. However, the Unseelie dancing badly isn't burning out my eyes any longer, so that's nice. My second request, why do you war with the Seelie?"

"Isn't it obvious?" he asked.

She shook her head. "I've had fruit meant to save my life stolen by an otter-thing and saved by an alligator of sorts, so excuse me if I draw a blank on the answer to your question. Can you tell me?"

"What is the reason for all wars waged?" he asked.

"Money? Politics? Sports?"

King Hamish Abernathy let out a breath. "The reason behind those is the one I'm getting at."

"I'm blonde," she stated. "Can you tell me and not play the guessing game?"

"You're smarter than you look," he countered.

"Thanks..."

"The reason that for hundreds of years I've waged war on the Seelie and refused to stop is simple, Paris Beaufont. It is because of love."

CHAPTER TWENTY-NINE

The court of Unseelie, who apparently wanted to see if Paris would go on a murdering rampage, gasped once more.

Seeing the annoyance on her face, King Hamish Abernathy pointed at them, his eyes on Paris. "I can kill them if you so desire."

"I think they need acting classes." Paris shook her head. "Like, give them a few more reactions in their arsenal. Maybe let them out of the Unseelie realm now and again so they get some diverse experiences. There's only so much one can learn from a bunch of gambling bunnies and goth friends."

"You think we should socialize with those blonde-haired do-gooders?" King Hamish Abernathy was offended.

"I've met the Seelie and wouldn't put them in a class of saints," Paris remarked, combing her hand over her chin and putting it all together. "So Queen Helena MacGillie..." She waited and watched the anger rush to the king's face, quickly followed by hurt and frustration. Then Paris dared to speak again. "She broke your heart, didn't she?"

"I have no heart," he murmured, but the look on his face contradicted his words. "She betrayed me, and for that, every year, I ensure that she suffers."

Of course, it was love that had broken apart the Unseelie and

Seelie. That was the fine line—it was between love and hate. It had created a war. But it was possible to mend it, and Paris hoped she really could do it. That would be the ultimate test as a fairy godmother in training.

"Her people are the ones who suffer," Paris began, "But she wants this truce with you, so she's obviously suffering too."

"She does?" King Hamish Abernathy said quickly, then covered his surprise with a stern expression. "Well, of course, she does. She's losing. More so each year."

"Then tell me what you need to end this war," Paris requested. "You have two demands. What are they?"

"I will tell you one," the Unseelie king stated. "But the other, well, you must simply guess."

Paris let out a frustrated breath. "These are things you want me to deliver to you and without them—"

"Without them, you don't get what you want, Paris Beaufont. If I don't get what I want, this war doesn't end."

Paris gulped. How did it come down to ending other people's problems to get what she wanted? Her life was incredibly strange and complex. "Fine, King Hamish Abernathy. What do you need to end this war?"

CHAPTER THIRTY

"I need Queen Helena MacGillie to give me two things," he stated with confidence.

They were getting somewhere, Paris thought. At least the Unseelie king was saying the Seelie's queen's name instead of calling her names.

"Okay, and the first one," Paris stated, knowing that he was only going to tell her one and the other would be a fun guessing game—if by fun one liked headaches and complex riddles.

"The first is that I want her to give me someone unique, as a gift," he answered.

"Did you say someone?"

"I did," he stated. "I want her to give me someone so unique that there is no one like her in the world."

"Again, did you say her?"

"I did," he repeated. "I want a halfling."

Paris gulped, not liking how this was going. "Halfling? Like half-fae and half-mortal? I know where the queen can find one of those."

He shook his head with a grin. "No, I'd like someone so unique that there's no one quite like her. And I don't want her to be only a halfling."

"What else?" Paris pretended to joke. "Also a vegan? Maybe a Capricorn? I don't know anyone like that."

"I want a half-magician, half-fairy who also has demon blood."

Paris didn't even grace this with a gasp like the Unseelie court would have. She simply groaned. "That's me. You want the Seelie queen to give you me. Can I state that's more than sadistic for a few reasons?"

"Why would you say that?" he sang, sounding to be enjoying this.

"Well, you're telling me that what ends this war is that the Seelie queen gives you me," Paris explained. "But you're telling me that, which means you could simply capture me. Then you have what you want."

He shook his head. "You forget this is about creating goodwill. About mending things. You and I, well, we've established that I won't harm you since you brought me the avocado. I can't capture you and keep you as a pet."

"Thank the avocado gods," Paris joked, not feeling humorous but trying to fake it.

"However, Queen Helena MacGillie...well, she can take you, a lowly fairy godmother, and turn you over to me as a gift to ease the wounds of war," he stated.

"So to end this bloody war, you want a halfling with demon blood as a trophy, given to you by the Seelie queen? Is that right?" Paris reiterated as if she was a waitress taking his order.

"That's right," he answered. "Are you going to tell her that's what I require?"

"Not a chance," Paris said at once.

He grinned on cue. "Then it appears that the war will continue."

"You don't want this to end, do you?" Paris accused. "Because you know that if I told Queen Helena MacGillie what you wanted to end the war, she'd realize that what Papa Creola's prophecy meant was that I'm the bartering chip. Then she'd capture me, give me to you, and you two would be happy forever after and your realms would live in peace. The last thing you want is to be happy and have peace, am I right?"

"Oh, look at the fairy godmother thinking she's got me figured out." He narrowed his bright blue eyes at her. "Yes. If you're how this ends, then it won't end unless you sacrifice yourself."

"You're a sadistic fruitcake," Paris said, causing the Unseelie court to gasp behind her.

She spun. "Oh, would you all shut up!"

"They think I'm going to murder you for your insult," King Hamish Abernathy said behind her.

She rotated. "But you won't because you know that I'm going to wrestle with being your prisoner so your and the Seelie realm will have peace. I gave you the avocado. You somehow want me to fix things with you and Queen Helena MacGillie, but you don't really, which is why you've made it almost impossible."

"It's not, though." He wore a wicked grin. "Just give yourself to her, and she'll give you to me as a peace offering."

"Easy-freaking-peasy," Paris sang sarcastically. "So since you've made this so easy, why don't you pony up the other thing you want from Queen Helena MacGillie to end this war."

He shook his head. "Oh, no. A deal's a deal. I'm not giving you that one. But I will tell you that if you get to the point where it will matter, that backstabbing, betraying Seelie queen will know what I want."

CHAPTER THIRTY-ONE

"An apology," Mae Ling said at once as Paris strode back and forth in Willow's office at Happily Ever After College.

"Of course." The headmistress tapped her feather quill on her desk. "Queen Helena MacGillie betrayed him. Who knows when or how long ago. The war between the Seelie and Unseelie has been going on forever. Those two are so prideful that I'm sure she was unwilling to apologize. It sounds like she did something to offend him."

"What are the chances she'll apologize?" Paris paused her pacing.

"Well, if there was one, she would've probably done it decades ago," Willow answered.

"It's not like it matters because as much as I want to help, I'm not going to live in a cage in the Unseelie realm for their peace," Paris declared.

"King Hamish Abernathy is afraid of a resolution," Mae Ling stated. "As you said, he's fearful of the dispute ending because then he'd be reunited with his lover, and sometimes it's easier to be alone than open one's heart."

"So those two have warred for centuries because they're afraid to love one another?" Paris questioned.

"It's not so strange," Willow explained. "Many do similar things to protect their heart. They're simply waging war on the battlefields of their hearts. But they truly love each other. Otherwise, they wouldn't keep it going. So we have to figure out a way to get them to forgive and mend their hearts."

"Well, we need new terms and conditions," Paris huffed. "Because me as a peace offering isn't working."

"I agree," Mae Ling stated. "Although you must be a part of it still. Papa Creola said so."

"He might've been throwing a curveball at us," Paris offered.

Mae Ling shook her head. "I don't think so."

"But the apology," Willow muttered, thinking. "That's another puzzle. I don't think Queen Helena MacGillie will apologize easily."

Something suddenly occurred to Paris. "What if she thought she was losing King Hamish Abernathy for good?"

The two fairy godmothers looked up at Paris in confusion.

"It sounds like she lost him long ago," Willow argued.

Paris shook her head. "No, because she's always had his attention. Yes, it was on the battlefields or when they were exchanging cannon fire, but they've been throwing their attention at each other for centuries. They knew they cared about each other because they spent all their efforts fighting. You only battle what hurts you, what you care about.

"What if Queen Helena MacGillie realized that making peace included two options? Either she gave him a peace offering, and he went away, never to terrorize her or her people again. Or she also apologized, and they were able to start anew.

"My guess is that the queen doesn't want to lose the king. Otherwise, she would've conceded defeat long ago. She wants him. She's not battling him. She's fighting *for* him. It's just that they speak a really messed up love language. It's our job as fairy godmothers to interpret it and get them saying something together that's a bit more functional.

"They want to be together. I know it. Otherwise, they wouldn't be going to such efforts. So we get the queen to see it, and she'll apologize because she doesn't want to lose her king."

"That makes perfect sense," Willow mused, her gaze off in thought.

"But we don't have the peace offering," Mae Ling stated.

"Yes, we can't have you sacrifice yourself," Willow said adamantly.

Paris nodded while chewing on her lip. "Yes, I haven't figured out that part yet, but there has to be a way."

Mae Ling gave her a hopeful look. "If anyone can figure it out, I have faith it will be you."

CHAPTER THIRTY-TWO

The morning sunlight seemed different when Paris stepped onto the Enchanted Grounds of Happily After College the next day. She didn't think anything had changed about how the rays of light slipped through the trees and spread across the grassy lawn. Paris knew deep down that things appeared different because she was different—nothing on the college grounds had changed...not really.

That night was the opening of the farm-to-table restaurant. Paris had tons to do, but she ignored the to-do list reciting in her head and made her way out over the green lawn, deciding she needed some time to meditate before everything demanded her attention.

The observatory in the distance looked the same as it always had— even after the Knees had graffitied it. Glancing over her shoulder, Paris glimpsed the entrance to the Serenity Garden, and it was also back to its new normal. She laughed, thinking of when Faraday had gotten himself trapped in there with the magitech waitstaff, turning the garden into something new.

That had been a dangerous affair, but everything had turned out for the best in the end. The fairy godmothers had realized they couldn't keep the AI butlers and maids imprisoned. They had to put them out of their misery.

As Paris walked, she spotted the stables to the left of Mirror Lake and guessed the large red building was the same as when she'd first entered Happily Ever After College. Thankfully her demon blood had excused Paris from equestrian studies since the horses sensed it in her and didn't like it. She never liked the idea of riding an animal...well, besides Lunis on the rare occasion. Oh, and Magnus the gargoyle, or George as Faraday liked to call him.

Her gaze drifted over to the tree that she'd magically climbed to survive a stampeding stallion. That had been moments after she'd been set free to stroll the Enchanted Grounds on her first day at Happily Ever After College. Before that, Paris hadn't ever climbed a tree since her Uncle John had raised her on Roya Lane.

The smile fell from her mouth as she remembered what happened after escaping the raging horse. That's when she'd looked down from the tree and laid eyes on Hemingway Noble for the first time. He seemed surprised to find a fairy godmother in training hanging out in a tree...in combat boots. Paris was surprised by how captivated she was from the first moment she looked into his eyes.

Her gaze drifted to the greenhouse, where Rory Laurens would be teaching that day's Magical Gardening classes. Paris wouldn't be attending—she had too much to do. She also didn't think she would if she didn't. Being in the greenhouse and having a gardening instructor who wasn't Hemingway, well, she wasn't ready.

The jack-of-all-trades for Happily Ever After College would be long gone on an adventure hunting down magical and rare plants for Astrid. Who knew where his travels would take him? Paris knew she could know firsthand and be by his side, but that wasn't the life she wanted. Without knowing it and to her total surprise, she wanted to work for FGA. A sentence she'd taken to get out of jail time had turned into her dream job, and she couldn't be more stunned by the events.

She was grateful that Hemingway had wanted her to travel with him. That's why she thought the words "I love you" were appropriately timed. If she couldn't be with him, at least he'd know how she felt about him. Apparently, he hadn't felt the same way. *Apparently, he only wanted a travel companion.* The pain of rejection twisted her heart.

Shaking off the emotion, Paris turned her attention to the Bewilder Forest—the place spawned by her blood. It was her forest. If she graduated, she'd be leaving it behind.

Paris spun in a full circle taking in the Enchanted Grounds, the various buildings, and the mansion in the distance. If Paris graduated, which she hoped to, she'd be leaving behind all of Happily Ever After College.

When she and Faraday stepped through the portal on that first day, she never expected to one day think of this place as her home. She never thought that she'd be sad to leave it one day. To Paris, she was simply fulfilling a requirement to stay out of further trouble. Although she'd fulfill her sentence after only a year or so, Paris hoped that didn't mean her time with the fairy godmothers was up.

She drew in a breath, enjoying the fresh spring air, although it was autumn outside the bubble that was Happily Ever After College. Paris didn't know what the future held for her. There were the prophecies, but even those were always in flux.

However, the one about her saving the fairy godmothers had been somewhat accurate already. She'd fallen in love and gotten her heart broken. It also said she had to graduate from Happily Ever After College and much of that would depended on the results of the restaurant opening that night.

Then there was her fate tied to the Seelie and Unseelie. Paris had never expected to be the one to create peace between the warring fairies. The twist that it would require her to give up her freedom and be a trophy of sorts to King Hamish Abernathy was the biggest shocker. Paris still didn't know how to approach that one. Everything was muddy, but she hoped that in time, things would become clear.

For now, Paris had her hands full. She needed to get to Little Pleasures and ensure that everything was running smoothly. Then if she had time, she might put on the new leather jacket her parents had sent for the occasion and comb her hair...the last part was doubtful. But she wanted to wear the new coat. It would be so much better than the frilly gown she'd have to wear if invited to the graduation ceremony. With all her heart, even if she had to wear a lacy dress, Paris hoped that soon she'd pass Happily Ever After College and become a fairy godmother...or something similar.

Saying a goodbye of sorts in her heart, Paris looked out at the quiet Enchanted Grounds. Students would be rousing in the mansion, many of them late risers. Paris didn't sleep much before and especially now. On that morning, it had allowed her to enjoy the quiet on the grounds of Happily Ever After College—a peace that she'd sorely miss when her life moved her somewhere else.

Paris closed her eyes, trying to imprint the scenery she'd seen in her mind's eye. She tried to memorize the way the gentle spring breeze caressed her skin. She tried to bottle a bit of the magic that was Happily Ever After College in her soul.

"Pare! Pare!" Faraday yelled. "We have a situation!"

CHAPTER THIRTY-THREE

Paris' eyes sprang open to find Faraday bounding across the grounds toward her, his puffy tail flying behind him like a flag.

"What is it?" Paris hurried in his direction, meeting him halfway.

The talking squirrel paused, panting and hunched over, trying to catch his breath.

"Is everything okay?" Paris looked between Faraday and the school, searching for one of the Knees or smoke or other signs of danger or an attack.

He nodded, his paws on his hips as he huffed, looking close to hyperventilating.

"Is anyone hurt? What's the situation?" she asked, frantic.

He held up one of his claws, indicating that he still needed another moment to catch his breath.

"You're really out of shape," Paris remarked, realizing that Faraday would have run a short distance from the mansion to reach her. "Maybe you should do a bit more cardio and fewer science experiments."

"My...science...experiments...are...important..." He panted between words.

"Okay, well, maybe we get you one of those treadmill desks," Paris joked. "That way you can create chemistry projects while clocking some miles."

"I don't think it would be safe to pour hydrogen fluoride while running on a treadmill," he seethed, apparently having recovered.

"You falling over from your tiny heart exploding also isn't safe," Paris argued.

He shook his head. "Not to mention that the movement could cause something like a piranha solution to combust."

"Again, trying to keep you from combusting," Paris stated. "Maybe at least lay off the cheese. Have you thought about going vegan like all your relatives?"

Faraday let out a long breath, his cheeks puffing out as if he'd stored nuts there. That wouldn't be the case though, since he was allergic. "My relatives were English, not squirrels."

"Okay, well, now that you don't look like you're going to pass out from a brief stroll across the grounds—"

"I ran down the roof from the third story of the mansion," Faraday interrupted, indicating the open window over an overhang. "Then I ran all the way here."

"Wow, you're like a parkour squirrel, jumping down the eaves of the roof like that," she teased, unable to control herself. "I didn't know you had those kinds of skills."

He offered her an annoyed glare. "And I ran all the way here."

She nodded, gauging the distance between her and the house. "Wow, a whole ten yards. You want to lie down?"

Faraday shook his head. "No, I ran down here, nearly breaking my neck climbing down the mansion—"

"Something that all other squirrels can do without breaking a sweat or hurting themselves," she cut in.

"I risked my life," he continued sternly, "to tell you that I think I've located the organization that made the undefeatable drones."

"Great job," Paris stated. "How do you know it's them and not a military base or a lab company that creates pharmaceuticals or a nuclear plant or some other kind of place that emits a lot of energy?"

"Because when we ran into the drones, I recorded their key defining components, then I isolated them and created a—"

Paris held up her hand, pausing the squirrel. "I'm a little pressed for time today, squirrel. Can we skip the scientific mumbo-jumbo and get to the part where you start speaking English?"

"I tagged the drones like one would a dog with a microchip," Faraday stated. "My tracking system has found the kennel where they hang out."

"See, it's not that hard. Congrats. I know this project has meant a lot to you. Can we schedule a time in the next few weeks to visit these doggies and do some reconnaissance on this place?"

Faraday shook his head adamantly. "That's the thing. When I found the location on the satellite, I did a bit more investigating and discovered an infrastructure anomaly suggesting there were loads of gamma rays radiating from—"

"Sorry, not sorry to interrupt, but again, I'm opening a business today," Paris cut in. "If you could give me the scientific explanations for dummies, that would be ideal."

"Gamma rays bad," he stated flatly, looking beat down.

"They're covering the dog kennel?"

"Yes, and my hunch is that they're remnants used to create something really bad..."

"Like, worse than the drones?" Paris asked.

"Yes, and from what I can tell, the facility has been recently abandoned," Faraday explained. "They even left behind the drones..."

"Well, it sounds like they had a nuclear meltdown," Paris stated.

"Maybe, but I'm not so sure. I think we need to go there right now and investigate. Find out what they created."

"Not that I don't want to waltz off to a place and swim in radiation, but remember that whole part where I told you that I have a big day? I'm launching my restaurant—tonight."

"I know, Pare. It's just that my instinct tells me this is really important. The longer we put between now and when we investigate, the more information we risk losing. If we get there now, we might discover what they were working on. If we wait, they might come back and destroy evidence. They might clean it up."

"Yeah, but there's that whole getting radiation poisoning problem," Paris countered. "I mean, it sounds like they left the facility for a reason. It's probably glowing with electro-whatever."

"Electromagnetism," he corrected. "I doubt it. But it will be dangerous. However, we know what we're working on. With my help, you can put a protective spell on us that will keep us safe, at least for a little while. Hopefully, that's enough to get us in there so we can look around."

"Fare...you know I want to help but—"

"You trust me, right?" he cut in.

"Of course, but I've got the final project, and I'm supposed to be looking for the Knees, not to mention that I have a huge problem with the Unseelie I haven't even told you about. This isn't the right time for me to go gallivanting on a side mission."

"It won't take long," he urged. "I promise. We portal there. Investigate, and we'll be back in time for me to put on a maître d' uniform. I'll help you at the restaurant. I'll do whatever you need. Please. I really think this is important. I know the timing isn't ideal, but my gut tells me that if we don't go now, we'll lose our chance."

Paris gave the squirrel a measured glare. It wasn't like Faraday to use words like "gut." He was scientific and calculating and didn't do things based on feelings. But something was radiating in his big brown eyes that Paris couldn't ignore. This was important to him, and that meant it was probably crucial to the world. Faraday's curiosity usually led him to essential places—albeit dangerous.

"Okay, fine," she said after deliberating. "But you're wearing a top hat and a monocle at the restaurant tonight."

He nodded victoriously. "You got it, Pare. I'm sure this won't be dangerous, and we'll be back in plenty of time."

"I highly doubt that, but I don't doubt that this will be supremely important and probably save others."

CHAPTER THIRTY-FOUR

Twenty-four hours earlier...

W ires snaked between three different gurneys. The three tooth
fairy dropouts lay lifeless on their beds, IVs plugged into
their veins delivering them magitech drugs, but that's not what would
bring them together. The drugs were part of making them one
person.

The magic from the Fang Wellspring was key. The demon blood
would be a component. The biggest part, Dr. Conrad Madden knew,
was the element that rained down overhead.

A strike of lightning lit up the sky. A moment later, the thunder
crackled all over the heavens, a companion to its predecessor.

The mad scientist threw his chin up to the sky, his mouth opening
wide as he laughed loudly—victoriously. His open eyes watched
through the lab's glass ceiling as the lightning streaked in different
directions. His arms spread out overhead, his back arched in victory.
This was his dream realized—finally, he'd brought something real to
life.

Even though fusing the two fairies and the magician had taken all
of the resources of Madden Operations, it had been worth it. Dr.

Conrad Madden was pretty sure that tonight's experiment would ruin the facilities, but it would be worth it. This was a scientific milestone.

As a magitech scientist, Dr. Conrad Madden had done many things. He'd created genetically altered monsters and indestructible drones and medicines that healed with dire consequences, but he'd never made a halfling with demon blood.

Tonight was unprecedented. Tonight would be the night that Dr. Conrad Madden made history—even if no one knew about it—and hopefully no one did.

The best part of the mad scientist's experiments was that no one knew to attribute credit to him. If they did, he'd be locked up. He'd be hunted. They'd try him for his crimes. But Dr. Conrad Madden was best at one other thing besides creating evil technology—escaping.

The sky finally went dark after the last of the brightness from the lightning died away, and with it, the power in Madden Operations blew out, one light at a time at first until the entire facility was dark.

Dr. Conrad Madden knew it. His empire, the facility he built on an island, was now dead. It was only a matter of time before the Fang Wellspring that was currently pouring into the main stage inside the lab would overflow, combined with the electromagnetic field he'd harnessed.

He always knew this would destroy the place—and he didn't care. The point was to create—to prove he could reign. Soon he'd get to where he was doing it all on his own, not commissioning projects for others to do so. Soon would be Dr. Conrad Madden's time...but not yet.

The lightning struck overhead once more, as he'd projected. It showed the canister of dark magic from the Fang Wellspring on the lab counter as it drained and spilled down into the IV. The fluid entered the tarp-covered body in the center of the lab, which connected to the other three.

No one knew what the magician and two fairies with demon blood would be, but Dr. Conrad Madden suspected she'd be horrible. Powerful, yes. But terrible, for sure. Would she be like Paris Beaufont? No. She'd be powerful, like her...

But otherwise like her, no.

She'd be the opposite.

The three Knees would make something very different when combined with demon blood. That was the thing. When you took the same ingredients and put them together scientifically, they created something different than if constructed organically.

An explosion rocked the opposite side of Madden Operations, making the island shake. The place would blow at some point. The level of electricity was too much. Dr. Conrad Madden could stay to see what came of his creations, but he couldn't risk it. He was pretty sure that his monster in the center of the room would kill him on the spot. She would kill anything that moved based on his calculations. She'd be devoid of reason. The best thing he could do was unplug the main source and flee the island, getting as far from it as possible. It wouldn't blow right away, but it would soon...

Running toward the covered body in the center of the lab, Dr. Conrad Madden reached out and grabbed a plug connected to the center of the platform. He didn't dare to look at the body under the sheet, although he was curious what form the three Knees would take when fused. He hoped that he could spy that from afar. For now, he had to get away before the monster awoke.

Dr. Conrad Madden turned and ran for the boat stationed by the docks. There was another one for the monster, but she wouldn't need it. She'd have powerful magic and be able to teleport at will if he'd done his job correctly, which he believed he had.

His chest ignited with anticipation as he ran for the boat. Dr. Conrad Madden simply couldn't believe what he'd accomplished. It didn't matter that he was running past a facility he'd founded that would soon sink into the ocean.

He simply couldn't wait to see Madden's monster, as he was calling her. She would be powerful. She would be incredible, a fusion of three parts. She would be ruthless.

CHAPTER THIRTY-FIVE

Twenty-four hours later...

"WHY do I get a distinct impression that this this place is about to blow?" Paris asked when she stepped through the portal onto the island. It quaked like lava was boiling under the surface and about to launch the small plot of land into the air, into a thousand tiny little bits.

There was a huge metal warehouse in the center of a small beach. Around it, smokestacks overflowed with green steam, and strange spindly equipment sat in place. The place didn't seem mortal, and it was definitely off the grid. Most importantly, it appeared that it was about to blow up from the inside out and take everything with it out of this world—Paris and Faraday included.

"Because I fear that it is about to blow." Faraday scurried forward like a deranged creature, sprinting for the facility that was smoking and shaking as if it might explode at any moment. "I think we have at least ten minutes by my calculations."

"Ten whole minutes," Paris joked, striding after the squirrel, keeping up easily. "Well, then, I'll take a squat and catch up on my email while you check things out on this definitely not suspect patch of land."

Faraday glanced over his shoulder as he continued forward. "Don't you dare, Pare. You stay with me. We're going to figure out what's going on here. Then we'll be gone before the radiation reaches lethal levels." He paused, glanced at a device in his paws, and nodded with confidence. "Yes, we have nine minutes and forty-seven seconds. Then we have to portal out of here because this place is going to blow then."

"I hope your calculations are accurate or I'm going to kick your furry butt."

"If my calculations aren't correct, you won't have to kick my tail." He entered the facility that was billowing with smoke, wires sparking, and machinery blowing steam into the air. "If I'm wrong, you'll have to take it up with me in the afterlife."

Paris glanced at the sky as they ran. "Oh, for the love of the angels. Should I kill him now or wait until we're safely back just to be ironic?"

CHAPTER THIRTY-SIX

"I really hope your calculations are correct, squirrel," Paris remarked when they entered the facility. She covered her mouth with the sleeve of her jacket. The chemical smoke in the air was thick, burned her eyes, and smelled strange.

"It's accurate." Faraday yelled to be heard over the furnace of noises around them as machinery seemed ready to blow. "This looks worse than it is."

"Worse than it is?" Paris asked dryly. "The whole place turns into a rocket when? According to your calculations?"

He glanced at the device in his paw. "Nine minutes and nine seconds."

"Loads of time," Paris spat. "So what are we looking for, Sherlock?"

"I don't know." He squinted through the smoke.

"That totally makes me feel better. Can you give me a hint of what I'm looking for?"

"Anything that will hint at—"

"Why the place is about to blow," Paris interrupted as her demon blood drew...no yanked her toward a set of double doors. Her father, Stefan, had said it would pull her toward evil, and she had to be careful because it could make her kill herself trying to blot it out. In this instance, she felt that it was hopefully pulling her toward what they were searching for.

Unbridled, she allowed her demon blood to lead the way. By the sound of scurrying claws on the tile floor, it seemed that Faraday was following her. She guessed he knew what was pulling her in the direction of denser smoke and more catastrophe.

If it were up to Paris, she wouldn't be going toward what appeared to be the epicenter of destruction. However, at her core, she felt that the clues Faraday was searching for were there.

With her head down to avoid the worst of the smoke, she moved forward. What was strange was Paris was mostly operating blindly. She hardly looked up to see where she was going. Instead, she felt the tug at her core and moved in that direction. To her astonishment, she never knocked into the stacks of equipment that she passed narrowly lined up in rows or into corners or anything else.

Only when she entered a large open room with giant machines making horrible hissing noises did she pause, feeling the first gripping fear since stepping onto the island—this time it was as paralyzing as the smoke wrapping around her. The demon blood had stopped Paris there.

This was it.

This was where her demon blood had led her. She wasn't sure if she wanted to find out what it had led her to.

CHAPTER THIRTY-SEVEN

"Is this a hospital?" Paris choked on the fumes and hoped that Faraday was close by to hear her question.

"Not as you'd expect," he said to her relief, climbing up onto some equipment nearby.

"Like, that it heals sick people," she guessed.

The large octagonal room they'd come to had three gurneys with covered bodies on them. In the center was a more prominent one, but there was nothing on it. Between the beds were tubes and wires, and around those were large glass cylindrical objects that billowed with a strange magical field.

Maybe it was Paris' magical blood, or it was the foreboding presence of the place that told her this facility was bad—really bad.

"Well, what do we do now?" Paris looked around, her eyes burning from the smoke.

"You look for something that tells us who designed this place," Faraday said. "Check out labels on the equipment. Ledgers. Anything that will tell us who's behind this."

Paris started for the far corner where there was a filing cabinet of records, she guessed. "What will you be doing?"

"I'm going to check out the cadavers and the medical notes beside them," he stated.

Paris grimaced. "For once, I think I have the easier job."

"Yeah, thankfully, it looks like they had to leave in a hurry, and some records were left behind." Faraday started to work. "They must have assumed that all evidence would go up in the fire."

"The fire that happens when?" Paris asked in a high-pitched squeal as she ransacked through a filing cabinet full of meaningless notes.

Faraday checked his device. "We have a whole seven minutes."

"Saying a 'whole' doesn't make me feel better," she remarked over her shoulder, continuing to search.

"Well, that's too bad because I was hoping it would since I was rounding up..."

CHAPTER THIRTY-EIGHT

Paris rummaged through the file cabinet with more fervor, knowing that they probably had less than six minutes. She didn't want to find out the hard way. However, she wanted to find out who was behind this. Her demon blood had led her there. She saw bodies under the sheets. Something bad had happened here...and Faraday had suspected it was important. Now she knew he was right.

Paris pulled out a thick folder and pulled it open, leafing through records of numbers and things that seemed inconsequential until she found a letterhead with a handwritten note. This seemed important. Her eyes scanned the contents, taking in the information, not making much sense of it but taking stock.

"Pare!" Faraday called from the far corner of the laboratory.

"What's up?" she replied.

"I think I figured out what's happened here." His voice shook with what seemed like fear.

"Yeah, I think I might have an inkling." She read the last of the note, putting things together.

"Oh?" he asked. "What did you find?"

"Well, I found your mad scientist." Her eyes darted to the top of the letterhead. "His name is Doctor Conrad Madden, and this is Madden

Operations. This project pertains to some weird Frankenstein-like stuff."

"Not like." Faraday ran toward her, a strange new fear in his eyes. "Exactly like Frankenstein. We have to get out of here now!"

He launched himself into the air and jumped into Paris' arms. Thankfully she caught him. With a fear unlike she'd felt in him before, he clawed onto her shoulder. "I'll explain everything. Portal us out of here right now…before it's too late."

Paris didn't ask any questions. That was a good thing because as she opened the portal and they stepped through, she caught sight of Madden Operations blowing up around them. Thankfully she closed the portal as the blast hit, sending them across the grounds of Happily Ever After College.

CHAPTER THIRTY-NINE

The perfect temperature and clean air were a welcomed relief after the heat and smoke on the island where they'd been. However, it all seemed like a sick joke after going from one extreme to the next.

"What did you find?" Paris crawled over to where Faraday lay a few yards away, noticing that the rodent's chest was rising and falling, indicating that he was alive, to her relief.

He looked at her sideways as if he was waking from a nap. "Oh, it's not good...not good at all, Pare."

"Well, you not telling me straight away isn't good for you, so tell me now." She stretched to a standing position and watched as the squirrel did the same.

"At first, I couldn't figure it out when I was reviewing the notes," he began. "The molecular data didn't match with what the—"

"I will turn you into jerky," Paris interrupted. "I have a restaurant opening in a few hours, my hair is full of soot, and I'm pretty certain that place ruined my favorite boots. Tell me what you learned and now, or you'll be on the menu at Little Pleasures."

"The Knees have figured out how to fuse into one person," he said in a mad rush.

"Wow, that's super bizarre." Paris was shocked. "I mean, I knew they were crazy, but that's one weird act of desperation. Why would they do that?"

"I'm guessing they realized that the only way to beat you, who they must believe is their main enemy and obstacle, is to become your shadow-self. So they've fused themselves, but they did it to become one. They used their parts to be like your parts, which is majority fairy, part-magician, and demon blood to create a truly formidable force."

Paris halted, swallowed, and assimilated the information. Then she turned to the squirrel and squatted to face him with a serious expression. "Did they succeed? This is very, very important. Did they create a replica of me?"

He bit his lip, put his paws in his mouth for a moment, yanked them out again, and looked to the side. "I'm afraid they did. There's a very dark version of you out there. Something that's part-fairy and part-magician with demon blood."

Paris threw her head back and laughed, realizing that Faraday was extremely confused but that things were finally going her way.

Her enemies might be helping her out for once.

CHAPTER FORTY

"Wait." Faraday straightened his bowtie. "You're telling me that your shadow-self rising to fight you is a good thing?"

Paris nodded, pulling on her brand-new leather jacket. She'd refused to talk to Faraday about all this and explain her side until they were clean. She couldn't risk wasting any more time and figured they could talk while getting ready. "The Unseelie king requires that the Seelie queen give him a halfling with demon blood to end the war... well, and an apology, but I'll figure out that part later. Anyway, I either had to sacrifice myself to be a sadistic king's pet or allow them to continue the war, thereby leaving the fairy godmothers and tooth fairies to continue their feud...but now..."

"But now," Faraday said, finishing her sentence, "The Knees have supplied you with a new option. You can give the Seelie queen your shadow-self. She's what the king requested."

He turned, looking around for the tiny comb on the dresser next to the mirror. "You could have also considered turning yourself over and escaping from the Unseelie realm."

"Says the rodent who wasn't watching a man willingly put his head in a lion's mouth in the Unseelie court," Paris remarked, combing her fingers through her hair. "I don't think it's a place that one easily escapes."

"Yeah, I guess I don't understand the context of that strange land, but I'd like to see it."

"I'll drop you off for a play date with my friend the talking alligator," she replied.

"I'm good," he chirped.

"Don't worry, Smeg is a vegetarian, but he'll talk your ear off about scientific theory or whatnot."

Faraday smiled, putting on his monocle as Paris requested. "Sounds like my kind of chap."

Paris couldn't help but smile at how handsome her sidekick looked. "So don't you see, although it seems that the Knees' act of desperation is a bad thing, it could end up good for me. The key is that I'll need to capture them...well, her, alive. I think I'll call her Evil Shadow-self. Maybe ESS."

"I like that," Faraday replied. "It is quite the compliment that they gave up their parts to become like you."

"Yeah, I'm so honored," she said dryly.

"Well, and Evil Shadow-self won't be exactly like you. I hypothesize that she'll be like you, but something really dark with diabolical magic."

"Hence why we're calling her Evil Shadow-self," Paris remarked.

"They used magic from the Fang Wellspring, and that can't yield positive results," Faraday continued to explain. "Not only that, but you can't simply fuse three people and think there won't be significant issues. It's unnatural."

"Not to mention, throw in a splash of demon blood and think that won't lead to problems."

Faraday nodded. "Yes, your mother used a genie's wish to fix your demon blood, using the fairy aspect of you to balance it out. However, you can't simply mix ingredients and think it will replicate something else."

"Yeah, as Mitch Hedberg said, 'They say the recipe for Sprite is lemon and lime, but I tried to make it at home, there's more to it than that.'"

"Yeah, I guess that's a good example." Faraday didn't look impressed by the joke.

"Anyway, this ESS business is good news for me," Paris stated. "I only need to capture her and turn her over to Queen Helena MacGillie. Now I have to capture one evil tooth fairy—"

"I'll remind you that this one will be more powerful than all of them combined," he interrupted.

"Yes, but still, it's easier to go after one person than three."

He gave her a doubtful look.

Paris waved him off. "Anyway, I get this stupid Frankenstein halfling, who is a me-wannabe and—"

"I need to point out that although modern culture thinks Frankenstein refers to the monster, it's the scientist," the squirrel interrupted.

"It's important for me to point out that I'm opening a business in about an hour, and I'm running late because you wanted me to go to an exploding island," Paris stated dryly, heading for the door to her room.

Faraday nodded, pulling the tiny top hat off the dresser and dutifully putting it on. "Right you are. I'll be the best maître d' you've ever seen tonight."

"I've never seen one, so my expectations are low."

"Well, still." He scurried for the door as she opened it for them. He looked up at her fondly. "Tonight is your night, Pare. Then tomorrow, we'll look into stopping this evil wannabe-Paris halfling. We'll fix all our problems as only we can do."

Paris smiled down at her friend, grateful that he was by her side. It did seem that everything was coming together. She hoped that her luck held—at least for the rest of the night.

Tomorrow she could hunt down her enemies...or enemy, as it were. Tonight, all Paris wanted was to enjoy a place meant to bring love to the world.

CHAPTER FORTY-ONE

As the sun shone above the mountains in Colorado, soon to make its descent for the night, lights twinkled on around the grounds of Little Pleasures.

Paris couldn't believe it. Things had magically come together—quite literally. They'd used magic to hang the twinkling lights in the trees and grow the produce and keep the bumble bats from murdering the surprise chickens.

Most importantly, it was renovation magic that constructed the farmhouse in record time. The idea that the structure was an organic being with feelings that could act out on its own accord made Paris a little nervous, but she hoped it would only reward its patrons and not throw anyone out that night...or any other.

The entire crew who had made Little Pleasures possible were all standing in front of Paris, looking at her expectantly. In less than an hour, the first service of the restaurant would begin, and with it, the grading of Paris' final assignment for Happily Ever After College.

It had all come down to this.

Soon portals would be opening to the farm, and magical races of all sorts would be arriving. Also, cars would be pulling up on the dirt road and dropping off mortals. King Rudolf had handled marketing for the farm-to-table restaurant at his insistence. Paris had worried that would mean something disastrous...time would tell.

It didn't matter as much if patrons packed the restaurant on its opening night. What Saint Valentine and the other faculty would be grading Paris on was execution and whether the business promoted love. They'd assigned an individual love meter to Little Pleasures, and it hung outside the farmhouse, currently showing zero.

Paris swallowed the tension in her throat and let out a tight cough, turning to face her crew.

"I want to thank everyone who has made this night possible," she began, her voice rising in volume as she spoke. "I know you all volunteered your time, talents, expertise, and energy for this restaurant."

"I thought we were getting paid," Ainsley said in a loud whisper to Quiet standing next to her.

"You haven't been paid in five hundred years," Mama Jamba chimed, standing next to Papa Creola.

Talk about pressure. Paris had Mother Nature and Father Time at the opening of her restaurant. She wasn't sure which part was harder to believe, the first or the latter.

"Don't think I'm not keeping track." Ainsley poked out her tongue at the older woman, who simply winked in reply.

"I really couldn't have done this without all of your help." Paris looked at Ainsley, the elf, who would be doing the cooking that night. Her gaze then darted to the gnome with a dirty face who had tended to the animals and farm, doing the work of ten people miraculously.

She smiled gratefully at Rory and Maddie Laurens, the giants who had helped to construct the buildings and would be helping with service. Finally, she gave her Uncle Clark and Chef Ash a thoughtful look, impressed with the work they'd done with the farmhouse and menu. Her Uncle Clark had proven to have quite the culinary knack, but more importantly, he appeared to love the art of cooking. It was a surprise since he didn't seem like the creative type in his stiff suit and polished appearance. That proved people could and would continuously surprise.

"This restaurant, I realize, was an ambitious endeavor for my final project at Happily Ever After College," Paris continued. "If it's successful tonight, I'll pass. The grade is mostly based on that." She pointed at the love meter in the distance. "If I've created something good and true, it'll promote love for friends, families, and couples. All I ask is that you do what you're supposed to with love in your heart because when we come from a place of goodness, that's sure to be our result."

"Well put, my dear," Mama Jamba cheered.

"After tonight," Paris went on. "What happens to this place is up to us. I'd like it to continue, but that will depend on what happens tonight. It will also depend on who wants to be a part of it. I know that many of you must go on to do other things." She glanced thoughtfully at Ainsley and Quiet. "But I know that some of you like the idea of serving in a way that keeps love flowing here." Paris smiled at Rory and Maddie.

"Regardless of what tomorrow brings, regardless of how much love the meter shows tonight," Paris said, her heart feeling full. "I'm grateful for all of your help, and that's brought so much love to my life. Thank you."

Something tugged on Paris' pant leg. She glanced down to find Faraday looking adorable in his suit and top hat. He pointed in the distance where a portal was opening, the blue light shimmering in the darkening grounds.

"Your first customers are arriving."

Paris gulped. It was go time.

CHAPTER FORTY-TWO

Paris wasn't sure who she expected to be her first guests but when the familiar faces were clear—she realized that she should've guessed.

Running for the portal, Paris held out her arms, hoping to keep her tears at bay. "Mom and Dad," she exclaimed, engulfing both her parents in a double embrace. They hugged her at once, a palpable joy radiating from them.

"Pare!" Liv said when they've separated, looking all around the farm. "You did all this? It's simply incredible."

Paris shook her head, pressing tears back from where they came from. "No, I didn't do anything. I simply had a vision, and a lot of talented people made it happen."

Her father gave her a proud look, his blue eyes radiating with love. "We usually are successful because of the devotion and work of those around us, but it was you who had the vision."

"What a vision this was," Liv remarked, doing a full circle, in total awe. "I can't believe, well, I can, but this was a huge undertaking. You're going to graduate at the top of your class."

Paris' eyes darted to the love meter, tension knitting her brow. "I don't know. It's not as simple as opening this place. It has to promote love. If the customers don't like their experience, if they don't enjoy their time with others, if Little Pleasures doesn't bring love to their hearts, well, then I fail."

"Well, you've set the scene with incredible ambiance, which your mother requires for a good dining experience." Stefan looked around at the pristine grounds and mountain range in the distance.

"Your food has to be the freshest of any place anywhere." Liv nodded at the garden and barn with animals.

"So you have a good foundation for creating love," Stefan added.

"And I have awesome people to serve and help." Paris smiled over her shoulder at the staff who'd broken away to take their stations in the kitchen, dining room, garden, or wherever else she'd need them for that night's experience.

"Yeah, you have a top-notch team," Stefan stated. "Is that Mama Jamba and Papa Creola taking a seat at a table?"

Paris glanced in the direction of the farmhouse where they'd set up picnic tables. Potted herbs sat in the center, and comfy pillows lined the benches. The large bulbs of twinkling lights in the trees overhead were like lightning bugs and hanging plants of pink and purple fuchsia dangled from the limbs.

"Yeah, Mama Jamba gave me the land and Papa Creola the name for the restaurant and grounds," Paris explained. "Aunt Sophia helped me to get all this help. She enlisted most of all the people here."

"Speaking of which, I hope you have a table that seats a dozen," Liv said as another portal opened. "By a dozen, I mean Sophia and Garfield."

Paris laughed, knowing that her mother was referring to Lunis, who she never called by his actual name. A wider grin spread on her face as the rider and her dragon stepped through the portal and onto the grounds of Little Pleasures.

CHAPTER FORTY-THREE

L iv and Stefan had taken Clark up on an offer to get a full tour of the farmhouse he'd help construct—leaving Paris to greet Sophia and Lunis.

Like her parents, they seemed impressed by the farm's progress in a short time.

"The restaurant is ready to go?" Sophia looked around in awe.

"We'll see." Paris' eyes darted to the love meter...it was still at zero. She guessed it wouldn't be operational until it was opening time.

Ten minutes...

"I hope your restaurant can cater to my allergies and food needs." Lunis swished his tail behind him with a cunning look in his eyes.

"I'm sure we can," Paris stated. "What are they?"

"I have a nut allergy."

"Not a problem." Paris indicated Faraday, who was scurrying for the restaurant's front to take his place as the maître d' for the night. "My sidekick does too."

"And I'm vegan," he continued.

She laughed. "I would say that a dragon who was vegan was weird if I hadn't met an alligator recently who was vegetarian."

"Oh, how is Smeg?" Sophia smiled.

"And I'm keto," Lunis continued.

"This is getting more challenging…" Paris muttered.

"Also, I'm lactose intolerant, gluten-free, soy avoidant, and allergic to sugar," Lunis went on.

"I think I have a piece of lettuce with your name on it," Paris sang, stifling her laughter.

"And also, he's a big fat liar," Sophia spat.

"And I have body image problems." He scowled at his rider. "Who would know why…"

"I'm sure we can find a bag of Doritos that fit your taste," Paris remarked, remembering how much the blue dragon liked the crunchy chips and the cheese dust.

"Oh, I think I might like this place. Let's hope the service is good. I had awful service the other day at a place." Lunis leaned forward, his large head coming in close to Paris in a conspiratorial way. "Incidentally, do you know how to save a drowning waiter?"

"Tell me." Paris waited for the punch line.

He smirked mischievously. "Just take your foot off his head."

"You can go ahead and kick us out now," Sophia stated dryly. "I won't be offended."

"I will," Lunis huffed. "They better serve dragons, or I'm filing a lawsuit. Just because we need the tables and chairs supersized doesn't mean we shouldn't be seated at restaurants. We're people too."

"No, you're not," Sophia argued.

"I think we have a nice outdoor dining space that will be perfect for you," Paris said diplomatically.

"I might get cold though," Lunis said, pretending to shiver suddenly. "With the sun setting, it's going to be freezing. The night air might make me sick."

"Get a jacket, dragon," Sophia ordered, hiding her amusement.

He pretended to sneeze. "I'm going to catch my death from cold out here. Pare, you sure I can't get a table by the fire inside?"

"I'm afraid we've already reserved that space." She maintained her smile.

"Yeah, for people who aren't dragons with thick hides and a propensity toward being demanding divas," Sophia joked.

He scoffed, throwing his snout in the air. "Well, I never...I'm giving this place a low rating on Yelp."

Sophia playfully slapped her dragon on the side. "You better not or I'm canceling your Disney Plus subscription."

Lunis whipped around and gawked at her. "You wouldn't?"

"I would," she shot back.

"Well, I'll behave then," he said good-naturedly. "Oh, and that reminds me..."

Sophia sighed, interrupting him momentarily. "I apologize in advance for whatever he says next."

"The other day, I ate at Mary Poppin's restaurant," Lunis began. "Super cauliflower cheese but the lobster was atrocious."

Sophia lowered her chin, regarding her dragon with mock contempt before giving Paris a slight smile. "On that note, we'll get out of your hair."

She kissed her niece on the cheek. "You'll do great, Paris."

Lunis nodded in the direction of the barn. "Come on already, Soph. I want to ride a goat."

Sophia shook her head, heading for the area with the animals—both magical and normal.

Paris laughed, about to warn them not to drink the milk, but a new shimmering portal caught her attention.

When the group that strode through the portal materialized, Paris immediately had one reaction.

CHAPTER FORTY-FOUR

"You have to get out of here!" Paris urged, running over to the portal and ushering Ramy Vance to go back the way he'd come.

"Oh, is this because I didn't make reservations?" He looked at King Rudolf Sweetwater beside him. "You said I didn't need them because I was with you."

The fae shrugged. "I don't work here."

"Well, if we need reservations, I'm leaving," Bep, the owner of the Rose Apothecary said, automatically annoyed. "I don't go to places that need to know to expect me. It's better when people don't know that I'm arriving."

"I'm sure that's true," Paul, the Great Librarian, said from beside the potions expert.

Paris hadn't expected all these familiar faces, but she was instantly grateful that they'd decided to come on the opening night of her restaurant. Well, she was happy that all but one of them had come.

"No," Paris stated. "It's not about the reservations. It's just that tonight is really important and people are grading me based on how much love I promote—"

"And Bep is sure to say something offensive to mess that up," Rudolf interrupted.

Paris shook her head. "No, it's just that—"

"Paul will probably monopolize the conversation with things he's read in books," Rudolf guessed.

"No, I thought that—"

"My devilishly good looks will make all the ladies who can't have me want to wallow in despair?" King Rudolf questioned, quite seriously.

"No, it's that death usually detracts from the love meter," Paris stated, indicating the love meter at the front of the farmhouse. "Ramy dying, which I think is inevitable, will be a downer on tonight's festivities."

"I promise not to die," Ramy said at once. "I'll be extra careful. I won't even use utensils."

"I'm afraid she's right, Ramy-Cans." Rudolf put his arm around the other guy's shoulder and led him back toward the portal. "How about I bring you a to-go order of shrimp to make you feel better?"

"I'm deathly allergic to shellfish." Ramy shrugged out from under Rudolf's arm and quickly made for the portal.

Rudolf waved, smiling wide. "Sounds good. I'll make it two orders, then."

Paris sighed with relief. One disaster averted. However, when another portal opened nearby and two people stepped through, Paris realized that she had another potential problem to avoid.

CHAPTER FORTY-FIVE

An assassination was certain to bring the mood down, Paris thought, rushing over to where Lee and Cat stood after stepping through the portal.

"You all have to promise to be on good behavior," Paris said in a rushed whisper, leaning in close to them.

Cat turned at once, shaking her head of red hair. "I knew I didn't want to come to this tonight."

Lee reached out and grabbed her wife's arm, keeping her from leaving. "We're staying. This event is to honor us."

"Ummm…no, it's my final project for college," Paris corrected.

"And who do you have to thank for your education?" Lee countered.

"My Uncle John," Paris answered.

"And?" Lee drew out the word.

"Ummm…my parents, my family, and the support and encouragement of many of my classmates and the faculty of Happily Ever After College."

Lee held up a finger. "Who was there for you when the world had turned its back on you and told you that you weren't good enough and that you'd never amount to anything?"

"I don't think that happened," Paris corrected.

Lee shrugged. "It was worth a shot. That works about half the time."

"Well, you all are supplying the bread and pastries, so I'm sure many would like the opportunity to meet the bakers," Paris began, mostly talking to herself. "But Lee, you have to promise not to kill anyone tonight."

"Promise is a strong word," Lee stated. "Can I give you a slight assurance with at least ten caveats?"

"I don't think that will work," Paris remarked.

Lee sighed. "Well, what if someone chews with their mouth open?"

"Try ignoring them," Paris offered.

The assassin baker gave her a sideways look. "I'm not sure I can do that. What if they talk loudly and send their food back?"

"Let that be my problem."

"But you've just graduated from preschool and—"

"Fairy godmother college and not yet, and especially I won't if you murder someone during the opening of my restaurant," Paris interrupted.

Lee glanced at her wife, then at Paris. "So no murders tonight? Is that what you're telling me?"

"I thought this was a murder mystery dinner," Cat complained, looking at Lee. "That's what you told me."

"Every night with me is a murder mystery," Lee stated.

"Look," Paris said sternly. "I'm going to need you to leave all of your weapons here if you're attending the opening. Otherwise, you have to leave."

"What do you want me to do, cut off my hands?" Lee asked, quite seriously.

When Paris didn't respond, not sure that she had a rejoinder, Lee held up her hands. "They're lethal weapons!"

"Yeah, I get it." Paris pointed at a nearby barrel on its end. "Put your weapons there if you want to eat here tonight."

"Fine," Lee huffed, trotting over. "It looks like you better go greet your guests. There are more coming through. Tell them the rules about chewing and not talking loudly. It's for their own good."

"I'm on it." Paris strode over to a portal as two friendly faces came through. She was grateful to finally have people attending her opening who wouldn't make bad jokes or die or murder someone, although there was no assurance they'd be on their best behavior.

CHAPTER FORTY-SIX

"Oh, talk about shabby chic." For a rare occasion, Christine wasn't in the blue fairy godmother gown that made her orangish-red hair bluish-gray. She wore a fashionable ensemble of tights, a jean skirt, and a button-down sweater.

"It's really beautiful, Pare," Penny said, also not wearing the gown. It was even stranger to see her actual hair color of brown and her in loose jeans and a blouse.

Christine formed her fingers together like they were the lens of a camera. "I could see this in a spread of *Home and Garden*. It might even be cool enough for *In Style*. The hipsters are going to be lining up to eat at this place."

Paris shook her head. "Let's hope not. I don't think I have the patience for such things. Not to mention that my mother and aunt will probably murder any hipsters that come here."

"But this is organic farm-to-table where they can meet the chicken who laid their eggs," Christine argued. "This is a hipster's Mecca."

"Yeah, I thought about that," Paris muttered. "I've got that covered." She pointed at a sign beside the driveway that in bold letters read: "Everything here is cool, new, and trending. There's no vinyl. No craft beers. No beards. No arguments."

"Good thinking." Penny giggled. "That will deter them."

Paris nodded. "The last thing I needed was for a bunch of hipsters to be hanging out here, pretending it wasn't cool and they weren't having a good time. So they aren't welcome. Only people who need more love in their life. Or are open to enjoying love. Not those who want to be cool by not being cool and pretending they don't like their life but say things like, 'Chillax' and 'YOLO.'"

"She deserves an A," Christine declared. "I hope the food here is good because I'm starving. If it's not, I'm sending it back."

Lee jerked her head to the side, looking over at them. On the surface of the barrel were at least half a dozen different weapons, and she was still pulling them from various hidden spots. "What did you say, Red?"

Christine grimaced, looking Lee up and down, and glanced at Paris. "Is that person talking to me?"

Paris shook her head. "Lee, you and Cat will be dining al fresco tonight." She turned her attention back to Christine and Penny, feigning a smile. "You two will have a nice cozy table inside by the fire."

"Sounds romantic," Christine said dreamily. "Is Chef Ash here?"

Paris nodded. "He's here for tonight, helping to ensure that the menu goes off without a hitch. Maybe you two can hurry inside and see how he's doing, and maybe meet and greet with some of the guests who have already arrived."

"Oh, anyone who I would know?" Christine asked.

"Well, yes, but they know you rather than you knowing them," Paris stated.

"I don't get it," Christine said in confusion.

"You know, like your creator, Mother Nature. Then there's the guy who's been running your life," Paris muttered dryly.

"My father," Christine and Penny said in unison.

Paris drew back, momentarily put off. "Yeah, no. But sort of. Your first daddy. Father Time."

"Cool," Christine stated. "Do you think I can get their autographs?"

"That's probably a hard no," Paris answered. "But my mom and dad are in there and my aunt and her dragon. And the king of the fae."

"Oh, my angels!" Christine stated. "I can't believe it. I get to meet him?"

"The dragon?" Paris questioned. "Or you mean, King Rudolf Sweetwater?"

"No, I mean your dad," Christine stated. "I hear he's hot."

She grabbed Penny's hand and hauled her toward the house. "Make me look good. Laugh at all my jokes."

Paris waved at their backs as they retreated. "He's married, you know. And my mom will pretty much erase you in an instant, so be careful."

She didn't think her friends heard her as they retreated toward the farmhouse. That was fine because another portal had opened and a familiar figure stepped through. Paris hoped someone else would follow them, which was why she looked so disappointed when the portal closed—leaving the lone person standing there on the darkening farm.

CHAPTER FORTY-SEVEN

"Were you expecting someone else?" Astrid asked when Paris kept looking behind her, thinking that the portal might reopen to reveal someone else joining her.

"No..." she said half-heartedly and added, "I mean, no. I mean, welcome to Little Pleasures. I'm so glad you came."

"Well, how could I not?" Astrid, the owner of the Glowing Orchid, admired the farm of fruits and vegetables still visible in the waning light. "I had to see how my magical seeds performed, and it appears that they did very well. I look forward to tasting the fruits of our labor." She snickered. "A pun intended there."

"The seeds really were amazing," Paris admitted.

"Well, I bet that Hemingway's green thumb came into play with their success."

At the mention of his name, Paris couldn't help but lose the fake smile.

"What's wrong, dear?" Astrid asked. "Did I say something wrong?"

"No, but it was Hemingway who I can thank for getting the farm going," Paris stated. "I wish he was here to see how his hard work paid off."

"Yes, I can understand that," Astrid admitted. "If it makes you feel better, he's sent correspondence saying how much he's enjoying his travels. Also, he's already sent back many specimens that I think will be incredibly useful. He's doing fantastic work."

"That's wonderful to hear." Paris tried to inject enthusiasm into her voice. "I knew he'd do a great job."

"Yes, but the question is, was that news you were expecting to hear?" Without another word, Astrid swept away, leaving Paris stuttering.

The truth was, she half-hoped—no, fully hoped—that Hemingway would be able to attend the opening of her restaurant that night. But she realized then that his travels would keep him away. She half-hated herself for thinking he would've made the extra effort to be there, knowing that was impossible for him. He'd moved on. She loved him, but he, well, he didn't love her. The sooner she realized that, the sooner she embraced her future.

No sooner had she thought those thoughts than the man who would decide her fate stepped through a shimmering blue portal, followed by two other figures.

CHAPTER FORTY-EIGHT

L ike the last time she'd seen him, Saint Valentine had dressed impeccably. Flanked by Headmistress Willow Starr and Mae Ling, the leader of the fairy godmothers looked strong and distinguished. Saint Valentine was wearing a black suit that easily cost as much as the farmhouse—if it were for sale, which it wasn't. He'd slicked back his salt-and-pepper hair and kept his bright blue eyes unmistakably centered on Paris.

He held up his arm to the headmistress, offering it to her, his ornately engraved silver cane in his hand. Willow took it, and he led her forward, Mae Ling in stride with them.

The headmistress wore her usual blue gown with its pink sash. Paris instantly wondered if she didn't wear the outfit that proved she was a fairy godmother after graduation, if she'd be considered one. Then her eyes went to Mae Ling, who was in her usual attire—black pants and a blouse to match. She and Paris apparently went to the same store.

Paris reasoned that others didn't challenge Mae Ling as a fairy godmother even though she didn't dress the same. However, Mae Ling was a different species of fairy, it seemed. She was a definite enigma, and Paris didn't see that changing any time soon.

"Miss Paris Beaufont," Saint Valentine said in his melodic voice, holding out his free hand to her. "It's a pleasure to be here tonight and see your restaurant."

She held out her hand and allowed him to plant a soft, polite kiss upon its back. "Thank you. I'm excited about the opening."

"I think we all are." Saint Valentine released her hand and looked around at the twinkling stars illuminating the farm and restaurant. "I didn't expect anything so…"

His sentence trailed away, and Paris took it upon herself to fill in the blank in her head. *So ostentatious. So grandiose. So doomed to fail.*

She swallowed, trying to keep the doubt from surfacing on her face.

"Soooo impressive," Saint Valentine continued. "I knew we could expect great things from you. I also expect that you won't do things like other fairy godmothers. But I've never seen anything quite like this for a final project. A restaurant, yes, we've graded that many times. A farm. Yes, I've seen a few of those done by students. A garden, of course. But an entire farm-to-table restaurant on one plot of land? This is an entire experience."

Paris pulled in a breath, her eyes skipping to Mae Ling, who gave a minute nod of encouragement, her eyes seeming to say, "Go on, talk now, child."

"That was the idea," Paris began, her voice faltering at first. "Families can come here and visit the animals, and we'll even have a 'You Pick' for the farm during the day. They can harvest apples in the winter, berries in the summer, and vegetables most of the year. Then patrons can grab a drink at the outside bar or an appetizer at the picnic tables. For those who want a formal dining experience, they can have a three-course meal inside the farmhouse."

Saint Valentine's chuckle was full of warmth and made his blue eyes twinkle. "There's something for everyone."

"I know the project is supposed to create romantic love—"

"That's the assumption most make," Saint Valentine interrupted.

"Well, my intent was to build something that would create love for more than couples," Paris explained. "I wanted something that would help love to blossom for all people. Gardens and animals and food, well, they all bring people together. There is hopefully something for everyone that will make their heart sing."

Repeating Hemingway's words when explaining why he was leaving brought a sudden twinge of pain to Paris' heart. She thought that with everything going on, she could ignore the heartache, but it followed her around despite all her distractions.

"A splendid idea! I think the only thing you missed was musical entertainment," Saint Valentine said and magically, the folk band that Paris hired to perform that night started playing. That meant it was time to open the restaurant.

The sounds of banjos and guitars filled the cool autumn air with warmth.

Everyone looked at the farmhouse where the band was playing, and patrons were filing into the restaurant.

Saint Valentine laughed again, a sound full of satisfaction and surprise. "Well, it appears that you thought of everything. What charming music."

"I thought in the summer, we could have movies on the lawn," Paris explained, pointing at the grassy area. "There's no reason not to go big when we have so many options."

Saint Valentine stepped forward, releasing Willow's arm. Paris didn't pull away when he reached out and cupped her chin. "The thing I don't think you're aware of is everyone has the opportunity to go big, as you put it. Most don't. They stay small. I don't think small would ever suit you."

Paris smiled despite his fingers holding her chin. "Thank you, sir. I hope you enjoy your experiences here tonight."

"Oh, I assume I will." Saint Valentine stepped back and looked sideways at the fairy godmothers. "Well, shall we, ladies? It appears the restaurant is open."

They both nodded. Paris was about to set off for the farmhouse alongside them, but another portal opened, making her pause. Then her heart leapt with total joy when she laid her eyes on the person who stepped through.

CHAPTER FORTY-NINE

The tears broke free from Paris' eyes as she ran for the man who stepped through the portal, throwing her arms around him at once. Another figure quickly followed him, but Paris didn't give her much notice. She simply held Uncle John close, happy to see him—but his appearance unleashed all the emotions she'd been bottling up for days.

"Oh, Pare, are you okay?" Uncle John held her tightly, his shirt quickly wet with her tears. She nodded against his shoulder.

"I'm so happy to see you." She hadn't expected this kind of reaction from herself. All her life, or the part she could remember, Uncle John had been her rock. It had been them against the world—all alone. She never questioned why that was, but she also didn't take his unconditional love for granted.

Now Paris knew the truth about her parents, why her family had stayed away, and she had them all around her—lavishing her with love. However, that didn't negate the bond she shared with Uncle John. He'd given up everything to protect and raise her.

All her life, Uncle John was all she knew. And he was enough. His laughter. His compassion. His wisdom. It had all been Paris' strengths growing up, and if she was anything great now, it was because of the man before her.

She peeled away, wiping her tears and trying to contain her emotions. He looked her over as if she might be hurt, then smiled, followed by a chuckle.

"You've overdone it, haven't you?" he guessed. "Now you're exhausted and brimming with emotions."

Paris nodded, partially covering her face with her hands. "Yeah, you know me so well."

"Oh, Pare, I can't even imagine how much stress you've had with all that you've had going on." He pulled his eyes off her and looked around the farm. "No wonder your state of exhaustion. Look at what you've done."

Suddenly Paris felt like a little girl again, and she'd shown Uncle John a watercolor picture that she'd painted. She looked up, studying his expression and anticipating his reaction.

"You like it?" she asked, her voice sounding small. "I call it Little Pleasures. The food is all organic, and I have a few dishes with you in mind."

"Like it?" He looked at her. "Pare, I've never been prouder of someone in my entire life. That's saying a lot because I've seen your mother do some extraordinary things. But this, well, you created magic unlike I've witnessed before."

She blushed. "Well, you haven't tried the spinach enchiladas yet."

He laughed, surprise in his eyes. "You have spinach enchiladas? Those are my—"

"Favorite," she interrupted. "Of course, I know that."

Uncle John chuckled again. "My favorite used to be steak enchiladas, but your mother put a swift halt to that. Don't tell her, but I prefer spinach now."

"I'm glad because they're much better for you."

"That was Liv's idea," Uncle John imparted in a whisper. "Little did she know that she'd give me the best reason to take better care of myself." He put his arms around her again, holding her tightly.

Paris looked over Uncle John's shoulder and noticed the other person who'd stepped through the portal. She'd been too distracted by her reunion with Uncle John to notice Alicia standing awkwardly behind them.

"Hi!" Paris squeaked, releasing Uncle John and hurrying over to Alicia. "I'm so glad you made it."

"Of course, I wouldn't miss this for the world." Alicia's thick accent made her words sound extra sweet.

When Paris released Alicia from a hug, she noticed a flash of something that caught her eyes. Peering down, she saw a sparkle on Alicia's hand. A sudden realization hit Paris.

"You got engaged!" she exclaimed, looking at the brunette.

Alicia nodded proudly.

Paris spun, looking at her Uncle John. "To him!"

He nodded, his eyes brimming with excitement. "It's something I've wanted since...well, the moment I met that woman." Uncle John smiled at Alicia, unmistakably in love with her. It radiated off him and made him glow with happiness.

Again Paris threw her arms around his shoulders, hugging him once more. "This is fantastic news. I'm so happy for you two."

"Thank you," he replied. "I think we owe it to you, throwing us back together."

Paris shook her head, stepping back. "You two were always going to find your way back to each other. I was a character in your story."

"Pare, you've always been the light of my life. To call yourself a character is overly simplifying things."

"Well, I'm grateful that you're together." Paris looked between the two. "You're getting married. That's amazing. I'll want details."

"You'll be the first to hear them," Uncle John stated. "But tonight is your night, and we can't wait to see what an amazing place you've created."

"It really is magical." Alicia looked proudly out at the grounds. The music from the folk band filled the air and laughter could also be heard as diners congregated under the twinkling trees. "It's so magical that it seems like the perfect place to get married."

"Oh, what a wonderful idea." Uncle John's surprise sprang to his face.

"Here? You two?" Paris was also surprised.

"Well, if it's okay with you," Uncle John said with a cautious smile. "Not tonight, of course. I don't have my tux yet."

Alicia laughed. "Nor do I have a dress."

"Yes, I would be beyond honored," Paris stated. "Again, you might want to wait until you try the food."

"Pare, I have no doubt that everything is going to be perfect from start to finish." Uncle John held out his arm to her. "Will you please do us the honor of leading us to your restaurant, Little Pleasures?"

Paris took her uncle's arm and nodded, again feeling like a little girl playing make-believe. But *this* was all real. And it was perfect... well, almost perfect.

CHAPTER FIFTY

The love meter outside the farmhouse had risen when Paris led Uncle John and Alicia into the restaurant. It now was sitting at fifteen percent. In the first few minutes that Little Pleasures had been open, it had increased love levels by fifteen percent.

For Paris, that wasn't good or bad. She'd expected a spike like that when the band started playing, and patrons knew that they'd soon get food and drink. The key was would it continue to go up, or would something happen, and it plummeted? Would it even go in the negative? The risk with the restaurant was that it could bring people together and give them a delightful experience. It could also bring people together for complications and stress. Excitement and anticipation were a double-edged sword.

At the threshold to her restaurant, she paused as a row of headlights shone on the road leading to Little Pleasures. It wasn't a lot of cars, but it was enough to get her attention.

"What's that about?" Uncle John noticed the cars too.

"Customers," Paris answered. "Mortals."

"Oh, well, this place is about to be even more exciting," Uncle John said enthusiastically.

"Yeah," Paris agreed. "It appears that King Rudolf came through with the marketing."

"For as bad of a reputation as that fae gets, I've never known him to let a Beaufont down." Alicia tugged on Uncle John's sleeve. "I think we better grab a table before there's a wait."

"Wait," Paris said, sounding like she was asking them to wait. She shook her head. "I realized that if patrons have a long wait, they'll be annoyed, and that will decrease the love meter."

"Pare, I'm sure that people won't mind waiting for an experience like this," Uncle John said consolingly.

"That's the thing." Worry constricted Paris' insides as the cars began parking. There were at least a dozen of them and more headlights barreling down the road. "Waiting is very stressful."

"It doesn't have to be," King Rudolf sang, gliding out the front door, carrying a tray with little plates of appetizers.

"What are you doing?" Paris asked.

"I'm giving out samples of the food." He flashed her a toothy grin. "That way, the waiting guests get an idea of the great tastes they're about to have. And everyone loves something free."

"Oh, that's a good idea." Paris felt mild relief. "What about after the samples are gone, and they grow impatient?"

"Well, then you'll be happy that I brought my knives," Lee buzzed out the door behind King Rudolf.

"No killing people," Paris stated tersely.

"I know." Lee trotted for the barrel where she'd left her weapons, looking over her shoulder at Paris. "I'm going to juggle them. It's super entertaining."

"Is that safe?" Paris asked.

"I'm a professional," Lee answered. "Of course it is."

"The boutique shop is open," Bep called from a side door where the store was. "Come and get your Heals Pills. Never before not sold on Roya Lane, this is mortals' opportunity at getting this miracle product."

Paris held her breath, disbelieving that things were going so smoothly, but it was all thanks to her friends coming to the rescue, as they so often did.

She watched as the mortals exited their cars and made their way in different directions. Some headed off to explore the gardens and barn with various animals—the twinkling strings of lights overhead illuminating the areas. Or they took samples from Rudolf or watched Lee's knife-juggling. Some made their way for the boutique, and others hung around the band and listened to the delightful music. The few who came straight for the restaurant had their eyes wide and smiles on their faces as they took in the beautiful farmhouse.

Paris glanced at the love meter. *Thirty percent.* She let out a breath, hoping it continued to go up, but she had a long night ahead of her and a lot of love to spread to get a passing grade.

CHAPTER FIFTY-ONE

"This is delicious!"

"Wow, I've never tasted anything so fresh!"

"Oh, look at that!"

The voices of the patrons in the restaurant greeted Paris' ears when she entered the farmhouse. Everywhere she looked, people were sampling their dishes and smiling or talking excitedly. Many were staring at the modern country décor that was comforting but with a unique flair.

Next to the hostess stand was an old bike with a basket full of flowers leaning against the wall. An art installation of bottle caps was on the far wall. They created a mosaic of a field of flowers and sunset sky. Although the tables and chairs were mix-matched, they worked together, creating an array of different colors, textures, and designs.

The entire restaurant was exactly what Paris had envisioned. It wasn't fancy, and it wasn't a dive. It was something relatable, relaxing, and fun. It was eclectic and full of personality. She hoped it was the right environment to help love blossom and bloom.

"Have you tried Christina's Wrong Name Souffle?" a patron asked the person across from them.

"I won't have room for that since I must eat all of Penny's Pocket Pita," their companion replied.

Paris smiled as she watched Maddy easily trot between tables, delivering orders. Ainsley appeared to be getting food out hot and fresh, and the dining room was buzzing with excitement.

"I didn't think I could love you anymore," Liv said at Paris' back. She turned to find her mother and her father beaming at her. "Then I had the Beaufont Nachos and nearly passed out."

Stefan laughed. "I thought she was going to get rid of me and marry the tray of nachos."

"I still might." Liv elbowed her husband. "Seriously, Pare, those were amazing. The freshness of the jalapeños and cilantro partnered with the creamy cheese and homemade chips was enough to give me a religious experience."

"Can I quote you on that?" a guy asked, who was standing nearby. "I'm a food critic for the *New York Times* and think that description just about takes the cake."

"Or rather the nachos," Liv stated. "Go right ahead. This is my daughter's restaurant, Paris Beaufont." She held out a presenting hand to her.

"Nice to meet you, Paris," the guy said. "I'd love the chance to do an interview sometime soon."

"Absolutely." Paris took the thick business card he handed her.

"I'll be in touch." The reporter strode out with a happy grin on his face.

"I think he had a lot of milk," Stefan whispered to Paris. "If you know what I mean."

"I do." She snickered.

"Hey, the cheese on the nachos," Liv began. "What was that made from? Those special cow's milk?"

"Do you really want to know?" Paris questioned.

"Hey, drunken nachos isn't such a bad idea," she retorted. "And of course it was my daughter who created them."

"With the help of my friends." Paris looked around and noticed that the restaurant was starting to empty. It had been a long dinner service, and it would soon be time to close Little Pleasures down for the night.

"Well, again, amazing job." Liv hugged her daughter. "I'm sure you'll be exhausted after all this, but congratulations on such an incredibly successful final project. I know you'll have passed."

"I hope so." Paris realized that in the last several hours, she'd been too busy to check the love meter. She had no idea if it had gotten to a passing level. Or some girlfriend might have broken up with her boyfriend because he double-dipped in the fry sauce, and the love meter might be dangerously low without a way to recover.

"I know so." Stefan also hugged his daughter.

They waved goodbye without another word, making for the exit. Paris appreciated their support and encouragement, but they were her parents after all. Of course, they would think everything she did was great. Still, there were many factors they didn't see or know about when it came to creating love as a fairy godmother.

Paris glanced over her shoulder at the dining room where most were paying their checks or yawning, tired from the food and music and excitement. If the food was too expensive, they might leave and fight with their friends. Maybe they'd argue before leaving the table because they were nickel and diming each other on how to split it. Or perhaps they would be so tired from the food that they'd be cranky.

Paris suddenly worried that this whole restaurant idea was too big. Too risky. That she'd overplayed her hand, and she was going to fail epically.

"Miss Beaufont," Saint Valentine said behind her.

She turned to find the very distinguished man standing by the doorway.

He held out his hand to the entrance with a smile playing at the corners of his mouth. "Would you mind walking me out?"

Paris nodded, realizing this was it. Her moment of doom. When her fate was sealed—for good.

CHAPTER FIFTY-TWO

"As I mentioned before," Saint Valentine began when they were out of the farmhouse and in the cool night air. "I've never seen a final project done on this scale."

Paris halted, turned to face him, and put her hands together pleadingly. "I'm sorry, I went too big, and I realize that bigger isn't better and that I could have done something small that was great instead of something huge that was mediocre."

He arched an eyebrow at her. "You think this was mediocre?"

She scrunched up her nose, catching sight of the band packing up for the night before looking back at Saint Valentine before her. "Bad... it was bad."

"What did you see in there?" He pointed at the restaurant.

"I saw people tired and full and paying up their checks," Paris stated. "There were probably other things I didn't see like fights and the results of overindulgence or jealousy. If I did a delivery business, this wouldn't have happened."

"Do you know what I saw?" Saint Valentine paused and waited for her reaction.

She shrugged, feeling suddenly small.

"Anytime people step out for an evening, they risk fights and jealousy and overindulgence," he began. "So you're not wrong there. Some will go home like that tonight. But also, when people step out of their comfort zone, they run into their true love. They fall head over heels again with the person they've been married to for a decade or rekindle a friendship.

"I saw people sparking new friendships and reconnecting with family members. I saw people sharing fun experiences that will bond them for years to come. I saw things that I hadn't seen in quite some time. I saw love sprouting up around me in many different ways across numerous types of people, and it was simply magical."

"Oh…" Paris didn't know what to say, and she felt silly for it.

"That's only what I saw," Saint Valentine said matter-of-factly. "The question is what the love meter recorded and for that, we'll have to consult it together."

He strode down the walkway to the front of the restaurant where the love meter was. With a sharp turn, he pivoted to face it and eyed it, an unreadable expression on his face. Paris joined him a moment later but kept her eyes low, afraid to see the results of her final project.

"Go on then," Saint Valentine urged. "Delaying seeing how you performed won't make this any easier."

Paris gulped, sucked in a breath, and pressed her eyes shut tightly.

Then she opened them and looked up, and for a moment, she thought she was dreaming. She expected to have failed—that the love meter hadn't registered enough for a passing score. But she never expected this.

CHAPTER FIFTY-THREE

"Is it broken?" Paris blinked at the love meter. The red indicator that ticked along, usually pointing at a number, had disappeared.

"I think it might be, in a way." Saint Valentine chuckled as if this was funny.

Paris resisted the urge to shoot him a look of offense. This was her life and her failure, and it wasn't funny to her. The love meter was so low that it wasn't even registering.

"Well, next time, I'll open a florist shop like everyone else." The feeling of failure already made Paris sick to her stomach. Or maybe it was the food, she thought in horror. *Great, I've given a few hundred people and myself food poisoning.*

Briefly, she imagined a new class at Happily Ever After College called "What Not to Do," taught by Paris Beaufont. Bringing herself back to reality, she realized that Saint Valentine was giving her a look that was halfway between annoyed and amused. Paris wasn't sure which one of those she preferred.

"Next time?" he asked. "Whatever do you mean?"

"Well, since the farm-to-table was an epic failure, I'm saying that for my next final project, I'll do something better."

"Oh, I see," he stated. "I'm not used to dealing with magicians. Fairies act much different."

"I'm a fairy," Paris argued.

"Yes, and you're also a magician," he countered. "As you know, that makes you more analytical, practical, and less prone to whimsy. It also means that you're subject to attacks from your ego."

Now Paris was offended. Her mouth popped open and her hands fisted by her hips. "I'll have you know—"

His laughter cut her off. "And magicians are much more likely to rebel than a fairy."

"Well, that's because magicians have a backbone," Paris argued, disbelieving she was having this heated discussion with the supreme leader of FGA. She was probably going to get kicked out rather than fail. Then it would be jail time for her. Paris wanted to feel sorry for herself that it had all come down to that.

"You do have a backbone, given to you by your confidence drawn from your objective nature," Saint Valentine said good-naturedly. "Conversely, fairies don't have as much of an ego. We tend to think that everything we do is wonderful or good enough. Our confidence, I dare say, is a bit subjectively inflated. Also, we aren't as ambitious as magicians in that regard. I think you've proven that eloquently tonight."

"Well, it appears my magician side was my downfall tonight," Paris said, trying not to sound dejected but feeling that way.

"Your magician part made you spiral to new heights with your project, really risking everything. It made you think holistically about creating love for all people instead of focusing on a single aspect, like pairing lovers together. It also made you doubt yourself every step of the way, meaning that you probably haven't slept and are exhausted, busy trying to find solutions for problems that don't even exist yet."

Paris nodded. "All of that sounds accurate."

"Conversely," he continued. "Your fairy part drove the project toward creative avenues. You grew a garden and adopted animals. You built a farmhouse, and you innovated recipes. Those are all things that appeal to fairies due to our imaginative nature."

Paris couldn't help but laugh a little. "I guess I'm suffering from my multiple personalities conflicting."

"I wouldn't call it suffering."

"Oh?"

Saint Valentine shook his head. "There's no one like you in the world. Never before have we seen a fairy godmother approach things the way you do. Because of that, you get results that we've never seen before. Paris, your project broke the love meter because tonight's festivities created so much love that it was off the scale. The meter simply wasn't designed to record an increase of this magnitude. It's unprecedented. You aren't suffering from your different parts conflicting. You're thriving on a level I haven't witnessed before."

Paris' eyes widened. Her mouth fell open. Her heart gave a loud *thud*. She thought it had stopped, but then it started beating wildly as the blood rushed to the surface of her skin, making her hot. This wasn't what she expected...at all.

"S-S-So I passed?" Paris felt incredibly stupid, but she didn't know what else to say.

Saint Valentine nodded thoughtfully. "Oh, yes, I'd say so. I estimate that Little Pleasures increased love by over two hundred percent, at least, since that's as high as the meter goes. Not only did you pass, but I would vote that you keep this place open for good. It promotes love in a way that should have far-reaching effects."

Paris nodded, swallowed, and knitted her hands together. She would need to hire replacements for Ainsley and Quiet. Although she had some ideas of how to go about doing that, it would still be a challenge. Still, the notion that the restaurant was a success was making her consider all sorts of things. This wasn't her final project anymore —it was an ongoing business.

"The real challenge for me is not deciding whether you passed or not," Saint Valentine continued. "I think we know that's an easy answer. The hard part will be trying to decide in which department to place you as a fairy godmother."

"About that..." Paris began nervously.

"Yes?" He arched a curious eyebrow at her. "Do you have preferences on the departments? Are you familiar with FGA's structure?"

Paris nodded. "Yes, I've been studying it, and that's the thing…"

"What's the thing?" Saint Valentine questioned.

She sucked in a breath, pulling the courage from deep down to say the next part. "Well, now that I know I've passed, I don't want to be a fairy godmother at all."

CHAPTER FIFTY-FOUR

"I apologize." Saint Valentine shook his head in confusion. "I think I misunderstood. You were worried about passing, but you don't want to be a fairy godmother. Can you please explain what I'm missing?"

"I know it sounds crazy," Paris began, mustering the courage to make this bold request, "but based on what you've said and my assessment, I would rather...well, I..."

"You what?" The lines on his forehead showed his confusion.

"I want to be an agent at FGA," Paris said in a rush, knowing that she had to spit it out.

"Oh." Saint Valentine drew the word out. "That's quite unexpected...even for you, Paris."

"I realize fairy godmothers are excellent in the field at setting the scene and throwing people together and matchmaking. But my research of FGA tells me that the agents are the ones who assign the cases. In most instances, they do the initial work, research, and setup. Then they assign a fairy godmother to go in and seal the deal, if you will."

He nodded. "That's a correct assessment of how things work at FGA."

"Well, you see," Paris continued. "I was thinking. Like you said, as a magician, I take a more holistic approach. I'm pragmatic and always looking for solutions. I think I'm better suited for being an agent because of that."

"Agents are roles filled by males," Saint Valentine argued. "Due to their nurturing nature, females have always been fairy godmothers."

"I get it, but just because that's the way it's always been, it doesn't mean that it can't change," Paris countered. "The agents are males because as fairies, they're often more leadership-oriented. I'm part-magician, and we're often leaders regardless of our gender."

"That's true." Saint Valentine appeared to be deliberating.

Paris hoped that she hadn't blown it all with this bold request. It might have made more sense to become a fairy godmother, get used to FGA, then ask for such an opportunity. However, for Paris, being a fairy godmother didn't feel right.

She wasn't the nurturing mother-like figure who Cinderellas were supposed to trust to fix their problems. She wanted to be the tough agent who solved the world's problems by taking down large obstacles to love. Then she could send her fairy godmothers in to sew up the seams and match-make.

Still, she realized she'd asked to skip ten levels for promotion to a job that women didn't hold. What next? Would she pose the notion that fairy godmothers could be men? Fairy godfathers? *It wasn't such a bad idea.*

Paris liked the idea of diversity in FGA. That would be the best way to evolve in the modern world. Diverse thinking was how they'd find innovative solutions.

Men knew best how men thought. Wouldn't that be important for helping Prince Charmings? What if fairy godmothers were missing something important continuously because they could only see things from a female's perspective?

More importantly, what if agents weren't assigning cases right some of the time because their male perspective limited them? What if they shook things up and approached them differently?

Paris didn't say all she was thinking because she thought that Saint

Valentine had probably read between the lines and seen this was what she was getting at. As a magician and fairy, Paris was best suited for a more practical leadership role, where she could employ creative solutions holistically.

She drew in a breath, wishing that Saint Valentine would say something soon. Finally, he granted that wish.

"I'm not sure about this," he said, his voice even. "I'm not sure if FGA is ready. I can tell you that there will be a lot of push back on something like this from the board."

"But you've taken back control from them," she argued.

"I've put them in their place, but that doesn't mean I have total control," he countered. "The board is supposed to be part of the checks and balances system. They can still push back if they want, and I'm afraid they simply aren't ready for something so extreme. We're evolving, but not to something like this."

"Oh…" Paris lowered her chin, trying to keep the disappointment off her face.

"Let me think about this," Saint Valentine stated, his tone sturdy. "I don't disagree that you'd make an excellent leader. I think you'd also make a great fairy godmother, although following protocol from your lead agent seems doubtful."

Thankfully he laughed, breaking the tension. Paris offered a smile.

"I'll see you at the graduation ceremony, which I hope you realize you'll be attending after tonight's performance," he continued. "I'll have an update for you then when I make my assignments of the fairy godmothers to departments. I can't make any promises, but I'll try to see if there's a department that will suit your unique nature. Please temper your expectations, but know that I want to use your talents to the best of my abilities."

Paris nodded. "I get that you have limitations with the board. I appreciate you hearing my bold request."

He smiled, his blue eyes sparkling. "I should've expected such a proposal from you, I realize now."

"I guess so," Paris said a bit sheepishly.

Saint Valentine looked around the grounds. Most people had gone home for the night. All they could hear were the crickets. The lights inside the farmhouse had been extinguished, making the stars pop out more in the dark Colorado sky.

"Wonderful job tonight, Paris Beaufont. Regardless of where you end up at FGA, I suspect you'll go on to do great things."

"Thank you, sir." The chill of the night air seeped into her being. "I really hope so."

"I know so." His eyes twinkled before he turned and strode for the drive.

CHAPTER FIFTY-FIVE

"It's quiet here at night." Faraday looked out at the Rocky Mountains with Paris—the farmhouse empty and dark behind them. The sliver of a moon cast enough light to illuminate the grassy lawn spreading before them and trees in the distance.

She wanted to smile and appreciate it all, but something didn't feel right to her. "Yeah, it's too quiet."

"You sound ungrateful," he chirped, scratching behind his ear.

"No, it's just that something seems wrong." Paris scanned the grounds from the porch on the backside of the farmhouse. "Like, there should be a coyote or the crickets from earlier or something."

When Saint Valentine had left Little Pleasures, there had been a few little noises. There had been a little ambient light. Now, it was still and quiet and mostly dark as Paris and Faraday looked out from the back porch. It wrapped around the farmhouse, and this side faced the thick woods and steep mountains that rose into the sky, framed by twinkling stars.

Although it seemed like a peaceful autumn night, Paris knew that meant something was wrong. She felt it in her chest.

"Are you sure that you're not worried about embracing your destiny at FGA?" Faraday asked.

She turned to face the talking squirrel who had removed his suit and hat, making him easier to look at without squealing from his adorableness. "You think that the quiet and stillness of the night are upsetting me because it's forcing me to think about my future at FGA?"

"I think it's easy for us to go, go, go, but when things settle down, we struggle because then we have to face the reality of our lives," he stated matter-of-factly.

"I like the reality of my life," she argued.

"What if Saint Valentine makes you a fairy godmother?" he questioned.

"Well, that's what I'm supposed to be, isn't it?"

"But it's not what you want to be," he argued.

"I'll be fine, regardless. I won't be in jail, so that's a plus," Paris stated so adamantly that she had to admit she was trying to convince more than the squirrel.

"You can talk to me, Pare."

"I'm fine," she stated. "The restaurant was a huge success. I'll graduate as a fairy godmother, according to Saint Valentine. Little Pleasures will go on to create love. I couldn't be happier."

"Except that you feel something is wrong," he observed, looking at her sideways.

"Fare, something is wrong," she whispered, looking out at the dark grounds, sensing an evil unlike she'd felt before. "I feel it at my core."

"Because you don't want to be a fairy godmother?" he asked.

A cackle, loud and sharp, ripped through the darkness, assaulting their ears. It was close. Then again, it could have been on the far side of the mountain range. It was hard to know since the cold night air made noise travel.

Paris straightened. Beside her, so did Faraday. They silently looked at each other, a foreboding dread in their eyes.

Then she mouthed, "Something is wrong."

He soundlessly replied, "Someone is out there."

"One, two, three," the high-pitched voice screamed, cutting through the night air. The outline of a dark figure appeared in front of the woods. Then it disappeared, running into the thick trees. "You'll never catch me!"

Without seeing her completely, Paris knew that was ESS—Paris' shadow-self. The monster had come after her. She was luring her into the forest. Alone. Paris knew the science experiment of a creature was incredibly dangerous and powerful.

Paris didn't hesitate. Neither did Faraday beside her. They both jumped off the porch and set out toward Evil Shadow-self—who they knew was the combination of the tooth fairies and magician who had come together to try to defeat Paris and her demon blood.

The former Knees had come after Paris. They wanted a fight. They were going to get one.

Little did Madden's monster know, Paris' ultimate plan was to trap ESS and offer her to the Seelie queen, thereby ending a long war. All Paris had to do was be better than Evil Shadow-self, but that was the challenging part since Madden built the monster to defeat her.

CHAPTER FIFTY-SIX

The grass was slippery with dew, but Paris' footing was solid. Her strides were long, and she made incredible progress thanks to her demon blood. However, as she sped across the dark grounds toward the even darker woods, she reminded herself that her evil shadow-self also had demon blood. That meant ESS was fast.

Paris didn't know what else that would mean. She hadn't gotten a good glimpse of the figure before she taunted her and ran for the woods.

Beside Paris and easily keeping up was Faraday, bounding in long leaps over the grass. Weaponless and exhausted from the long day, Paris didn't know what she and the squirrel would do to capture her shadow-self. However, she couldn't let this opportunity to catch ESS go. Turning the Knees over to Queen Helena MacGillie was crucial to fix relations between the tooth fairies and fairy godmothers. She wished that she had a moment to prepare for this battle.

That's how life went, though. Paris slowed as she neared the forest. One didn't get the opportunity to rest before the big fight. Usually, it was sprung on someone when they weren't expecting it. The true victor had to rise to the occasion or admit defeat. Paris wasn't going to do the latter.

Halting, Paris and Faraday studied the dark woods ahead of them. Running straight into a dense forest wasn't smart. Paris needed a strategy, even if ESS had sprung all of this on her.

She pushed the exhaustion away, inviting in the adrenaline as she eyed the forest. Her heightened senses picked up the slight footsteps roughly twenty yards inside the tree line. There was a cackle to the right. Paris jerked her head in that direction and narrowed her eyes, willing them to adjust to the darkness.

Then another sharp laugh cut through the air, this time to the left.

How did the monster move so quickly from one end of the woods to the other without making noise?

She leaned forward, picking up on footsteps still to the right.

ESS hadn't moved. She'd used magic to throw her voice. She was playing with Paris and trying to trick her. However, Paris refused to be fooled by three dumb tooth fairy dropouts. They wanted to fight her and win so badly that they became one.

Paris knew exactly how she would defeat the Knees. She was going to do the one thing they didn't expect—not fight back.

CHAPTER FIFTY-SEVEN

"Oh, well." Paris yawned as she shrugged at Faraday. "I don't know where that freak could be. What do you say we turn in for the night? I'm beat."

The rustling in the forest paused. ESS was listening...

Faraday's eyes widened with alarm, but then he put together what she was doing. Paris could charge into the dark forest, playing right into ESS' hands, or she could draw her out.

Faraday nodded slowly. "Yeah, I could use some sleep after being on my feet all night."

"Yeah, and I don't feel like ruining my nice night with looking at that horrendous monster in the forest." Paris dared to turn around. "She's bound to look like a real cow."

Faraday laughed, but that elicited a different reaction from ESS in the woods. A scream full of rage cut through the night air. Paris resisted the urge to look toward the piercing noise. Instead, she casually glanced down at the squirrel.

"She even sounds ugly...well, uglier," Paris muttered, knowing full well that Madden's monster could hear her.

Another snicker fell from the squirrel's mouth. He knew that Paris was taunting the Knees. The question was, would it work?

Her evil shadow-self had gotten a head start, charging into the forest. ESS probably hoped that Paris would run in there blindly, tripping over logs in the dark and falling into whatever trap the monster set up for her. Paris planned on running after the weird science experiment, but only when she had her eyes on her.

Then she was going to tackle the monster and gently subdue her. Although she might give her a black eye or two. Still, she'd keep her alive. That's how she had to deliver ESS to Queen Helena MacGillie.

A high-pitched growl shot through the autumn night, making a chill run down Paris' back. However, she covered it by pretending to laugh.

"Sounds like wolf-girl is hungry," Paris remarked, keeping the spot where the sound came from in her peripheral vision. "I bet she eats enough for three."

"Then she'll surely become obese soon," Faraday stated matter-of-factly.

"I don't think it will matter," Paris imparted. "The bear she breeds with will probably want her to have a little extra blubber."

There was a rush of noise as the monster charged forward, *crunching* over leaves and branches. Then a *whoosh* of air when ESS halted by the tree line.

A hiss shot from the Knees' mouth, and in her side vision, Paris caught sight of the weird creature—pale and grotesque.

"We are incredible," the monster said in a scratchy voice. "You will bow to our greatness, but that still won't save you from your fate."

CHAPTER FIFTY-EIGHT

Quite simply, Paris' evil shadow-self was grotesque.

ESS might be equal parts of Paris: magician, fairy, and demon, but she didn't look like the dark version of her. She looked like a hideous form of the halfling.

It was as if the experiment had smushed the Knees' three faces together. Their features competed with each other rather than one taking a specific role. Their nose, for instance, was like a compilation of all of theirs. It was pointy like Courtney's but wide like Whitney's and also crooked like Sidney's.

No wonder they were easily outraged when I made fun of their appearance. Paris looked the strange creature over. Evil Shadow-self had a gaunt face, her cheekbones severely protruding. The monster's mouth was uneven, her lips large at the ends and thin in the middle. Most revolting about her face were the red eyes that glowed as they regarded Paris with definite evil intent.

Evil Shadow-self's hair was long and short in places and grew in patches, with several bald spots on her head. Her arms were also different lengths, and her legs were too. When she started forward, it made for a strange movement, like a praying mantis coming after its prey. Paris realized then that even with their demon blood, she could outrun the Knees.

She could defeat this deranged monster.

Raising her palm, Paris quickly shot a stunning spell at ESS, planning to paralyze her. Then she could cart her off to Queen Helena MacGillie, and all her problems would be over.

However, to her shock and severe disappointment, the spell hit the creature, and volts of electricity spread out over the surface of her face and arms and chest like a spider's web. The spell ricocheted off and away, completely ineffective. The creature appeared to have a forcefield protecting her.

The Knees cackled loudly, appearing to smile, but the gesture was revolting on her deformed face. "Nice try," the monster said in a deep, demonic voice. "Now, our turn."

She held up her bony hand that was strange in itself with fingers of varying lengths, the thumb longer than all the rest. "Get ready to die, halfling."

Paris jerked her gaze down, looking at Faraday for help.

His eyes widened, and he mouthed one word, terror radiating off him suddenly. "Run!"

CHAPTER FIFTY-NINE

It was loud inside the Knees' head. That's what the newspapers and authorities had been calling her, so that was the name she adopted for herself.

The problem the three women didn't anticipate when they morphed into one was who would be in charge. They figured that since they were becoming one person, they'd all be in control. The reality was they all could take the reins and control their body but one of the others could also overpower them. Even more jarring was that all their thoughts streamed through their head at once, creating an overwhelming disturbance, like multiple voices screaming simultaneously.

We'll take her down once and for all, Whitney said in their head, raising the Knees' hand into the air, aiming it at Paris Beaufont.

Our magic is unstable, Sidney argued in a rush. *It backfired last time.*

She's right, Courtney agreed. *Let's charge after her. We're fast.*

We use magic, Whitney urged, their hand shaking as the other two parts of the Knees fought her internally.

We attack her using our strength, Sidney fought, trying to push forward, but Whitney held them in place, knowing what she intended to do. They nearly stumbled to the ground, their balance thrown off by the resistance. Their hand jerked up and down as though Knees couldn't decide what to do with it.

The halfling and squirrel a few yards away gave them a strange look, no doubt confused by the weird display.

Let us move, Whit. Courtney fought against the magician not allowing them to run.

Let me hit her with a spell, Whitney argued. *I can do it. I know how to use magic better than you two.*

It's two against one, Sidney countered. *Let us go!*

Fine, Whitney acquiesced, giving them control of their legs. However, she also stole the opportunity to use magic and jerked their hand back into the air, and shot a spell straight at Paris Beaufont.

CHAPTER SIXTY

The bright red light shot from Knees' hand and straight for Paris. She hardly had enough time to dive for the grass to avoid being struck by the spell. It was no doubt meant to cut her in two or blow her up. Thankfully she didn't have the misfortune of learning what the magic did because it passed over her as she rolled on the ground, tumbling in the opposite direction from the monster.

Paris wasn't sure what she was seeing when the weird experiment started after her. ESS' hand had shot into the air and down again, her chin jerking back and forth like she was arguing internally. Paris realized that's what was happening exactly.

Three people couldn't be stuck together without wrestling for control. They were what they intended, three different parts: magician, fairy, and demon. Unlike Paris, it appeared that the monster was separate parts, not all mixed, playing off each other's strengths.

Paris was a vegetable soup, all pureed together, none of her parts identifiable from the others. Her evil shadow-self was a mixed vegetable kabob, each piece separate from the other, as though they'd all been skewered and charred together—frying them as one.

Paris popped up to her feet, searching the grass for Faraday. The squirrel had run for the edge of the woods. He was searching for something in the tree area, but she couldn't fathom what.

Quickly she assessed her options. It appeared that she couldn't shoot spells at the Knees because of a weird forcefield covering her from when she fused. Maybe Faraday was trying to figure out how to break that magic, although it appeared he was rustling through leaves.

Not able to rely on her magic, Paris realized she would have to fall back on her first mode of defense.

She lunged low and raised her fists.

Reading her body language and realizing Paris was inviting the monster to a fight, the gross creature lumbered forward, although several times she stumbled back as if changing her mind. However, her fists came up as she neared and it appeared they were about to have a good old throwdown.

CHAPTER SIXTY-ONE

Faraday caught sight of Paris preparing to fight and froze—his eyes widening suddenly. "No!" he yelled, his paws in the air frantic.

Paris paused, blinking at the strange reaction to her defending herself. That was long enough for the manic creature to lumber forward and stagger sideways. Then seeming to get control of her limbs, ESS raised her hand again.

Paris knew what was coming next and launched herself to the side in Faraday's direction as another red shot of light streaked over her head. This time she saw the damage it would've done to her as the spell scorched the earth.

"What's the deal, squirrel?" Paris called after jumping to her feet and looking over her shoulder briefly at Faraday. The monster was trying to turn, but pivoting appeared to be a bit much for her, as if she couldn't figure out which way to turn.

"I don't think you can touch her," Faraday urged. "I think the electrical force that's shielding her from your spells will shock you."

"Okay." Paris drew out the word as she lunged low, watching as the monster wrestled with itself, raising her hand and swiftly throwing it back down. She turned to the side and back again as if doing a weird dance. "What am I supposed to do? I can't hit her with my fists or a spell."

"I'm working on it." Faraday continued to rummage in the ground cover by the tree line.

"What are you doing?" Paris kept an eye on the monster.

"I'm trying to find a vine or something we can use to tie her up."

"Good call." Paris gulped as the creature finally figured out how to turn and face her.

"Ready to die, Paris?" Knees asked, her voice like gravel.

"Not really," Paris casually remarked as ESS raised her hand again.

This time the spell that shot from her fingertips wasn't a neat stream of light. It was a blanket of red. Paris immediately knew there would be no ducking the curse. All she could do was try to outrun it.

Picking up Faraday, Paris ran straight into the woods, the heat from the spell racing after her. She kicked it into high gear, hoping that her feet carried her faster than the magic could get to them.

CHAPTER SIXTY-TWO

The chill of the forest hit Paris like she was entering a walk-in freezer. The mist from her breath shot from her mouth as she exhaled, running fast. It was hard to see where they were going, but Paris tried to keep her eyes focused on the opening ahead. There wasn't one so she simply leapt over logs and large rocks and wove around trees.

Behind her, she heard the monster pursuing, although she didn't sound as though she was moving as gracefully as Paris—or as fast. Paris realized one reason why when a blast of red light illuminated the forest behind her.

Glancing over her shoulder, Paris caught the spell's trajectory and jumped behind a large tree trunk as the combat magic shot through the air. The flash of heat hit Paris in the face, and the force of the spell picked her and Faraday up and threw them several feet. She landed on her back on a patch of soft earth. It cushioned her fall, although the assault had knocked the air out of her lungs. The whole thing would have been a lot worse if not for the tree trunk shielding them.

However, the attack had lost Paris precious time, and to her horror, she caught sight of the monster stomping forward. The creature's red glowing eyes made her look even more ominous as she came around the tree, stalking in Paris' direction.

Scrambling to her feet, Paris tucked Faraday under her arm and sprinted as fast as she could farther into the forest. She wasn't paying attention to where she was going. And she was so far off a path that she constantly tripped over bushes and sticks, trampling through the dense forest.

"That way," Faraday said when a clearing became somewhat visible ahead. The illumination thankfully-slash-unthankfully was because of another flash of red light as Knees sent another spell in their direction.

Paris dove to avoid it and jumped down a hill into what appeared to be a large ditch. However, it was clear with no trees and gave them an open path, which she needed to get some distance from the monster. Then they could form a plan since so far, nothing she'd tried could subdue ESS.

Picking up speed, Paris ran without obstacles, the squirrel in her arms and flashes of red in the distance. Chancing a look over her shoulder, she caught sight of Knees tripping down the incline she'd jumped, not descending as gracefully as she did. That's when Paris realized where they were.

"This is a dry creek," Paris stated, noticing the high banks on either side of them.

"I haven't had much of a chance to explore the land, but there's an old mining area up ahead." Faraday's claws pierced Paris' arm.

She nodded. "Maybe we can find some supplies there or an option to gain an advantage."

"Yes, we need a moment to strategize. Then we can take the advantage."

Paris was starting to feel a slight bit of hope when lightning streaked overhead followed by a clap of thunder.

Although Paris didn't know much about the terrain in Colorado, she knew enough to know that one place you didn't want to be in a thunderstorm was a dry creek. This area was known for its flash floods, and nothing filled up faster than a shallow creek.

CHAPTER SIXTY-THREE

"We need to get out of here," Faraday said in a rush.

"I know," Paris replied between breaths, her legs kicking harder. "Dry creeks. Flash floods. I've read about these stories. We aren't safe here."

"No, not us," Faraday said, climbing up to Paris' shoulder looking over it at their pursuer. "We have to get Knees to safety."

"Huh?" Paris nearly slowed, not having expected that from the squirrel.

"Well, you don't want her harmed, right?" Faraday questioned as if they were having a casual debate and not running from Frankenstein's monster's cousin.

"Yes, I need her...alive..."

"And you need her as a halfling with demon blood, like you," Faraday added as another streak of lightning lit their path ahead, followed by a loud *clap* of thunder that promised rain soon. The air felt suddenly heavy with moisture like it did before a torrential downpour.

"Right." Paris tried to decide if she should chance jumping up onto the bank and navigating through the overgrown forest or staying on the clear path that could soon flood with rain. She was an easy target for ESS behind her, but she appeared to be using her efforts to catch up rather than shoot spells. The problem was that when the monster wanted to, she could be quite fast, and she was gaining on Paris.

"I haven't done much work exploring Dr. Madden's notes," Faraday imparted, "but from what little I could understand, it was electricity that fused the three Knees and demon blood."

"Right," Paris repeated. "The lightning, like with Frankenstein's monster."

"Exactly," Faraday chirped. "The thing that could separate them is the same that put them together."

Paris felt the electrical current in the air as the implications of what Faraday was saying set in. "Do you mean that if that monster gets struck by lightning or electrocuted by charged water, then she'll—"

"She'd split apart and won't be a halfling with demon blood anymore," Faraday interrupted in a rush. "I'm not sure what she'll be, but she won't be what the Unseelie king wants to end the war."

"So in a weird turn of events, I need to keep her safe—not only alive," Paris remarked, veering out of the dry creek as the first fat rain droplets started to fall.

CHAPTER SIXTY-FOUR

B ecause Paris' sidekick was a nerd, he'd told her all about this area of Colorado. She knew that each year lightning struck the mountains around there over seven hundred times. She knew that the combination of flash flooding and lightning made for an electrical breeding ground. Not only was being in a flood area dangerous, but the chances of an electrical shock were exponential.

"We need to get to higher ground," Paris said, stumbling to climb up the bank with Faraday in her arms.

Sensing this, the squirrel wiggled free and ran ahead of her, leading the way. "We need to get somewhere dry. Even a small shock that is carried through the air or across the wet grounds could be enough to sever the three women and their demon blood."

The rain had fallen hard and heavy, soaking Paris at once. It also made it hard for her to see Faraday as he hopped over logs and bushes, progressing up a steep hill. The only advantage of this weather was that it made it harder for her pursuer to see her. However, peering briefly over her shoulder, Paris caught sight of ESS—her glowing red eyes showed her location. She wasn't too far behind, working on climbing out of the dry creek, following them.

Unfortunately, the rain and threat of electrocution weren't a deterrent for Knees. She hardly slowed as she held up her hand and yelled. A moment later, a giant tree beside Paris split as if electricity had struck it—but in actuality, it was magic.

It cracked and fell in her direction. Not sure of the trunk's trajectory, Paris picked up the speed. The tree fell with a loud *thud*, rocking the ground under them, nearly making Paris eat dirt as she stumbled forward.

She glanced over her shoulder and watched as her evil shadow-self hopped over the freshly fallen tree like it was a fun obstacle course and continued like a mad soldier. The rain only enlivened the monster.

Lightning shot down in the forest and lit up the sky and their surroundings. An explosion nearby rocked Paris again, making her throw up her arm to shield her eyes from the sudden brightness. The lightning had struck a tree, but thankfully, the soaked forest wasn't going to catch on fire easily. However, as they got higher, they also risked getting hit by lightning or electrocuted.

"In there," Faraday said. The explosion of light had shown him a path to a nearby cave.

Paris climbed up a steep hill hand over feet, following the squirrel who made quick work of getting up to the cave opening. She checked over her shoulder. Thankfully ESS was following them. Unfortunately, she was much closer than before, making quick progress—catching up with Paris.

CHAPTER SIXTY-FIVE

The dry cave was welcome after being in the drenched forest—the rain had assaulted Paris in the face and made the trek even more difficult. The problem now was that it was dark, much too dark to see without magic.

Realizing that it would give her location away but deciding it was worth it, Paris created a light orb to show their way. She'd be an easy target if she knocked herself out running into a cave wall.

To her relief, the cave wasn't a dead end. At least not from where she stood. Three different tunnels led in different directions. Faraday, also grateful for the light, ran over to the first tunnel.

"Let me figure out which one has an outlet," Faraday stated. "Keep a lookout and try to keep ESS back."

"Right, without killing her or getting her electrocuted," Paris remarked.

"Exactly." Faraday knocked on the tunnel wall, put his ear to it, and listened. He pulled away and ran to the second one. "We want her to follow us. I think if we get her to the mining area, we can contain her."

"I hope you're right." Paris looked out and saw the monster climbing up the steep hill in their direction. She pointed at her, sending a spell down that eroded the dirt, making the creature slide to the bottom where she started. She screamed and thrashed in the rain but wasn't deterred and continued the trek after getting to her feet. "That thing is really powerful. She's intent on killing me no matter what."

Faraday pressed his ear to the second tunnel wall, then started for the last. "Yes, and taking down that tree was no small use of magic. I'm afraid to tell you that you won't be able to overpower her."

"Which means I'll have to outsmart her." Paris watched as the monster climbed, making progress in their direction.

"Thankfully, that shouldn't be hard for us." Faraday pointed at the first tunnel. "We need to go down that one."

"Okay, but how do we ensure that she knows which way we went?" Paris realized they were playing a very dangerous game of cat and mouse.

"We wait until the last possible moment and run. She'll see the light from your orb and know which direction to go."

Paris nodded, glancing down the hill outside the cave where it was still raining hard. She could already hear the sound of water rushing in the creek in the distance. She was grateful that they weren't still down there. However, as she peered down the dark cave tunnel they were about to enter, she wasn't confident that where they were heading didn't hold more dangers. She was sure it would have challenges.

CHAPTER SIXTY-SIX

The light from the orb wasn't great. It only illuminated the space ahead by about five or so feet. That meant that although Paris wanted to run, she kept moving at an even pace, simply walking fast. That was getting increasingly more difficult as the howling started behind them, echoing through the cave tunnel.

That haunting sound paired with the drumming of rain overhead was a chilling combination that made Paris' blood beat wildly.

"How far does this tunnel go?" Paris murmured, wondering what their next course of action was. It would end hopefully next to the mining area. That would lend them some new options.

Still, Paris was starting to doubt what she could do to capture this monster who had an electric force field around her, making it impossible to hit her with a spell or a fist. She hoped that Faraday had some bright ideas—since that was kind of his job.

He ran over to the wall and knocked, putting his ear next to it immediately. "Not much farther. The rain should let up soon."

"How do you know?" Paris thought the hammering of rain overhead was getting louder.

"Because that's how these flash floods work," Faraday explained, continuing to scamper forward. "It rains hard and fast for a short time. One has to weather the quick storm and not get pulled away in the current. If you do that, you're fine. But it only takes one bad decision to be in the wrong place and time when one of those electric floods passes through."

"Okay, that makes me feel marginally better." Paris looked over her shoulder and see saw the shadow of the pursuing monster. ESS was following, which was good. She was gaining on them, which was bad. Paris picked up her speed. Faraday, sensing the same as her, also hurried more, his tail billowing behind him.

The squirrel sniffed the air as they hopped over small stones and veered around cave walls. "There's fresh air up ahead. We're almost to the end of the tunnel."

"Good." Paris suddenly ducked, nearly running into a low part of the ceiling.

Faraday sped up, then halted. Paris slowed after catching the look of horror in his eyes. The orb illuminated the space between them but nothing ahead.

"What is it?" Paris asked. "The exit is up ahead?" She squinted past him. "I don't see it. Where is it?"

He pointed down. "It's there. We have to jump."

CHAPTER SIXTY-SEVEN

Paris halted before she slid down a steep slope. The smell of fresh water and the sound of it moving were all around her. It took a moment for the orb's light to illuminate the area around them, but she realized that below them was a small lake of sorts. The cave over them shielded it, but in the distance, she saw a bit of light through an opening.

"We have to jump into that lake?" Paris checked over her shoulder. They were running out of time. The monster was close.

"And swim," Faraday added matter-of-factly. "The land should be past that archway there." He pointed at where the ambient light was winking roughly fifty feet away.

"Remember that whole lightning and electricity problem," Paris stated. "That's a bunch of water, a conduit if I remember correctly."

He nodded quickly. "You remember correctly. The lightning storm seems to have dissipated, so we should be okay. We need to jump now, though, because we have to swim and get ahead of ESS."

"How do you know that it's deep enough to jump?" Paris peered over the edge and looked down into the pool of clear cave water.

"I don't, but we're out of options."

Faraday was right because the creature rounded the corner, her mouth open and red eyes murderous. Her speed picked up at the sight of Paris.

Without hesitation, Paris plugged her nose and threw herself off the side of the cliff, taking the ten-foot jump into the mysterious water below, hoping it was deep enough.

CHAPTER SIXTY-EIGHT

The water was freezing, nestled in the cold cave basin. Paris sucked in a breath as soon as she kicked up to the surface, grateful not to have met a shallow bottom. Immediately she kicked for the other side, where the cave opening promised an exit.

However, another loud *splash* met her ears. The monster was after her, not wasting any time or allowing her to get any distance. The only thing that made Paris feel better was that Faraday was making fast progress. He was a quick swimmer for a little squirrel with a fluffy tail.

Within a few hard strokes, Paris found the pool's edge and pulled herself onto the rocky shore. Faraday had already shaken himself and scurried for the exit. He appeared to be surveying the area when Paris pulled herself out and shrugged off her leather jacket, leaving it behind. She couldn't have it weighing her down. However, it saddened her that tonight's adventures had ruined the brand-new garment her parents gave her for the restaurant's opening, and she had to leave it behind.

Better it than her. She checked over her shoulder.

Thankfully, ESS appeared to be as uncoordinated with swimming as she was with walking. Paris pictured that the multiple personalities inside her were fighting for control, making her go in different directions and causing her movements to be less than graceful.

"Where to?" Paris huffed and looked around. They were still in the forested area, although the trees were less dense. The rain had let up, but she heard the sound of water churning through the forest.

An area to the south was partly illuminated by the stars and moon trying to peek out. Faraday pointed in that direction. "That's where the abandoned mining area is. It's our best bet."

"Okay, lead the way." Paris glanced back in the direction of the creature splashing around. Knees thrashed, and for a moment, Paris thought she might drown. She tensed, wondering if she would have to jump in and save her in an ironic turn of events. Paris needed the science experiment alive. Unconscious would be ideal—but alive.

Thankfully it appeared that the monster recovered as she neared the shore area where she could get some footing. Paris didn't wait around any longer to see that she was okay. Instead, she raced after Faraday, realizing that she'd given ESS enough time to trail them to the mining area.

Paris hoped that it lent them an option for capturing the creature. Otherwise, she wasn't sure what they were going to do. She couldn't keep up the chase all night.

CHAPTER SIXTY-NINE

The ground was soft from the rain and made running difficult. However, Paris pushed on, making her way to a small set of buildings surrounded by big machinery.

"What are we looking for?" Paris whispered to Faraday as she pursued him.

"A way to trap her," he stated.

"But not kill her," Paris added.

"Exactly," he stated. "Try this door." He pointed at the first building they came to. "I think this is a furnace room."

"Well, I'm not sure if that will work." Paris pushed down on the door handle, but it was locked. She held up her finger. "I have magic. Shall I?"

Faraday glanced in the direction of the cave mouth where the beast had emerged, dripping wet and looking especially ugly. He shook his head. "You're right. That's probably not the right place to set a trap. What we need are some tools." He scurried between the buildings and stopped at the next door. "Try this one."

Paris checked the handle. It was also locked. She peered in through the dusty window and squinted. "I think that's a set of communal places. I see tables and chairs."

Faraday shook his head again. "That won't work."

"It would help if you told me what you're looking for, squirrel."

"I don't know," he stated. "Something that will hold her until you can get her to the queen. Or something to undo the force field protecting her. I'll know when I see it."

"Hey," Paris began, following the squirrel. "Why didn't the water mess with the electrical force field? Could it have made things worse and fried her, or could it be gone?"

He paused, thinking. "Unfortunately, I think because of its magitech that it's separate from ESS. It's probably simply a part of her recent regeneration and will fade, but in the meantime, it makes it impossible for you to touch her without getting shocked or hit her with a spell. It's like an eggshell encasing her."

"It wasn't affected by the water? I thought electricity and water weren't friends."

"Again, magitech doesn't have the same rules as other things. Plus, the Fang Wellspring is fueling a lot of what she is, and that doesn't follow the same universal rules."

"But if she gets electrocuted then…"

"Then I hypothesize that she'll split." Faraday paused by the last building on that row. "Okay, try this door. I think this is our best bet."

Paris turned the doorknob and found the building open to her relief. Then she poked her head inside and looked around, her chest tightening at the sight.

CHAPTER SEVENTY

"I t's full of tools," Paris said in a whisper.

"Perfect," Faraday stated.

Paris shook her head and created a light orb to show Faraday the space. "No, I don't think so. Going in there is a death trap."

He poked his head in as the light covered all of the objects hanging on the wall. There were axes of various sizes. Chisels. Hammers. Picks. Knives. Large nails. Tons and tons of sharp instruments.

"Perfect!" Faraday chirped, bounding into the large building.

"Perfect," Paris stated, following him against her better judgment. "If that monster comes in here, I'm pretty much dead. I've given her a hundred ways to kill me, and I can't do anything to retaliate. All I can do is shield myself since I can't hurt her."

"We could find something in here to gain the advantage." Faraday disappeared. "I need a chance to look around."

"I wish you'd tell me what this thing was that could help us," Paris said as she heard footsteps outside the building. The science experiment was close. Moments from finding them...in a building full of sharp objects, and Paris couldn't use any of them on her enemy. Instead, she'd surely be part of ESS' target practice. Paris quickly wondered when she had her last tetanus shot.

"I don't know what I'm looking for," Faraday stated. "I will once I find it."

"Brilliant," Paris muttered as a clawing rapped at the door like the beast decided to have manners all of a sudden and knock before entering. Paris wondered if she could tell her that they were closed or to go away. Or throw herself up against the door. Or use magic. While she was considering her options, the door handle turned.

"Buy me some time," Faraday said from a darkened corner, still rummaging around. "I'll find us a way to capture that baddie."

Paris pulled in a breath, trying to decide how to survive an angry monster that she needed to keep alive while surrounded by sharp weapons.

CHAPTER SEVENTY-ONE

"Heeeyyyy giiiiirrrl," Paris sang when her very unattractive shadow-self stepped through the door into the weapon room. ESS was dripping wet, her black hair clinging to her white face, making her look even scarier, if possible.

"I've been meaning to ask." Paris backed up, noticing there was a door on the other side of the room. "Those boots you're wearing, where did you get them?"

The monster grunted, her red eyes intensifying as she fisted her hands beside her and trudged forward like a possessed bull.

"Like, an Army-Navy store?" Paris continued to back up, trying to figure out her options. She had to defend herself but couldn't attack. This was like a complex equation. After this, she was going to skin that squirrel.

The science experiment grunted, twitching her head violently to the side. Paris tensed, wondering if ESS was suffering from an aneurism, but she recovered and growled once more, her way of saying, "I'm good."

"Or maybe a cool thrift store?" Paris continued to question, trying to stall the only way she knew how.

Knees marched forward, holding up both hands as though she

planned to strangle Paris. Thankfully the beast was limping badly and bleeding in places, not moving with as much agility as before. She was also wrestling internally again, her arms darting up and down like she couldn't figure out if she wanted to end Paris or invite her on a shopping spree.

Paris easily ducked to the side, trying to pick a spot in the warehouse that didn't have as many weapons on the wall. "Sooooo it's pretty cool that you're a halfling and get to join the club."

The creature yelled, her face turning an awful shade of red. Suddenly ten different sharp tools telekinetically flew off the wall and hovered in the air next to the monster. All of them pointed in Paris' direction.

"Club of two. You and me," Paris said in a squeaky voice, realizing that she might have to kill the thing in front of her. It would ruin things with the Seelie and Unseelie, but that was better than dying.

The monster looked like it needed to be put out of its misery as it limped forward, the sharp weapons moving along with her at an uneven pace.

Paris held up her hands, pretending to surrender. She was creating an invisible shield in case ESS released the weapons and fired at her. It wouldn't hold for long, but hopefully long enough.

"Hey, I'm not fighting you," Paris stated as she lowered her hands. "I think we got off on the wrong foot."

The creature stepped forward, and Paris noticed how mangled one of her feet was, pointed to the side. She gulped. "Did I say foot? I meant...hey, are you a Scorpio? I've always thought that was a cool zodiac sign..."

The monster yelled again, this time so loudly that it rattled the weapons on the wall. The ones in the air beside the monster shot forward a few inches. Paris held up her hands, pretending to reinforce the surrender act, but she was keeping up her shield.

She heard the door open behind her, felt a draft of wind, and saw the monster's eyes dart over her shoulder.

Then Faraday said, "I've got it. Let's go! Hurry."

Paris didn't hesitate. She turned and ran for the other door, knowing that she couldn't keep up this act much longer—face-to-face with the beast. The weapons all shot forward straight in her direction. Checking over her shoulder, Paris saw as they all hit her invisible barrier where they fell at once, clattering at the monster's mangled feet.

CHAPTER SEVENTY-TWO

Knowing that Knees would be in hot pursuit, Paris raced as fast as she could out the door, searching for Faraday. The shield would hold the monster back, but only for a few seconds. It would act like a sticky place that pulled her back briefly before she broke through, especially with her strength and charged anger.

The squirrel was a fair distance ahead, up a hill and holding something bulky that Paris couldn't make out from that distance in the dark. Faraday waved at her. "Come on. We need to get up here."

"Why?" Paris ran after him. "Where?"

"Up there." He turned and sprinted to the edge of a cliff.

"Again, why?" Paris called after him, looking over her shoulder. As she suspected, the monster had broken free and looked madder than hell as she charged out of the building. Apparently, Knees was the resourceful type and had thought to grab a large ax on her way out of the weapons room.

"Just get up here," Faraday encouraged.

"Are you going to tell me what your plan is?" Paris realized that the cliff broke suddenly and dropped off sharply to dizzying heights.

"No time," Faraday stated. "Just lure ESS up here."

"That's not a problem." Paris pointed at the monster lumbering in her direction, drooling and grunting. "She has a super big crush on me."

Faraday had moved off to the side of the cliff and was hiding out of the way. Paris didn't have a chance to see what he was carrying.

"What's the plan, squirrel?" Paris watched as Knees made her way up the hill, the sharp ax in her hands and murder in her demon eyes.

"Let her come after you and jump out of the way at the last minute."

"I feel like there needs to be an 'and then' to that statement." Paris knew the moment was upon them. The monster was so close.

"Then you'll—"

The squirrel's instructions were cut off by the loud, intruding scream of the science experiment as she charged forward, swinging the ax and seemingly energized by the night air.

CHAPTER SEVENTY-THREE

At lightning speed, the mammoth ax swung through the air at Paris. She ducked, wishing that she had the time to know Faraday's plan. Now she was playing to survive, and this game felt very, very real.

She jumped backward as Knees came at her, but she nearly tripped over the side of the cliff. Looking over her shoulder, she caught a glimpse of the dismally long fall it was to a rocky bottom below. Her heel was over the edge, and any bit of weight backward would send her over the edge.

Throwing her weight low, Paris barreled forward, under the creature's ax and arms and coming up on the other side of her. This fast motion confused the beast, and she looked out over the cliff as though thinking that Paris simply disappeared into thin air.

Paris realized then that the whole Frankenstein process probably robbed the already dumb tooth fairy dropouts of precious brain cells. The monster grunted, and Paris saw Faraday on a ledge, pointing at the cliff on the other side of ESS.

What did he want? Paris wondered. Did he want her to push the monster? That was what they'd been trying to avoid—killing the halfling who could end a war.

However, when the squirrel gestured the universal movement for "push," she figured that's what he intended, and she decided to trust him. If she couldn't trust the talking squirrel who put on a top hat for her that night, who could she trust?

Barreling back the direction she'd come from, she threw her arms out, ready to push them into the monster's back before she spun. Unfortunately, the creature was faster than she'd bargained for and swung around with the giant ax.

Paris dove to the side, rolling in the mud. ESS yelled, holding the ax over her head and bringing it down on Paris. Well, it would have connected if she didn't roll to the side. The blade hit the mud and splattered it everywhere. The monster pulled the weapon into the air again, going in for another chance to split Paris like a log.

She shot up to balance on her tailbone and swung her feet out, knocking Knees' legs out from under her. The creature fell straight to her back in the mud, the ax tumbling out of her hands. Paris went to grab for it, but it tumbled down the hill and away.

Away was good. Not in the monster's hands was better.

However, the creature recovered quickly and wrestled to her feet, but in a strange crouched position. Paris was still on her butt and trying to get up but kept slipping in the mud. That's why when Knees dove right at her head, she did the first thing she could think of and ducked.

The deformed halfling plunged straight over Paris and the edge of the cliff—to what was certainly her death.

CHAPTER SEVENTY-FOUR

Paris sucked in a breath, disbelieving she was regretful about her enemy's demise. It all happened so fast. But things were still moving fast as she watched the monster launch over the cliff. Knees attempted to catch herself, her arms flailing, her toes trying to catch the edge. Then her momentum took her down.

"Hurry!" Faraday yelled, throwing something into the air. "Tie her up."

Paris didn't know what was happening as she watched something long and brown spiral through the air in the direction of the mutant halfling. Then all of it came together. Faraday's plan. The cliff—and what he intended her to do.

Tying the monster up wouldn't have worked because she would've resisted, and she was too powerful to be stopped. However, falling over the side of the cliff, the beast was thinking of nothing but self-preservation, making it easier to bind her. It was genius, and the timing had to be perfect. It had to be right then.

Paris shot her finger in the air at the rope flying in the direction of the beast. The spell worked at once, coiling around ESS, tying her up tightly from her shoulders to her ankles. Then Paris yanked her hand to her chest, and the rope-constricted body jerked forward, pulling Knees back onto the cliff ledge, not about to fall to her doom.

Still, the monster was ungrateful about being saved from death and resisted as Paris magically laid her down on her side. Screams ripped from her crooked mouth and Paris considered looking around for a gag. However, she didn't have a chance because Faraday strode over carrying a stone and threw it down hard on the back of the science experiment's head, knocking her out at once. The screams stopped. The beast was out cold. And she was contained.

Faraday had figured out how to capture ESS even with her electrical shield and without hurting her...well, without hurting her too much. Knees would wake up with a bad headache, but she'd wake up. It just so happened that she'd wake up in the Unseelie court.

CHAPTER SEVENTY-FIVE

"What exactly am I looking at?" Queen Helena MacGillie asked with a repulsed look on her face as Paris and Willow magically lowered the unconscious body of Evil Shadow-self to the courtyard's surface.

Faraday had been able to dose the bound monster with chloroform to keep her passed out. When they couldn't use magic, old-school techniques of knocking someone out or using chemicals were lifesavers—literally. Exhausted from the long day and exceptionally taxing battle, Paris called on Willow as soon as she portaled to Happily Ever After College with a tied up monster in tow.

The fairy godmother's expression of shock when she met Paris by the vortex to the Seelie and Unseelie realm was priceless. Now for a second time, Paris had the pleasure of seeing surprised looks all around the Seelie court as the fairies all whispered and regarded the scene with a combination of amusement and offense.

"This is how you're going to make a truce with King Hamish Abernathy," Paris stated, feeling her legs shake from all the strenuous exertion. "I spoke with the Unseelie king about his demands to end the war. He stated that he wanted a gift from you."

The queen huffed. "Of course he does. That man knows how to

keep a grudge and won't be happy until I give him over my entire kingdom."

"He simply wants two things from you," Paris explained, indicating the ugly monster in front of her. Faraday stood close by with a rag and a bottle of chloroform in case the creature stirred. "He stated he wanted a halfling with demon blood for his collection."

Queen Helena MacGillie lowered her chin. "That would be you."

"It would've been me," Paris corrected. "However, the evil tooth fairies who have been attacking Happily Ever After College volunteered to become a science experiment of sorts. They were fused and dosed with demon blood."

"Is that even possible?" Queen Helena MacGillie gawked at the hideous beast lying in front of her.

"It appears so," Willow answered. "I don't think the results are quite favorable, but the fairies and magician used science, magitech, and magic from the Fang Wellspring to become one."

"Why would they do such a thing?" Queen Helena MacGillie looked horrified.

Paris sighed. "They thought that was how they'd beat me. I became their target after their last few attacks."

"Paris helped to rid the college of Bloody Mary—"

The rush of whispers and gasps interrupted Willow's explanation. She waited until the court had settled down again to continue.

Willow raised her chin and offered Paris a proud look. "Yes, one of the tooth fairies infiltrated our college, pretending to be a student, and summoned Bloody Mary. Thanks to Paris' demon blood and bravery, we were able to trap the ghost for good. The tooth fairies got away, but their identity was out, and the authorities wanted them. I concluded that they decided their best bet at revenge and survival was to become as powerful as Paris by combining all their powers."

"So that's not only one person?" the Seelie queen asked. "That's three people?"

"Yes, and when not tied up, she looks like it," Paris admitted.

"She's alive?" the queen questioned.

Paris nodded. "Yes, although I can't use magic on her because of an electric shield so Faraday is dosing her until I turn her over to you."

"This is what King Hamish Abernathy wants? That's what he said?" she asked.

"I believe he intended for you to give me to him to resolve this war," Paris explained.

"Of course," the Seelie queen said with sudden realization. "The note from Father Time said that you, Paris Beaufont, were the key to ending the war. That's what you told the king, didn't you?"

Paris nodded.

A glint of anger radiated in Queen Helena MacGillie's eyes. "So he decided that meant I had to give you to him as a peace offering. He does love to collect rare and weird things."

"And it would require that you capture me and turn me over," Paris explained.

"You weren't going to inform me that you were the pawn to be used to end the war," Queen Helena MacGillie guessed.

"I figured that would be the end of my freedom," Paris admitted.

"It would," the queen stated matter-of-factly. "Do you know how many Seelie I lose every year in this war? As wealthy as my kingdom is, we simply can't continue to fund these war efforts. Honestly, we're losing, and it's only a matter of time before the Unseelie take us over."

She sighed, suddenly looking exhausted. "I have to end this war. If that means abducting you and giving you as a gift, well, I would do it."

Paris gulped, not grateful for the Seelie queen's honesty. "Well, thankfully, I get to remain free, and you have what the king asked for."

"What exactly was King Hamish Abernathy's demand?" the queen asked.

"He said, 'I want the Seelie queen to give me a half-magician, half-fairy who also has demon blood,'" Paris answered.

A wicked smile rose on the queen's face. "He thought that would be you, and if you were the key to ending the war that you'd abandon the mission." She eyed the creature on the ground. "Based on what he asked for, this satisfies his demands, doesn't it?"

"It does," Paris stated. "And ESS, as I call her for Evil Shadow-self, is unique in her scientific creation. King Hamish Abernathy said he wanted someone who there was no one like in the world."

"Oh, and he's going to get it," the queen said triumphantly. "Of course, we're going to change her name. ESS doesn't roll off the tongue."

Paris nodded in agreement. "She's also called Knees, monster, science experiment, creature, and beast."

Queen Helena MacGillie considered these options. "Knees it is. Now, you said the king asked for two things from me. What is the second one?"

Paris drew in a breath, dreading telling the diabolical queen the next part. Thankfully, Headmistress Willow stepped forward. "We think we've figured that out, but you're going to have to tell us if we're correct."

CHAPTER SEVENTY-SIX

A worried expression jumped to the Seelie queen's face. "What is it you think that man wants from me?"

"Since he wouldn't tell us," Paris cut in, "we've had to guess."

Queen Helena MacGillie laughed suddenly. "He wouldn't tell you. That sounds like Hamish. It always has to be impossible with him."

"He said that you would know what he wants from you," Paris continued, bracing herself for the queen's reaction.

Anger flared in the queen's eyes again. "Oh, he won't stop until he gets what he thinks he deserves."

"Do you know what the Unseelie king wants from you to end this war?" Willow asked, her voice careful and her hands pressed together tightly in front of her.

"Of course I know," the queen answered shrilly. "It's been the same for centuries, although he also wants me to give him something crazy and impossible like a unicorn with two horns or a purple canary."

"Or a halfling with demon blood," Paris added.

"Exactly." The queen *thumped* her scepter in a rush of anger. "It's always something that doesn't exist or would be unviable to get my hands on even with my vast resources."

"Now you have the first thing he wants," Paris offered, indicating the passed out Knees.

"Yes, but the other thing...I'm not sure I can do it." The queen sounded very small suddenly.

"Does the king think you betrayed him?" the headmistress dared to ask.

Whispers broke out around the court.

Queen Helena MacGillie's fingers tightened on the staff. "That's none of your business."

"Is what he demands an apology?" Willow continued, being much bolder and braver than Paris had ever seen her.

The queen's mouth popped open, her eyes wide. The fairies in the court whispered even louder amongst themselves. "Again, that is none of your business, and one more intrusion into my affairs will cost you, Willow Starr."

Paris stepped forward, knowing that she was protected. She was still the one that Papa Creola foretold could end this war. "We're trying to help. I've obtained the hardest part of what King Hamish Abernathy asked for."

She pointed at the passed out halfling. "All you have to do is give him the other part. If that's an apology, it will cost you very little. You said that you couldn't afford to fight this war any longer. So why not end this if you have everything you need to?"

The queen looked halfway between livid and crestfallen. "Because he's making this all about him. He's making all the demands."

"He said you broke his heart," Paris stated matter-of-factly. "That's the reason for the war."

Much like the Unseelie court, the Seelie fairies didn't know this piece of information either based on their surprised reactions.

Paris threw up her hands at the fairies, her grumpiness from exhaustion getting the better of her. "Oh, come on, really? You all have about as diverse reactions as the Unseelie."

"How dare you," Queen Helena MacGillie scolded.

Paris didn't care if this got her the queen's reaction. She was tired and done with playing this diplomatic role for the spoiled Seelie and

Unseelie. "And you, just like King Hamish Abernathy, you never told your people why they're fighting."

She shrugged casually, sliding her eyes to the side. "It was none of their business. Just like it's none of yours."

"Look, I could not care less if you broke the man's heart," Paris stated. "I've given you the evil tooth fairies you've asked for. I've given you the way to end the war. It's up to you whether you do it." She folded her arms, giving the queen an impatient look. "I've honored my end of the agreement. Now it's your turn. You need to clean the Fang Wellspring."

Queen Helena MacGillie's eyes narrowed to slits. "How dare you order me around? I will have your head for such disrespect."

"I dare!" Paris exclaimed, thoroughly fed up. "I've had a mud fight with this deranged monster who was trying to chop my head off. If she didn't succeed, I don't think you will either. I risked my life and that of my squirrel to keep this criminal alive, to turn her over to you so that you would clean the wellspring.

"Also, I knew that the truce would only work if you had an alive halfling with demon blood, and as mentioned, I'm not up for grabs. So excuse me for what you see as disrespect, but I'm freaking exhausted, fed up with your war and stubbornness, and only want a resolution between the fairy godmothers and the tooth fairies. Are you going to honor your end of the agreement?"

The queen took a long moment to deliberate on this. Meanwhile, her subjects looked anxiously between her and Paris. Most appeared to be holding their breath. Finally, she twirled her scepter, and Knees disappeared.

A moment later, a large golden cage appeared in the corner of the court. Inside it was the deformed monster, although she wasn't bound anymore. Thankfully, she remained passed out. Faraday sighed and lowered the rag, finally able to take a break.

"Okay, fine." The queen relented. "I asked for you to turn over the culprits terrorizing the fairy godmothers. I will clean the Fang Wellspring."

"On an ongoing basis?" Willow asked.

The Seelie queen nodded. "Yes, I'll keep my word, as long as the fairy godmothers and tooth fairies get along and no longer have a rivalry."

Willow nodded. "If the wellspring is clean and supplies clean magic, I see no reason to disapprove of the tooth fairies."

"And your war with the Unseelie?" Paris asked although she realized she should quit while she was ahead.

"I'm not sure," the queen answered, looking off in thought suddenly. "I'll have to think about it. I don't want to war with them any longer, but what that man is asking me is to admit that everything was my fault. I didn't break things alone, and he's not the only one who got hurt."

"Maybe," Paris began slowly and carefully, "you can apologize for the part that you're responsible for. In relationships, usually one person isn't at fault for everything. Usually, it's a shared thing. If you say you're sorry for your end of it, maybe he will too."

"And if he doesn't?" the queen questioned.

"Then the war is still over," Paris stated. "You've given him what he wants. You can't afford to fight anymore, which means soon you'll be defeated and no longer have the king's attention. Wouldn't you rather end things on your terms? Wouldn't you rather not lose but have a truce?

"If he does defeat the Seelie, there will be no way to repair things. Really, at the end of this, you have to ask yourself if you're ready to lose the king for good. Don't apologize, and you'll lose. Apologize, and it's over, and you have a chance to save things. Maybe he'll apologize too, and you two can start over."

"As a fairy godmother in training, you show a lot of promise," the queen said in a low voice. "You've given me something to consider."

"So, will you end the war?" Paris asked.

"I will," Queen Helena MacGillie said with fortitude. "Whether there will be peace between the king and me again, that's yet to be determined."

CHAPTER SEVENTY-SEVEN

"You look incredible." Faraday peered over Paris' shoulder and stared at her reflection in the long mirror in her room. She had to admit that the blue ball gown was beautiful and made her look and feel like royalty—although technically she already was.

She twirled, the dress rising slightly from the movement. "It's really nice. Juergen did an amazing job."

"He did," Faraday admitted, "but it's the girl who makes the dress, or woman in this case."

Feeling the nervousness in her chest, Paris pressed her hands there as though trying to keep her body parts attached—rather than beating right out of her.

"Are you okay?" Faraday spotted her movement.

She nodded, blowing out a long, hot breath. "Yeah…it's just that…"

"You know that you're graduating," Faraday stated. "So you don't have to worry. You passed your exams. You got the highest score in the history of Happily Ever After College on your final project. The signature dish and final dance are all formalities at this point. You're golden."

Paris blew out another breath, pressing into her sternum with her fist, trying to relieve the pressure building in her chest. "I know, but even when we get what we thought we wanted, new worries take over."

"So now, instead of being worried about whether you'll graduate, you're worried about where Saint Valentine will place you," Faraday guessed.

"Yes," Paris affirmed. "This all marks a new chapter in my life. I'll be moving out of here, leaving this all behind. Starting a new life."

"That is a lot," Faraday stated. "We'll be adults, living on our own. Can we get a loft?"

Paris laughed. "Some of us are already adults. Some of us aren't people. We'll see. I haven't thought about housing yet. I have Uncle John's old place on Roya Lane. He can't go there or use it anymore, so it makes a lot of sense to live there, and it's full of good memories."

"Your parents offered for you to live with them in Los Angeles," Faraday reminded her.

"Yeah, and FGA is in New York City so we could always consider a brand-new place."

Faraday shivered with disgust. "If I get a vote, I say we don't live in a place where I'll be terrorized by pigeons regularly."

Paris chuckled. "Okay, fine. Of course, you get a vote."

He grinned bashfully at her. "I'm glad I do and that you're allowing me to tag along."

"Of course." Paris pursed her lips. "You didn't think this was a college dorm experience and when I graduated, you got booted, did you?"

He looked away suddenly, glancing out the window where the sun was setting on the Enchanted Grounds before the graduation ball. The entire college had been prepped and decorated for the night. They'd transformed the mansion and grounds and especially the ballroom for the festivities and the many guests they'd be hosting—mostly the families of the graduating students, but also many from FGA.

"I don't know, maybe a little," Faraday admitted after a moment. "I never like to take our situation for granted or make assumptions."

"Situation?" Paris challenged. "You mean the one where you're my best friend and better not desert me?"

He turned and looked at her directly, a wide grin unfurling on his furry face. "Thanks, Pare. That means a lot. You're my best friend too, but that may not mean as much coming from me since I'm a squirrel."

"The smartest, most reliable squirrel sidekick a girl could ask for," she countered.

He hopped down from the dresser and made for the door. "And your escort to the ball. Should I put on the top hat?"

Paris shook her head. "You're too cute in that outfit. Don't tell anyone I'm saying this, but I want people looking at me. Then I get credit for putting on this giant dress."

"I don't think it's possible for anyone to keep their eyes off you tonight."

Paris beamed, pulling in a breath and preparing herself for all that was in store for her tonight. It would be a time of celebration, of learning her future, and of saying goodbye to her past.

CHAPTER SEVENTY-EIGHT

Paris realized she should've expected the screaming when she descended the grand staircase in the fairy godmother mansion to meet the other graduating students. Christine was wearing a purple gown that was perfect with her orangey-red hair. It had a plunging neckline and a modern flair. Penny was wearing a more conservative navy blue dress. The other students expected to graduate all looked beautiful wearing their gowns designed by Juergen.

"You look so...girly." Christine fumbled to find the right word. Then her smile dropped, and she glanced down at the floor. "Guinevere Paris Beaufont, are you wearing combat boots?"

"You look like a princess." Paris deflected the question.

Christine huffed. "Compliments will get you everywhere in life but don't think I haven't noted how you almost wore the best dress tonight, only to ruin it as only you can."

"You know how I do things," Paris sang, peering through the crowd toward the ballroom. "What do we do now?"

"We're waiting to be called into the ballroom after all the guests are in there," Penny stated. "We'll form a procession, take our places in the center of the dance floor, then Saint Valentine will read our names and assign us in FGA."

"Then the best part starts," Christine said dreamily. "We get to eat."

Penny nodded. "We're supposed to sample each other's signature dishes, although Saint Valentine and the instructors already graded them as part of the final assessment."

"Then we dance?" Paris asked. "Is that graded?"

"If so, you'll fail," Christine teased. "That's more a of part of the celebration. Everyone watches as we start the big party with elegant ballroom dancing. Chef Ash has agreed to be my partner."

"My dad is going to be mine," Penny offered.

"My dad offered to," Paris admitted, "but I declined. He can dance with demons, but that man knows nothing about ballroom dancing."

Christine sighed. "He's so devilishly attractive. Why can't my dad kill demons for a living and carry a sword? Instead, he has a dad bod and wears Cookie Monster pajamas."

Paris laughed. "At least he gets weekends off. Thankfully, Wilfred has agreed to be my partner. I should be in good hands with him."

Penny and Christine exchanged looks of regret. They both felt what Paris wasn't saying, which was that it was heartbreaking for her that Hemingway wasn't there that night. He'd been so much a part of her life since coming to Happily Ever After College. Without him, well, there was a hole in her heart.

However, she couldn't admit that to herself or anyone right then. She'd deal with the heartache...well, maybe never. Still, that night was about her and her friends and making her family proud.

Paris knew that in the giant ballroom, her parents and family and friends were all ready to celebrate who she'd become. What she'd accomplished. And see her in a rare state—wearing an elegant and beautiful ball gown.

CHAPTER SEVENTY-NINE

All eyes seemed to be on Paris when she entered the grand ballroom—which somehow was even more beautiful than usual. It was always gorgeous with its huge chandeliers and muraled walls. However, tiny twinkling fairies buzzed around the ceiling, making it appear like it was glowing. There were fresh bouquets everywhere. At the front of the ballroom was a stage and beside it was a real orchestra, all its members dressed impeccably.

Sitting on the stage was Headmistress Willow in her blue gown with its pink sash, a few agents all dressed in their black suits, and Saint Valentine—looking as elegantly handsome as always.

Around the large ballroom's perimeter were hundreds of excited faces, all watching the line of women in beautiful ballgowns as they lined up in front of the stage. There were only a dozen of them graduating, so sitting wasn't necessary. Nor would it be practical in large dresses like what they were wearing. No, the ceremony would be fast. Then it would be time to dance and celebrate.

Paris spotted her parents, proudly waving. They weren't hard to pick out among the other parents wearing buttoned-up cardigans and blazers with patches on the elbows.

Liv and Stefan wore all black, long traveling cloaks covering their

Warrior outfits. Paris guessed that they'd probably come straight from a mission for this, but they were there, and that was all that ever mattered. It appeared that they'd left their swords behind, or at least out of sight.

Beside her parents were Uncle John and Alicia, and Aunt Sophia and Uncle Clark. All of them were looking at Paris like she was the most treasured person they'd ever seen. Right then, she felt like it.

Happily Ever After College had opened that night to allow others onto the grounds. It was probably weird for many to see their family members on the campus. Even stranger was Paris' next observation, which most others noticed at the same time.

"Is that a dragon?" someone asked with surprise.

"Oh, he's cute," another graduate stated.

"He's already magnetized," Paris muttered, noticing Lunis in the corner, not looking as inconspicuous as she thought he was attempting to be. Sitting on his shoulder and staring at her with his large brown eyes was Faraday. Paris laughed, grateful that even if her family wasn't the typical kind with ordinary human members, they were hers.

CHAPTER EIGHTY

"Thank you for joining us for the graduation of our new generation of fairy godmothers," Saint Valentine began from the front of the stage when everyone had taken their places. "I'm excited for this new group to join FGA. As the leader of this organization, I know how important it is to have excellent people in the right places. You may think that fairy godmothers match a couple or two, but what they do is far-reaching. It ripples out, creating long-lasting effects."

Paris looked around, catching sight of Mae Ling standing in the corner, removed from the other staff members as usual. Her gaze connected with Paris', and she winked. Paris smiled back, remembering when that unassuming woman burst into the sitting room on Paris' first day at the college and in a conspiratorial voice demanded that she be herself—even if that meant rebelling against everything.

Paris didn't know if she did that, although she always tried. She also didn't know if she'd saved the fairy godmothers as predicted. No doubt, Paris was graduating. She'd fallen in love and had her heart broken, as the prophecy stated.

Whether she saved the fairy godmothers, well, it was hard to know when there were always challenges. No longer was there a threat from the Knees. The Seelie queen had contained them in her court. Hopefully, relations between the tooth fairies and the fairy godmothers would improve.

Also, Paris and others had defeated Agent Ruby and taken care of many other dangers in her time at the college. Whether she saved them, well, she'd never know.

"For today's graduation ceremony," Saint Valentine continued. "I'm going to do things a bit differently. Usually, we go by alphabetical, but I'm going out of order, and you'll see why at the end."

This produced some excited whispers around the room.

"You see, at FGA, we're facing some challenging times," he continued over the noise. "We need to evolve or risk dying. For that reason, I've created some new departments, and today some of our graduates will be assigned to them."

Many of the women around Paris began elbowing each other with excitement. Paris wondered what this would mean for her. Would she be placed in the Dating App department? Or maybe Cyber Chat Rooms? Or maybe Hipster Nation? She shivered at the thought of the latter.

"Without further ado, let me announce the first graduate," Saint Valentine continued, holding out his hand. A rolled-up certificate appeared. "Please help me congratulate Hibiscus Embers in graduating from Happily Ever After College."

The ballroom filled with applause as a woman in a yellow gown made her way to the stage. As she shook Saint Valentine's hand and took her certificate, he bowed. "Hibiscus, after evaluating your final project, the board and I think you'd make a great addition to the Second Marriages Department."

Hibiscus seemed very happy about this and clasped the certificate to her chest and smiled at the crowd.

The ballroom erupted in more applause.

As the graduate descended the stage, Saint Valentine continued reading names, handing out certificates, and making assignments.

"Our next graduate is Christine Welsh," Saint Valentine said, waking Paris from a daydream of how she'd redecorate her new apartment. She realized that Faraday would have to give up his lab, but he could always come back to the college to use this one. It was his after all.

Christine breezed up to the stage and proudly took her certificate.

"Your final project was both helpful and creative," Saint Valentine stated. "Therefore, we've decided to assign you as a fairy godmother to the Fashion department. When a Cinderella or a Prince Charming needs help deciding on what will make them feel best for a date, you'll be enlisted."

"Woot!" Christine cheered, throwing her hands into the air.

When she'd taken her spot next to Paris, Saint Valentine picked up another certificate. He called Penny onto the stage and assigned her to the Practical Love department.

Paris did some quick counting in her head and realized that meant she was the only graduate left. Why had Saint Valentine left her until last? She immediately worried, a hundred conflicting thoughts streaming through her head. Suddenly, she wished she hadn't made the bold request to him on the opening night of her restaurant. He would've heard about her encounter with Knees, and maybe he would've concluded that a woman who could fight monsters wasn't suited for FGA.

Paris gulped, sucked in a breath, and held it.

"Our final graduate is very special in both how she came to be with us and what she's done since she's been here," Saint Valentine began, his blue eyes landing directly on Paris. This was it...there was no avoiding what happened next.

CHAPTER EIGHTY-ONE

"Please join me in welcoming Paris Beaufont to the stage," Saint Valentine said, followed by a roar of applause that Paris never expected. She tried not to trip on her dress as she made her way up the stairs.

When she stood in front of the elegant leader of FGA, she felt strange, as if suddenly she didn't know what to do with her hands. Before, she felt like all eyes were on her. Now she knew they were as she stood on the front of the stage.

"Paris is the first halfling to graduate from Happily Ever After College," Saint Valentine said to the crowd. "Her enrollment here was at first met with contention. If anyone doubts whether she deserves a place among the fairy godmothers, they only have to see the results of her final project. The love meter that grades those projects broke the night of her assessment because it couldn't record such a high increase."

Saint Valentine was interrupted by the many gasps around the ballroom followed by hushed whispers. He nodded, settling the crowd down. "It's true. No one can doubt that someone of Paris' caliber not only deserves a place in FGA but has earned a position befitting her skills. Therefore, with the approval of the board, I've decided that the best use of Paris' talents is as an agent for FGA."

The gasps turned to audible sounds of shock. Several exclaimed. Many sounded excited, but there were some sounds of disapproval around the room. What was clear was this was shocking news. However, Paris noticed her parents beaming on the far side of the room. A glance at Mae Ling gave Paris confidence. The encouraging nod from Headmistress Starr made Paris face forward again.

This was what she wanted. She'd gotten it. Somehow…

"Paris, I firmly believe that due to your critical nature, coupled with a creative spirit, you'll make a great agent," Saint Valentine continued. "I know it's unprecedented, but times are changing, and we must embrace it when it makes sense. Therefore I'm happy to award you a position as an agent in the Casual Romance Department."

Paris took the certificate, her mouth dry and all words escaping her. However, she was able to manage to mouth the phrase, "Thank you."

Saint Valentine nodded proudly. "I expect great things from you, Paris Beaufont."

CHAPTER EIGHTY-TWO

Paris was an agent for FGA. The very first female. She'd gotten everything she wanted...well, almost. Still, she'd gotten so much more than she ever expected. She would be researching cases and taking a holistic approach while supervising fairy godmothers and assigning missions. It was exactly what she wanted that she never knew she did.

With the graduation ceremony over, all the graduates lined up in the center of the ballroom as the orchestra started to play. It was time for the beautiful women in their dresses to dance. Then the real celebration would start. Paris couldn't wait to cheers with her family, share the good news with her friends, and move on to the next chapter of her life.

However, she couldn't deny that something—or rather someone—was still missing.

She shook off this feeling as the graduates' partners took their places in front of them. Paris managed a smile at Wilfred, who looked very distinguished in his three-piece suit with his white gloves. She took his hand when he offered it, pulling her snug and leading her in a waltz she'd practiced many times but still couldn't get right, especially in the large billowing ball gown. As excellent a dancer as Wilfred was, she only danced well with one person.

"Congratulations on the promotion." Wilfred led her around the dance floor, moving around the other twirling couples. Their families and friends watched from the sidelines, many of them smiling and taking pictures.

"Thank you. It was a surprise, but I'm very happy about it."

"You deserve it, Paris. I've spent many decades serving Happily Ever After College, and never have I met a person like you who has left an impression on me. I have a confession to make," Wilfred said in his polished British accent.

"Yes?"

"I think I'm experiencing something rare for me."

"Oh?"

"Yes, I realized before this ceremony started that I didn't want you and Faraday to leave," he admitted, his feet moving around the floor expertly, leading Paris in the dance.

"You didn't?"

Wilfred shook his head. "I'm going to miss you two."

Paris smiled. "Oh, well, we'll miss you too, Wilfred."

"But that's a human emotion," he argued. "I'm not human and not programmed to miss people."

Paris shrugged and smiled wider. "Well, I didn't make you laugh, but I made you miss me. I think I prefer it this way."

"I don't think I'm the only one who missed you." Wilfred's gaze flicked over her shoulder as he slowed and paused them in place.

Paris tilted her head and gave him a questioning look. "Why did you stop? The music is still going."

Someone tapped her on the shoulder. "Paris Beaufont, I hoped that I could interrupt. That I could have this dance."

CHAPTER EIGHTY-THREE

Paris couldn't breathe. She was pretty sure the corset of her dress was pinching the life out of her. Or it was simply shock.

She turned to find the person she knew belonged to the voice who'd said those words.

"Hemingway." Paris didn't feel in control of her voice. It was too shaky. Too full of emotion. Too excited.

He'd dressed unlike she'd ever seen him in an elegant suit and slicked back his usually wild brown hair. His tie was neat and perfectly in place. The unique flower in his lapel was as fresh as the look on his face.

Wilfred had released her, and now she felt him protectively standing behind her. Hemingway's blue eyes darted to the AI magitech butler and Paris. "I hoped to lead you in your graduation dance if that's okay."

His gaze darted back to Wilfred, and Paris glanced over her shoulder as if looking for permission and him to release her to a new partner. When Wilfred nodded and bowed, she felt relief.

Then there was also so much confusion. Paris turned back to Hemingway, shaking her head. "What are you doing here?"

"I'm making things right." He held up his hands, offering to be her dance partner, to lead her. "I believe the crowd wants to see us dance, so shall we?"

Paris glanced around, noticing that many around them were staring at the interruption. Deciding she didn't want to draw any more attention to herself that night, Paris nodded and stepped forward, taking Hemingway's hand.

The warmth of his fingers around hers was instantly welcoming. The way he moved her around the dance floor was magical. It was like they were one, flowing like water. Wilfred knew the moves and how to lead Paris. Hemingway knew *her* and how to direct her so she knew the moves too. She only ever wanted to dance with *him*—yet she guarded her heart, not understanding why he was there or for how long.

"You came back," Paris stated after they'd been quiet for a long moment. "For the graduation ceremony."

He shook his head, looking more handsome than she'd remembered. There was something new about him. Something better, as if he'd evolved. "You know why I left..."

"Because you'd always been at Happily Ever After College. I always got it, Hemingway."

"Right." He twirled them around the dance floor. "I thought I was missing something. That by seeing the world, I'd find what I was looking for. But life is ironic, Paris. Like with you. You came to Happily Ever After College to avoid punishment and found your destiny. Oh, and congratulations on becoming the first female agent in the history of FGA. The restaurant must have been a fantastic success."

"Thank you." Paris didn't trust her voice not to crack, so she kept her responses short. "It was."

"Pare, I left here and saw so much, so quickly. The entire time, I wished I had you to share it with. I realized that all along, I wasn't looking for something or someplace. I was always waiting for you to find me.

"You see, you're the reason I wanted to see the world. You're the reason I wanted to do something new. As soon as I did it without you, it was meaningless. You're my muse. How can I write without you? You're my inspiration, and without you, it's all meaningless."

Paris realized that she'd slowed. So had Hemingway. Suddenly, she felt like they were dancing alone on the floor. The music was only for them.

"But...I told you that..."

He halted and looked her deep in the eyes. "I'm sorry, Pare. I wanted you to go with me, and I was heartbroken when you didn't. Traveling the world had been *my* dream, but it wasn't yours. It was wrong of me to hold back from you even if I was disappointed. I should've told you what I'm telling you now. What I want to tell you."

Paris gripped Hemingway's hands, not caring that the orchestra playing indicated that the blur of movement around them meant others were joining them on the dance floor. She only had her eyes on Hemingway. And all her attention on his lips. "What do you want to tell me now?"

He released a nervous grin. "You mind if I steal the famous Hemingway's words for this one?"

She shook her head. "Go ahead."

Hemingway pulled her arms around him and smiled down at her. "'I love you for all that you are, all that you have been, all that you're yet to be.' Paris Beaufont, I'm not worthy of your affections, but give me a chance to prove that I can make you happy. Give me a chance to love you because nothing in this world would make me happier than you. I know that because I've been out there, and there is nothing quite like you on this planet."

Paris wanted to hold him tighter and kiss him on the packed dance floor. Instead, she stayed straight, held up her chin, and let out a breath. "But your dream. Your job..."

He shook his head. "I didn't like it so much. I'll admit it was fun at first. But a new bed every night and constant adventure..." Hemingway laughed. "Well, that last part seems more up your alley. Honestly, I like hard work and dirt under my fingernails and doing things that make a difference. And waking up to the same view—but a really good one. I'd like to wake up to the view of you."

"Hemingway, I'll be working at FGA," Paris stated.

"We don't have to figure it out right now. We're magical beings, though, and we have portal magic. We have options. We could be together."

"Are you sure?" Paris vibrated with emotions and so much doubt. "You gave up your job here."

He pulled her in close. "I've never been more sure of anything in my life, Pare. And hey, I hear you might need help with that fantastically successful restaurant. Maybe I can help. I know a thing or two about gardening."

Paris laughed and put her head on Hemingway's shoulder, happier at that moment than she'd ever remembered—ever thought possible. She peered up at him, their faces close. "You really want this?"

He nodded, looking deep into her eyes. "I want you. I want us. I want this."

Paris didn't have to ask what "this" was. It was clear. It was the kind of love she needed to create for others. It was the things of storybooks and happy endings. It was true love.

She tilted her chin, and if anyone saw the kiss that followed, Paris didn't care. All that mattered was the spark of magic that radiated between Hemingway Noble and Paris Beaufont as they sealed their love in a kiss—the first of many, many more.

CHAPTER EIGHTY-FOUR

"This cheeseball is fantastic!" Liv Beaufont exclaimed, her eyes popping open with delight.

Paris smiled and held up her glass of champagne. "Thank you. I made that."

"Wow." Uncle John took a sample of food from the buffet table of signature dishes. "So many talents, all rolled into one person."

Paris blushed, looking around at her family and feeling grateful. "Well, I have all of you to thank for your support."

"I don't know," Lunis muttered, indicating Liv and Stefan. "Those two were gone for most of your childhood. You mostly have me to thank."

"How do you figure?" Sophia asked.

"Well, because I was supporting her through silent moral support," the dragon answered.

"Yeah, I don't think so," Clark countered.

Paris used this opportunity to approach her uncle as the group broke into pairs to talk. "Hey, Uncle Clark. I wanted to ask you something."

"Of course," he stated at once.

"Well, I know your job as a Councilor keeps you busy," she began.

"But I need to replace Ainsley as the restaurant's chef. I know it's a lot to ask, but if you were interested—"

"Are you serious?" Clark interrupted, his eyes wide with excitement. "I've wanted the opportunity for something like this for so long. Really, I only need to be at the House of Fourteen for meetings. I can do all the rest of the work remotely."

Paris clapped. "So you'll do it? You'll be the head chef for Little Pleasures?"

"Of course," he exclaimed.

"What's up, Clark?" Liv turned to face him. "Are you gearing up to reorganize your tie collection? I know how excited you were the last time you needed to do that."

He shook his head. "No, Paris has asked me to be the chef at her farm-to-table restaurant, and I've accepted."

"Cheers, mate." Stefan held up his drink to him. "That's great."

"Really great!" Liv was excited.

"So cool," Sophia agreed.

"Very excited for you." Uncle John smiled sideways at Alicia.

"I have some good news," Liv began, hiding a grin. "The college here has asked me to teach on a part-time basis. The recent events have indicated that fairy godmothers could benefit from combat magic courses."

"Oh, that's amazing!" Paris smiled at Hemingway, realizing this was the beginning of so many good changes. He beamed at her.

"Really cool," Sophia stated. "Lunis and I will be teaching a class on magical animals when Bermuda isn't available. It seems that things are evolving."

"They are," Faraday said proudly.

"Well, then we should toast," Lunis declared, waving Wilfred over who was carrying a tray of champagne flutes, full to the brim. "Everyone take one. We have lots to be grateful for. We need to make a toast."

Everyone passed around champagne until all had one. Then they held up their glasses and looked at each other, wondering who would make the actual toast.

A cough echoed from the floor. "Fine, I'll do it." Plato gave them all an annoyed glare as he pursed his lips before he continued, "To Paris, who exceeded expectations at Happily Ever After College. To the Beaufonts, who have found new ways to help the world. And to the rest of us, who get to be part of the action and watch from the sidelines—amazed by how these magicians save the world with their giant hearts. And lastly, to family."

Liv smiled at her familiar, an unmistakable fondness in her eyes. "Familia Est Sempiternum."

"Familia Est Sempiternum," Plato repeated.

"Cheers!" everyone exclaimed, clinking their glasses together and taking a sip, everyone wearing smiles.

"Oh, that's good juice," Lunis said, not having taken a drink.

"It's champagne," Sophia corrected with a pursed expression.

"How am I supposed to know?" Lunis countered. "The last time I drank juice, I lost two hours of my life because the bottle said, 'concentrate.'"

Sophia groaned. Liv shook her head. Clark, John, and Alicia all grimaced. Stefan dropped his head. Paris glanced at Hemingway, sharing in the awfulness of the joke. Even Faraday and Plato shook their heads at each other.

However, a strange sound broke out. It was from the magitech AI butler. Wilfred's eyes sparkled. He nearly dropped the empty tray. Then with his free hand, he covered his midsection and did something Paris had never witnessed. He buckled over, laughing at the awful joke.

"Seriously, that's the joke that gets you to laugh?" Paris was offended and also hiding her amusement. However, Wilfred's laughter was infectious, and against her better judgment, she laughed too. The others soon joined her, entertained more by an AI made to laugh by a prehistoric dragon than the actual joke.

Life was strange like that.

CHAPTER EIGHTY-FIVE

"Paris, would you join me over here," Headmistress Willow Starr requested when Paris made her way through the crowd.

She nodded, splitting from her group of friends and family, but Faraday followed her. He'd been so excited by the festivities that he'd hardly left her side since graduation. Paris eased through the thick crowd of people, following the fairy godmother until she paused at a table in the corner of the ballroom. There she turned, holding a presenting hand at two people seated close to one another, holding hands.

Paris could hardly believe who she saw cuddled together. Together was the main word. And cuddled. Together.

"Queen Helena MacGillie and King Hamish Abernathy?" Paris looked between the two who appeared ordinary when not in their regal courts and surrounded by strangeness. And cuddling...together.

"Paris, because of what you said, because of what we did, the Seelie and Unseelie have ended their long war," Willow stated proudly.

Paris looked at the lovers' hands intertwined on the table and read in between the lines. Much more had happened than a war ending. Love had blossomed...again.

Smiling, Paris said, "That's amazing. I'm so happy. And Knees? How is she or them or it?"

The king and queen laughed like they were fun-loving people and not the type to murder on a whim.

"Oh, she's atrocious," King Hamish Abernathy answered. "And perfect for my collection. My favorite thing that Helena has given me. Well, besides all her love and affection."

"I'm glad you like her for your museum," the Seelie queen stated.

He leaned in and kissed her cheek. "It feels complete now. Just like me and my life and our kingdom."

"Just like all that," Queen Helena MacGillie said, turning her attention directly on the king, seemingly dismissing Willow and Paris.

They strode off with Faraday following.

"Well, that situation seems to have resolved itself." Paris was totally surprised by what she'd witnessed.

"That's the thing about you." Willow put her finger on her nose. "When you get involved, trouble happens, followed by change. Those two have loved and warred for centuries. Then all of a sudden, you enter the picture, and they find a way back to each other."

The headmistress put her arms around Paris and hugged her tightly, a real hug, full of love and healing and meaning. When she pulled away, there was a thoughtful look in her eyes.

"I expect big things from you at FGA," Willow stated. "That's not a demand. That's not me putting pressure on you. That's simply the way it is. You don't do what you've done in the short amount of time here with the fairy godmothers without those around you expecting greatness. That's the bar you set. I can't wait to see what you do."

Paris smiled at the fairy godmother, not knowing what to say. She therefore smiled and said the only two words that seemed necessary. "Thank you."

CHAPTER EIGHTY-SIX

"When we move into the farmhouse, can I have my own room?" Faraday asked when Willow left Paris to meet and greet with someone else.

"How do you know we're moving into the farmhouse?" Paris questioned the squirrel.

"Because Hemingway is back," he answered.

"So?" she asked.

"So, I would deduce that if your uncle Clark is the chef, that's because you have someone to replace Quiet," he explained. "That would be the guy who swept you off your feet at the ball."

Paris narrowed her eyes at the squirrel sitting on the bar table, staring at her defiantly. "I didn't get swept…okay, this is a ball, but I'm not wearing glass slippers."

"Combat boots. I saw that bad decision like everyone else."

She rolled her eyes. "Yes, Hemingway will be taking care of the farm at Little Pleasures."

"Which makes the most sense as far as where we live," Faraday stated. "I mean, the commute is the same regardless with portal magic. You don't want to go backward, and that's what living on Roya Lane would be. You can't move in with your parents. You're trying to pretend to be an adult."

"I am an adult." She stuck out her tongue.

"Point proven. You and I don't like city life so New York is out. The farm, well, that's us. That's Hemingway. That's perfect. So can I have my own room?"

Paris nodded, grateful her best friend was with her wherever she was. "Yes, but your lab stays here. I don't want you blowing up my restaurant."

"Fair enough. Just open portals for me when I need to come back here."

"Deal. Maybe we can find a contraption to get you back here on your own."

"Good idea," he chirped. "I'll work on that when I'm not tracking down an evil mad scientist."

"Oh, Madden?" Paris asked, curious about the crazy doctor who created Knees.

"Yeah, I haven't tracked him down yet, but I will," Faraday stated. "I hope you'll help me get to him before he unleashes his next diabolical experiment."

"Fare, I think you always know the answer to that even if it endangers my life or gets me in trouble. Even if it costs me greatly, if you need my help, I'm totally in. Always and forever."

He smiled at her, his bushy tail twitching. "Right back at you, Pare. I always have your back. Forever and always."

CHAPTER EIGHTY-SEVEN

"She's going to need a lot of supervision." Father Time watched the Happily Ever After Mansion from the edge of the Bewilder Forest. From there, he could see through the large open windows of the grand ballroom where the party-goers were dancing and singing and celebrating. Among them, at the center of all toasts, was Paris Beaufont.

"I know," Mother Nature sang, looking at Paris Beaufont in her blue dress, swaying in the arms of the man she loved.

"She can screw this up if we're not careful," Papa Creola continued, always so serious.

"I know," Mama Jamba repeated.

"You put a lot of faith in one person," Papa Creola continued, eyeing the guests in the ballroom.

"As you did with yours," Mama Jamba stated, watching as Liv Beaufont hugged her daughter, bidding her farewell.

"She's never let me down," Papa Creola argued. "She saved me and my butt a hundred times."

"So will her daughter," Mama Jamba said with confidence, watching as the party split apart, people starting to file away and go home.

"If she doesn't... If she doesn't measure up..."

"Then we'll lose love," Mama Jamba acknowledged, suddenly serious. "I get the stakes. I know what I've risked. My planet. My people. And what they're good at—creating love. I've wagered it all on one halfling, and I stand by it. She'll be the change we've been waiting for."

"I hope you're right," Papa Creola said, his tone haunting.

"Don't you worry, Papa. Paris Beaufont is going to be the best agent FGA has ever had. She's going to fulfill her destiny. She'll save the fairy godmothers and then some. She's going to ensure we all live happily...ever...after."

Father Time nodded, always having confidence in his partner on this planet, in this world, in this universe. They'd created it together and put together the key players that would keep it going when people and events challenged it.

Paris Beaufont had proven to be a formidable force. She'd already saved so many and created so much love. Found happiness with her family and friends.

The halfling was the thing of legends. She'd already done so much. Still, Father Time and Mother Nature knew that Paris Beaufont's journey had *just* begun. Her destiny included things that would change the course of the planet.

Paris was in charge of love, which meant she'd be charting a new future for the globe.

THE UNCONVENTIONAL AGENT
BEAUFONT

Paris' story continues in a new series from Sarah and Michael called, **The Unconventional Agent Beaufont**. Book one is *The Extraordinary Fixer*.

The Fairy Godmother Agency has been operating without a need to change for
    centuries—*until now.*

Why?

Because Love is dying...

Can the agency adapt to how love works in a modern world?

When a young halfling with snark, an attitude, and a criminal record breaks into the ranks of agents at FGA a lot of members aren't happy.

Unfortunately, those upset can't argue Agent Paris Beaufont's results are incredible.

She just doesn't follow the rules to get things done.

For some incredible results just aren't enough!

Corruption has insinuated itself deep inside the ranks of agents at FGA.

Many believe that tradition is what makes love go 'round.

Are they wrong? Will changing the old ways stop love from blossoming in the world?

Can Agent Beaufont shatter the beliefs that have kept FGA from evolving?

The fate of love depends on it.

Claim your copy today!

THE MYSTERIOUS PLATO (A BEAUFONT SHORT STORY BOOK 1)

Who would suspect that one of the most powerful entities in the world is a black and white cat?

Few know that most historical events in the last several centuries were orchestrated by this innocuous feline. Plato isn't an ordinary cat. He's a magical lynx with extraordinary powers.

When a series of dangerous activities break out in a small city

in Mexico, is it by design that the magical creature is present? Is Plato really coordinating everything?

Plato isn't the only one staying in this Mexican city or at the boutique hotel. Other magical creatures are working to stop the bad guys.

That's what Beaufonts and their sidekicks do.

Can Plato, a dragon, and a talking squirrel save this coastal city?

Claim your copy of this Beaufont Short Story today!

SARAH'S AUTHOR NOTES
OCTOBER 5, 2021

A huge thank you to all of you for reading this entire series. I'm not sure if you realize this, but your buying, reading and reviewing my books literally changed my life. It makes it so I can continue to do what I love. It makes me happy. Really happy.

So apparently, I sort of left you all dangling from a cliff after my last author notes. I got messages from readers who were like, "Wellllll, did the Scotsman put up with your writing habits or what?"

The short answer is *yes*.

But we all know that I don't do short answers. So let me tell you how writing these stories turns me into a psycho-pants. Yes, I coined the term psycho-pants and you can use it in place of psychopath. You're welcome.

So when I write, I become the character. Usually that just means that I delude myself into thinking that I can win a fist fight and do magic. I can't...

There was this one time in high school when my exe-best friend tried to fight me in the parking lot of the Sack-A-Burger. The whole school turned out to watch Bonnie (her name hasn't been changed because I hold grudges) fight me. Apparently I have a tendency to mouth off...who knew. My exe-husband used to tell me that it would get me punched. Not by him. He meant by someone at a concert or crowded bar or at the grocery store. So far, he's been wrong.

Anyway, Bonnie challenged me to a fight and everyone was like, "Fight! Fight! Fight!" But I'm five foot nothing and like my face the way it is. So when she pushed me down on the gravel in the parking lot I didn't channel a Beaufont and kick butt. I simply got up and walked away. Yep, I can't fight.

Oh, wow, you didn't think I could derail this much. You should know better by now.

Okay, so besides from deluding myself into thinking I can fight and do magic, I also suffer the heart break of my characters. In this one, when Hemingway left, well, I cried a lot and listened to JP Saxe break-up music nonstop. And the Scotsman probably suffered from this depression of mine. He even said at one point, "Maybe you don't have to feel the character's pain to write it."

Maybe. But I do because that's how I work.

Some of you know that the Scotsman is an author too.

Side note: He keeps teasing me for calling him the Scotsman in these notes and on social media. He's like, should I call you "the American"?

Short answer is no.

See, I can be brief.

I've been calling him Scotsman for so long, I can't stop now. And everyone gets nicknames in the author notes. Well, not Bonnie. She gets called out.

Anyway, the Scotsman writes awesome science fiction but his process isn't the same as mine. He doesn't immerse himself the same way I do and he still write very compelling books. But this is how I work and I'm not changing even if my character's stories send me spiraling into depressions. They always recover and therefore I do too. And we can't start pretending that there aren't shades of my life written into these stories. I mean, we all know that I talk to squirrels and barf if I watch a rom-com.

So in an attempt to give the people who love me a break from my psycho-pants, I'm taking three months off from writing. This series is complete, although Paris' story continues at FGA—as I'm guessing you've figured out after that ending. I'll start writing that series in January. But for about four years, I've churned out a book every month. Yes, that's 48 books in 48 months. Many times I wrote the book inside of two weeks, taking a week off to stare at the ceiling and another one to pretend I was writing a book.

The Scotsman and Lydia and my friends have put up with my crazy schedule, writing for twelve hours a day or muttering incoherently to myself or not living in the real world. I decided that it would be good for my health and family for me to finally take some real time off. And you all won't dump me...will you?

The Unconventional Agent Beaufont will come out in February 2022. And in the meantime, I've got some Plato, Lunis and Faraday short stories—inspired by my time in Mexico.

Oooh and I've got other plans for during my time off. I'm going to finish Netflix. I'm going to become a Pinterest mom. I'm going to learn to play the piano. And I'm going to take alllll of the Master Classes starting with Massimo. I'm keto so it makes sense that I take a class on how to make pasta from the best Italian chef. But really, I just love food because, well, it's food. But also cooking tells us about history, geography and people.

I'm sure you'll see the inspiration in the next story. The farm to table restaurant will be a central setting in the new series.

So to pull you all back over the cliff, the Scotsman was very supportive of my writing and craziness. I think he'll put up with a lot of my psycho-pants, but I'll try not to challenge that notion. I'm very grateful to have the most supportive people in my life, encouraging me to do what I love so much.

And now we have to talk about Bird Killer and how I plan to make his life just a little more difficult. All this time off is bound to give me an opportunity to be an extra pain in the ass. So I have the huge honor of finally doing a presentation at the 20Booksto50k conference this year. I have only pestered Martelle for all the time we've known each other for such an opportunity. And the squeaky wheel...

Let's actually hope that he picked me because I have experiences in writing that others can learn from. The subtitle to my presentation is, "Learn From My Mistakes." The main title is, "I'm Either Making Anderle Look Good or Really Bad."

The really fun part of this presentation in Las Vegas is that it's *right* before MA's keynote address. And I plan on revealing secrets about things I've stolen and telling really bad jokes. So when Mike takes the stage right after me, the audience is either going to be seriously relieved that they don't have to look at me anymore, welcoming Manderle with huge applause *oooooor* they'll be reeling from the trauma of my bad jokes and having their own psycho-pants episodes and therefore not at all listening to anything that follows.

We'll see…

But in all seriousness, I'm beyond grateful for the opportunity, for all that Michael has done for me and that he continues to put up with my psycho-pants. Thanks, MA. Let's do this book thing again real soon.

Much love and Peace,

Tiny Ninja

MICHAEL'S AUTHOR NOTES
OCTOBER 22, 2021

Thank you for not only reading this story but these author notes as well.

I'm in Frankfurt, Germany at the moment, just finishing up with the Frankfurt Buchmesse (Bookfair). The time here is 5:55 PM, which is about 9:55 AM back in Las Vegas.

I feel like I'm going to pass out.

I spent the morning with the esteemed Jens Schulze, who handles all things German translations, and after that, I went to go look for art supplies. Why? I'm glad you asked.

There is a new tool for drawing called Mental Canvas (https://mentalcanvas.com) which I decided I wanted to play with and see if it was something LMBPN might be able to use for telling stories and entertaining.

Except over the years, my hands have started shaking worse and worse. So, my handwriting is just this side of atrocious. You can sort of read my handwriting if I write...large.

Or, I could twist this to say I have the perfect handwriting to be a doctor. If there was ever a role for TV (just showing hands) where the purpose was to write a script for medicine that could not possibly be read?

I'm your man.

Fortunately, I can still type.

I provide that background because I wanted to try out the drawing software (it allows you to create 2d drawings in 3d space. Pretty cool stuff.) But I can't draw a straight line to save my life.

I remember from many decades ago that art supplies have little plastic templates along with the standard rulers and figured that would work. Check out the handy Google maps and ten minutes later, I'm walking about a half-mile away to go to a German art store.

I was able to find the templates but stumbled over finding tape I might need to tape something to the front of my iPad. While I haven't needed the tape (so far), the plastic templates have been a bit of a problem. Why? I'm glad you asked.

The problem is they are slippery as hell. I can't place the ruler or templates on the iPad without them slipping around as I try to use them. It seems friction is pretty damned useful.

<Sigh>

I might have to try using the tape to provide a bit of friction to the plastic.

I'll save you the time but I also needed to go by an Apple store to pick up an Apple Pencil 2 (to replace the one I lost about 6 months ago. I'm sure that little shit will show up on Tuesday, now that I've replaced it.)

Speaking of Apple, they have released their new laptops with the advanced chips. I'm a bit annoyed as I'm going to be out of the country a lot over the next few months and I can't come up with a good justification to purchase the Pro laptop yet. They aren't exactly cheap and yeah… No new laptop for me right now .

Perhaps someone will release some amazing software that requires the extra juice (please)? I'd like to play with one of them. Until that happens, I'll focus on…

Mental Canvas! I know you were wondering how the end of this story goes.

It goes like this:

• I can't draw a straight line…with a ruler!

• The canvases, scenes, and templates aren't easy to understand–or even working at the moment. I have an email sent in to customer support. I'd like to figure the template issue out.

• If I am understanding it correctly, each new plane of drawing (like lining up multiple canvases behind each other) is required to display each 2d drawing plane in 3d space. Which means I would have to have a *shit*load of canvases to make anything halfway descriptive.

• You can't easily get canvases to match up on perpendicular planes. Makes the effort to build a building rather difficult.

• Have I mentioned I suck at drawing? Yeah, it's not only my shaky hands. I really need to go back to grade school and go through art classes again.

At the end of this day, I have decided that I am so good at this art thing that I'd better go write another book. ;-)

I'll harass Noffke in the next book. #Probably.

Have a great week or weekend, and talk to you next time!

Michael

ACKNOWLEDGMENTS

SARAH NOFFKE

I have so many people to thank who make this all possible. Firstly, thanks to Mike, who really pushes me to be a better writer, coming up with the best ideas, not just the really good ones. We work together pretty well, I'd say. I wonder what he'd say... Anyway, MA gave me the opportunity to write with LBMPN a few years ago and it's been life changing. He's very supportive and really cares. Thanks Bird Killer.

A huge thank you to the LBMPN team who work tirelessly so that I have less stress. Thanks to Steve and Kelly for making my life easier and being on top of everything. Thanks to Tracey and Lynne for fixing all my editing mistakes. A big thank you to the JIT team whose feedback at the 11th hour before publishing is invaluable. Thank you to my alpha readers Juergen and Martin. Thank you to everyone who makes getting the books to the reader possible. I really can't do this without you. And you make it so much more fun.

Thank you to my daughter, Lydia, who inspires my stories over and over again. She's my muse and we are always discussing story. She's an avid reader and listens to the Liv Beaufont series at night and reads the Sophia Beaufont books with me before bed. She also reads other authors, which I guess is okay. But my point is that she's supportive of me in so many ways. I need to stay immersed in this universe and remember all the details. There are 12 book in each series so there's a lot to remember. And Lydia loves my stories and then also supports me by listening and reading them so I can keep crafting. But also, she puts up with me when I go all psycho pants during a big crunch of a deadline. I will be the first to admit that I'm pretty intense a day or two before a book is due. And she always just smiles and says, "Mommy, you can do it."

Thank you to my family, the Scotsman and all my friends. You all are always so supportive of me and for that, I'm infinitely grateful. I really couldn't do this without the encouragement of those I love. On the really tough writing days, the Scotsman points out all the things that I don't see, like my dedication to the craft or how much readers are enjoying the books. I don't know what I did to have the most loving and thoughtful people in the world in my corner, but I'm going to do everything to keep them and hopefully keep making them proud.

And finally, thank you to you the reader. Without you I wouldn't be able to do what I love. Your support means so much to me and my family. Thank you from the bottom of my heart.

Love,
Tiny Ninja

BOOKS BY SARAH NOFFKE

Sarah Noffke writes YA and NA science fiction, fantasy, paranormal and urban fantasy. In addition to being an author, she is a mother, podcaster and professor. Noffke holds a Masters of Management and teaches college business/writing courses. Most of her students have no idea that she toils away her hours crafting fictional characters. www.sarahnoffke.com

Check out other work by Sarah author here.

Ghost Squadron:

Formation #1:

   Kill the bad guys. Save the Galaxy. All in a hard day's work.

   After ten years of wandering the outer rim of the galaxy, Eddie Teach is a man without a purpose. He was one of the toughest pilots in the Federation, but now he's just a regular guy, getting into bar fights and making a difference wherever he can. It's not the same as flying a ship and saving colonies, but it'll have to do.

   That is, until General Lance Reynolds tracks Eddie down and offers him a job. There are bad people out there, plotting terrible things, killing innocent people, and destroying entire colonies. **Someone has to stop them.**

Eddie, along with the genetically-enhanced combat pilot Julianna Fregin and her trusty E.I. named Pip, must recruit a diverse team of specialists, both human and alien. They'll need to master their new Q-Ship, one of the most powerful strike ships ever constructed. And finally, they'll have to stop a faceless enemy so powerful, it threatens to destroy the entire Federation.

All in a day's work, right?

Experience this exciting military sci-fi saga and the latest addition to the expanded Kurtherian Gambit Universe. If you're a fan of Mass Effect, Firefly, or Star Wars, you'll love this riveting new space opera.

NOTE: If cursing is a problem, then this might not be for you.

Check out the entire series here.

The Precious Galaxy Series:

Corruption #1

A new evil lurks in the darkness.

After an explosion, the crew of a battlecruiser mysteriously disappears.

Bailey and Lewis, complete strangers, find themselves suddenly onboard the damaged ship. Lewis hasn't worked a case in years, not since the final one broke his spirit and his bank account. The last thing Bailey remembers is preparing to take down a fugitive on Onyx Station.

Mysteries are harder to solve when there's no evidence left behind.

Bailey and Lewis don't know how they got onboard *Ricky Bobby* or why. However, they quickly learn that whatever was responsible for the explosion and disappearance of the crew is still on the ship.

Monsters are real and what this one can do changes everything.

The new team bands together to discover what happened and how to fight the monster lurking in the bottom of the battlecruiser.

Will they find the missing crew? Or will the monster end them all?

The Soul Stone Mage Series:

House of Enchanted #1:
The Kingdom of Virgo has lived in peace for thousands of years...until now.

The humans from Terran have always been real assholes to the witches of Virgo. Now a silent war is brewing, and the timing couldn't be worse. Princess Azure will soon be crowned queen of the Kingdom of Virgo.

In the Dark Forest a powerful potion-maker has been murdered.

Charmsgood was the only wizard who could stop a deadly virus plaguing Virgo. He also knew about the devastation the people from Terran had done to the forest.

Azure must protect her people. Mend the Dark Forest. Create alliances with savage beasts. No biggie, right?

But on coronation day everything changes. Princess Azure isn't who she thought she was and that's a big freaking problem.

Welcome to The Revelations of Oriceran. Check out the entire series here.

The Lucidites Series:

Awoken, #1:
Around the world humans are hallucinating after sleepless nights.

In a sterile, underground institute the forecasters keep reporting the same events.

And in the backwoods of Texas, a sixteen-year-old girl is about to be caught up in a fierce, ethereal battle.

Meet Roya Stark. She drowns every night in her dreams, spends her hours reading classic literature to avoid her family's ridicule, and is prone to premonitions—which are becoming more frequent. And now her dreams are filled with strangers offering to reveal what she has always wanted to know: Who is she? That's the question that haunts her, and she's about to find out. But will Roya live to regret learning the truth?

Stunned, #2

Revived, #3

The Reverians Series:

Defects, #1:

In the happy, clean community of Austin Valley, everything appears to be perfect. Seventeen-year-old Em Fuller, however, fears something is askew. Em is one of the new generation of Dream Travelers. For some reason, the gods have not seen fit to gift all of them with their expected special abilities. Em is a Defect—one of the unfortunate Dream Travelers not gifted with a psychic power. Desperate to do whatever it takes to earn her gift, she endures painful daily injections along with commands from her overbearing, loveless father. One of the few bright spots in her life is the return of a friend she had thought dead—but with his return comes the knowledge of a shocking, unforgivable truth. The society Em thought was protecting her has actually been betraying her, but she has no idea how to break away from its authority without hurting everyone she loves.

Rebels, #2

Warriors, #3

Vagabond Circus Series:

Suspended, #1:

When a stranger joins the cast of Vagabond Circus—a circus that is run by Dream Travelers and features real magic—mysterious events start happening. The once orderly grounds of the circus become riddled with hidden threats. And the ringmaster realizes not only are his circus and its magic at risk, but also his very life.

Vagabond Circus caters to the skeptics. Without skeptics, it would close its doors. This is because Vagabond Circus runs for two reasons and only two reasons: first and foremost to provide the lost and lonely Dream Travelers a place to be illustrious. And secondly, to show the nonbelievers that there's still magic in the world. If they believe, then they care, and if they care, then they don't destroy. They stop the small abuse that day-by-day breaks down humanity's spirit. If Vagabond Circus makes one skeptic believe in magic, then they halt the cycle, just a little bit. They allow a little more love into this world. That's Dr. Dave Raydon's mission. And that's why this ringmaster recruits. That's why he directs. That's why he puts on a show that makes people question their beliefs. He wants the world to believe in magic once again.

Paralyzed, #2

Released, #3

Ren Series:

Ren: The Man Behind the Monster, #1:

Born with the power to control minds, hypnotize others, and read thoughts, Ren Lewis, is certain of one thing: God made a mistake. No one should be born with so much power. A monster awoke in him the same year he received his gifts. At ten years old. A prepubescent boy with the ability to control others might merely abuse his powers, but Ren allowed it to corrupt him. And since he can have and do anything he wants, Ren should be happy. However, his journey teaches him that harboring so much power doesn't bring happiness, it steals it. Once this realization sets in, Ren makes up his mind to do the one thing that can bring his tortured soul some peace. He must kill the monster.

Note This book is NA and has strong language, violence and sexual references.

Ren: God's Little Monster, #2

Ren: The Monster Inside the Monster, #3

Ren: The Monster's Adventure, #3.5

Ren: The Monster's Death

Olento Research Series:

Alpha Wolf, #1:
Twelve men went missing.

Six months later they awake from drug-induced stupors to find themselves locked in a lab.

And on the night of a new moon, eleven of those men, possessed by new—and inhuman—powers, break out of their prison and race through the streets of Los Angeles until they disappear one by one into the night.

Olento Research wants its experiments back. Its CEO, Mika Lenna, will tear every city apart until he has his werewolves imprisoned once again. He didn't undertake a huge risk just to lose his would-be assassins.

However, the Lucidite Institute's main mission is to save the world from injustices. Now, it's Adelaide's job to find these mutated men and protect them and society, and fast. Already around the nation, wolflike men are being spotted. Attacks on innocent women are happening. And then, Adelaide realizes what her next step must be: She has to find the alpha wolf first. Only once she's located him can she stop whoever is behind this experiment to create wild beasts out of human beings.

Lone Wolf, #2
Rabid Wolf, #3
Bad Wolf, #4

CONNECT WITH THE AUTHORS

Connect with Sarah and sign up for her email list here:

http://www.sarahnoffke.com/connect/

Michael Anderle Social

Website: http://lmbpn.com

Email List: http://lmbpn.com/email/

https://www.facebook.com/LMBPNPublishing

https://twitter.com/MichaelAnderle

https://www.instagram.com/lmbpn_publishing/

https://www.bookbub.com/authors/michael-anderle

BOOKS BY MICHAEL ANDERLE

www.ingramcontent.com/pod-product-compliance
Lightning Source LLC
Chambersburg PA
CBHW020409110726
47899CB00006B/1907